Letters to an
Aspiring Physician

Letters to an Aspiring Physician

Reflecting on a Career in Medicine

COMMENTARY BY Edward J Drawbaugh MD
FOREWORD BY Amy E Theriault MA
AFTERWORD BY Brian D Wong MD

T MICHAEL WHITE MD
A HealthCare Value Professional

ISBN: 1976449855
ISBN 13: 9781976449857
Library of Congress Control Number: 2017914646
CreateSpace Independent Publishing Platform
North Charleston, South Carolina

Letters to an Aspiring Physician is biographical fiction. Although stories are invented, to the best of my ability, perceptions and perspectives are accurate and true.

DR. MIKE WHITE

Also by T Michael White MD

Unsafe to Safe
An Impatient Proposal for Safer Medical Care

A Crystal Spring Thanksgiving
A Little Girl Plays 'Manly' Golf

Safer Medical Care for You and Yours
Six Tools for Safe, Effective, Compassionate Care

Table of Contents

I. Finding Momentum

- *"Let him that would move the world, first move himself."* Socrates
- *"All mankind is divided into three classes: those who are immovable; those who are movable and those who move."* Benjamin Franklin
- *Man is the creature of circumstances. Circumstances are the creatures of men."* Benjamin Disraeli
- *"Don't be afraid to take a big step when one is indicated. You can't cross a chasm in two small jumps."* David Lloyd George
- *"Trust only movement. Life happens at the level of event not of words."* Alfred Adler
- *"You may have the loftiest goals, the highest ideals, the noblest dreams, but remember this, nothing works unless to do."* Nido Qubein
- *"Wisdom is knowing what to do next, skill is knowing how to do it and virtue is doing it."* David Star Jordan
- *"I know of no more encouraging fact than the unquestionable ability of man to elevate his life by a conscious endeavor."* Henry David Thoreau
- *"Satisfaction lies in the effort, not in the attainment."* Mohandas Gandhi
- *"The will to do, the soul to dare."* Sir Walter Scott
- *"Lives of great men all remind us we can make our lives sublime and, departing, leave behind us footprints on the sands of time."* Henry Wadsworth Longfellow

1

Millennials

"Don't lie to anyone, but particularly don't lie to millennials.
They just know. They can smell it.
Be yourself: if you are old, be old."

John Green

The FountainHead WhiteHouse
Aspiring Physicians,

1. *Hello.*
2. *Thank you for all you do daily so well for so many.*
3. *Towards a common understanding...*

———

Several millennials in my life have been kind enough to give *Letters to an Aspiring Physician* a glance — glance is what I am told millennials do.
Uniformly they see value for the individual considering a career, especially a career in medicine. Uniformly they express concern that those who might

benefit the most may not overcome inertia — a tendency to do nothing — to find momentum — the impetus and driving force necessary for change.

My millennials advise I make it all more interesting — that I skinny it down and just get their/your generation to the stories — what an idea. I am remembering…

- Einstein allegedly observed, "The most powerful force in the universe is a charismatic story." I choose to believe this as in my career and life, it has always been so.
- Iconic sportswriter Frank Deford (a hero — it is good to have heroes), conveys the same sentiment — changing his word 'sport' to 'medicine' — "But I also believe that the one thing that's largely gone out is what made *medicine* such fertile literary territory — the characters, the tales, the humor, the pain, what Hollywood calls 'the arc.' That is, stories. We have, all by ourselves, ceded that one neat thing about *medicine* that we owned."

Recognizing my millennials are right, my message is in the composite stories — the tales, narratives, accounts, anecdotes, yarns, spiels, rumors, gossip, whispers, speculations, fictions — that listening, observing, imagining and living compel me to share. Therefore, despite my obsessive-compulsive personality (and the OCPs of my similarly afflicted editors and publishers) which obligates me to provide a structure to thoughts, meeting millennials in the middle, I encourage you to randomly explore the text. For example, and without being prescriptive, I observe that *#2 Addendum — Art and Science, #12 The First Time, #14 'Better Angels' Called* and/or *#38 Compassion* may be logical places to begin to get a feel.

———————

4. *Are our generations so different? I think not. I stand with Satchel Paige, "Age is a question of mind over matter. If you don't mind, it doesn't matter."*

5. *For sure, if it is right for you, our generation needs brilliant 'Better Angel' you to step up to the honor, privilege and responsibility of caring for a most grateful us.*
6. *Thank you for considering.*
7. *Other Thoughts?*

Respectfully submitted,
Dr. Mike White

———

2

Addendum — Art and Science

"Perfect is the Enemy of Good"

Apocryphal

The FountainHead WhiteHouse
Aspiring Physicians,

1. *Hello.*
2. *Thank you for all you do daily so well for so many,*
3. *An addendum?   What an unusual way to start a book.   After review, it feels like a fitting and just, quirky start.*
4. *Since the long-ago contentment of mid-career medicine, I have felt pressured to write a book, something like — The Ten (or is it the One-Hundred?) Things I Wish They Told Me before I Entered Medical School.*
5. *There is a matryoshka doll-like nest of concepts I feel compelled to convey:*
   - *Congenitally, I am a perfectionist,*
   - *I will be wrongly trained that, as a physician, I must be perfect,*
   - *I will be wrongly trained that the strong perfect handle things and the weak imperfect call for help,*
   - *I will make mistakes,*

- *Provided my pathological congenital perfectionism and misdirected training, my mistakes will be cruelly and eternally painful; therefore,*
- *I must I must take care to be trained to deal with my mistakes and my pain.*

6. *Within this context and without undue searching, a few career mistakes do too readily come to mind (the more painful are forever repressed). Examples include:*
   - *In the interest of efficiency, I fail to lead my resident team on compassionate rounds on an obtunded dying patient,*
   - *A lady skillfully feigning Crohn's Disease beats me out of a narcotic prescription,*
   - *One weekend on call, an addicted dentist claims to be caring for a suffering, dying mother and beats me out of a vile of meperidine,*
   - *A lady with pheochromocytoma is finally diagnosed by my brilliant covering physician while I (lucky for her) am on vacation,*
   - *A gentleman proves to have colon cancer despite two negative colonoscopies,*
   - *A neighbor/friend/patient's sleep is disturbed by severe bilateral carpal tunnel syndrome which I am slow to diagnose and treat relieve,*
   - *I consider a young lady to have the autoimmune sicca syndrome (dry eyes and dry mouth) when, in actuality, she is suffering the oral complications of self-induced vomiting and*
   - *I too long considered a patient with spinal stenosis to have peripheral vascular disease.*

   Sparing you perseveration, the list goes on.

7. *My bias is to encourage you, if you desire, to pursue the honor, privilege and responsibility of a physician's career. When I was deciding, I could envision the infinite magical moments — they were all there. Looking back, I wish I had known more about the anxious moments. The knowledge would not have changed my direction; however, it would have prepared me and perhaps left me, at times, feeling less alone.*

8. *Perhaps my next book will be — A Compendium of The Joys of Medicine — a millennial snoozer for sure. At this time, with your interest at heart, and with my heart full of joy, I must share the robust, complexity the honor, privilege*

and responsibility a career in medicine will bring to you. Consider, as an example, the spirit of this composite fiction conveyed to me by colleagues through the years...

Art and Science

Upon leaving residency, I took up private practice in a small town. On July 1st when I became the third internist in the community, the two others immediately left town for prolonged, well-deserved vacations and left the responsibility of the hospital and the community to me for six weeks. Immersed without orientation, I immediately simultaneously discovered:

- I had been well trained as a general internist,
- The hospital emergency department was open for all comers,
- The hospital did not have subspecialty (for example, cardiology, pulmonary or neurology) coverage. Therefore, as a general internist, I would have tremendous responsibility for complex acute care,
- Without negotiation about prolonged vacations, my career had been placed in jeopardy. If I were not up to this unreasonable overwhelming challenge, it would be immediately become transparently obvious to the community (especially the hospital's nurses) and my practice would be doomed before started,
- I was, in fact, up to the task. When the two internists returned six weeks later, I had won over the hospital, the nurses and the community and
- I recognized that going forward, I would not practice hospital medicine without, at a minimum, available cardiology and pulmonary specialists.

On my fifth straight weekend (and next-to-last) on call [note: an unconscionable burden], at 10 p.m. a middle-aged lady with everything to live for, suffered a heart attack and presented to our emergency room. The moonlighting emergency room physician detected heart failure, reflexly (perhaps wrongly) gave the patient a diuretic and admitted the patient to my care in the intensive care unit. I was at the bedside almost immediately and found a patient with massive cardiac damage in cardiogenic shock, hypotensive, anuric and electrically unstable. Based upon my internal medicine (3 years shy of a cardiologist's) training, I recognized her prognosis to be grave and went about stabilizing as best I could acute conditions and ensuring his comfort.

Through all of this, she was entirely lucid and she and I developed an immediate strong personal attachment. Her vibrant and impressive, yet stunned, partner spent every moment at her bedside and joined our intense bond. From our non-verbal communications, the quite spiritual patient knew her chances were slim and she began to prepare for "crossing over." In delicate but frank conversations with her partner, I helped with an understanding of grave prognosis.

To no avail, I spent significant early Sunday morning effort pleading with consulting cardiologists to come to the bedside. At the same time, I arranged for a cardiac transport team to come from the university hospital and transport my patient to their major cardiac center. When they arrived at 2 a.m., she became extremely unstable. Tending to her every need, I reviewed findings and options with the transport team; we judged prognosis for recovery was zero; we judged she would surely die among strangers in the heart mobile and we decided to preserve her dignity and allow her to die among family and friends. It being my call, I sent the transport team back without her. Within an hour, she succumbed with her partner and her dedicated, compassionate nurses and physician at the bedside. Immediately, the partner became the focus of our team's ministrations — in these circumstances the near and dear become the patient. We did our best. With great sadness, we, crushed, parted early that Sunday morning.

The next day with too little sleep, I tended to the other forty patients on my hospital service. As I made rounds, I came to understand that my deceased patient's relatives in another state were irately questioning the care provided to their family icon. "How could she die without a cardiologist?" was their justified question. Having given the patient my all, in an exhausted state, I was devastated. I asked a cardiologist (who had not been available in the wee hours) to review the chart. To my relief, he found "no deficiencies.".

On Monday, I met with the hospital's dedicated and effective president/chief executive officer and told him that if he were to maintain an emergency department and intensive care unit that were open to "all comers," as a requirement for my staying in the community, he must immediately recruit cardiology and pulmonary specialists — so that each of our complex patients would have the 'benefit of clergy.' Without hesitation, he agreed.

As the years have gone by, with the benefit of wisdom and experience, I have come to understand it was most unusual for a most junior physician to forcefully confront hospital leadership regarding patient-centered care in this way.

As a happy ending, I would like to relate that the partner and the relatives made an appointment to see me to express their comfort with and gratitude for my efforts. Regrettably, I cannot. As close as I can come to finding the closure I seek:

- There was never any posturing towards a law suit. For this I am eternally grateful to the family as the legal process, win or lose, would have devastated an already devastated, idealistic me.
- The president/chief executive officer was as good as his word and our hospital quickly invested in and transitioned to complex modern care. For this I am most grateful.
- Six months later, while I was exuberantly and too noisily entering a restaurant with friends, the patient's partner, leaving alone, and I came face to face. Without a word, the partner looked down and away and quietly (sadly? agonizingly?) exited the premises leaving me to imperfectly wonder:
  - Did I too painfully remind of that Saturday evening and Sunday morning?
  - Were there acute and painful reminders that the exuberant and too noisy life I was enjoying had been unfairly stolen from them?
  - Was I not yet forgiven for perceived imperfect care?
- To this day, I remain painfully haunted by wouldas, couldas, shouldas:
  - If only the emergency medicine physician and I had sent the patient directly from the emergency department to the university.

- If only a cardiologist (i.e., 'benefit of clergy') had been available.
- Should I have placed the patient in the transport van and placed a semblance of death with the 'benefit of clergy' (The Science) ahead of very personal, compassionate care (The Art)?
- If this case had happened on my first weekend on call — before developing clinical street cred with nursing and community — my reputation and career trajectory would have taken an entirely different, likely disastrous arc.
- Did the wonderful partner ever cease suffering?
- Have I been too hard on myself? Have I not been hard enough?

Soon specialists were on staff and regularly rounding in the intensive care unit. Trained as a medical student by my professionally and personally fine senior resident, Dr. Sal Pipito, to understand, "Your eyes cannot see what your brain does not know," every patient ill enough to be admitted to my medicine service was provided the 'benefit of clergy' — a relevant subspecialty consultation.

———

9. *Aspiring Physicians, after review, using the always infallible 'retrospectoscope,' I recognize there may have been a safer path for the physician that evening — futile transfer to the university. But, as the story is told, I perceive the correct path was taken. The patient's dignity was preserved.*
10. *At the same time, if the partner's long-term well-being was primary, perhaps transfer was in order. Personally at peace with the story's denouement, I will leave this for others to parse.*
11. *Other thoughts?*

Respectfully submitted,
Dr. Mike White

———

3

Dedication

"To those who inspired this book and will never read it."

ANONYMOUS

The definition of dedication: 1) the quality of being dedicated or committed to a task or purpose — clearly the reader's responsibility and 2) the words with which a book or other artistic work is dedicated — my responsibility. My task should be easy.

There are plenty of examples out there. The above quoted example intrigues me.

Seriously, this book might be dedicated to you — one with the goods and the courage to aspire to become a physician. At the same time, it might be dedicated to our 'Better Angels' who, as they care for us so well, inspire those that aspire.

Then there is a long line of individuals who have guided me (sometimes successfully) from where I was to where I needed to be. This book might be dedicated to them: Dr. Sherman (paradigm); Pharmacist Aumiller (wisdom); Professor Sheffer (kind advocacy); Drs. Cassidy, Firth, Goodman, Lamb, Scharfman, Steinhart, Tartaglia and Cantone (art and science); Dr. Bernene (probity); Dr. Alfonsi (judgment); Dr. Howard (vitality); Mr. Price (friendship); P/CEO Jones (enablement); Dr. Crosby (quality); Dr. Moyer (structure); Professor Anderson (learning/teaching); Ms. Kleppick (resolute); P/CEO Ott (culture); Dr. Leach (shift); Dr. Ahmad (grace); Ms. Navarra (faith); Dr. Roth (horizons); Mr. Lieber (fortification); Mr. Studer (implementation); Mr. Hirsch (mindfulness); Dr. Wong (consummate); Drs. Kellis, Ghobrial, Godse, Condit, Drawbaugh and Hightower (constancy); Editor Theriault (balance); Artist Haught (images); Reverend Dodson and Dr. Leff (connections) and Nurses Forsythe, Lasek, Theriault, Anderson, Como, Gaudy, Rotz, Lyons, Williams, Towe and Amalfitano (safe, timely, efficient, effective, equitable, patient-centered care).

After review, remembering those that guided me, this book is dedicated to those that will assist you find your way.

Dr. Mike White

———

4

PREFACE

"I graduated Phi Beta Goddamn Kappa from that school."

DAVID BROMBERG

The FountainHead WhiteHouse
Aspiring Physicians,

1. *Hello.*
2. *Thank you for all you do daily so well for so many.*
3. *As prelude…*

———

"I am a very lucky human because I have always been able to do what I want to do — what I enjoy doing. And, further, I have been able to do it the way I want to do it. You cannot ask for more than that out of life."

Those are not my words. They belong to citizen, entrepreneur, father, genius, hero, husband, luthier, mentor, musician, philosopher and poet David Bromberg. But they could be my words — he just beat me to them. They could be your words. I sincerely want them to be.

If you have been attracted to this tome by the title *Letters to an Aspiring Physician*, I encourage you to aspire. However, unlike me a hundred years ago, I wish for you to proceed towards medicine informed. Despite my letter-carrier/musician father's pleadings against, I insisted on enrolling in the school of hard knocks and graduated Phi Beta Goddamn Kappa. I went forward counting on blind luck. While I did OK — it is true in golf and life that you make your luck — information would have stacked my deck. I want better for you. As you move forward, I want you informed.

Many in medical education have told me my perceptions, which reflect my realities, represent important, meaningful work that makes a difference. Many aspiring have conveyed that my coaching, both when right and when wrong, has been useful. So, I encourage you to give this book a quick turn. As I do so, I am confident it will enable some — perhaps you — a hundred years from now, to say, "Having chosen medicine, I became a very lucky human. I have always been able to do what I wanted to do — what I enjoyed doing. And, further, I have been able to do it the way I wanted to do it. I could not have asked for more than that out of life."

——-•——-

4. *As you move forward, enjoy every moment.*
5. *Other thoughts?*

Respectfully submitted,
Dr. Mike White

——-•——-

5

University of Pikeville
Dear Aspiring Physicians,

Letters to an Aspiring Physician by Dr. T. Michael White is a compilation of letters to pre-medical students from a uniquely experienced physician, clinician, educator, quality improvement leader and patient safety advocate. It provides guidance on specific aspects of career development, like choosing a residency, and gives the reader the scaffolding needed to build a personal and professional framework for approaching your medical career. This framework can be used to guide the development of your knowledge, experience and career path. Dr. White has helped shape many physician careers and will undoubtedly guide many more with this work.

Some themes are woven through multiple letters and serve as an anchor, keeping the reader to a unified, faithful view of an unfolding career that often feels beyond one's control. As Dr. White describes, his career took some unanticipated turns but the outcome was ultimately satisfying. The use of personal stories about successes, failures and incompletes is reassuring to readers. The letters contain lessons for each of us on the pre-med path. Each missive funnels into the concept of job versus vocation, ensuring we can fulfill our commitment to medicine for as long as we choose. Some include becoming a patient advocate, developing a dedication to patient safety and quality improvement, fostering commitment to other physicians and colleagues, and setting personal and professional priorities. At times, Dr. White relates what he has learned by closely watching the tribulations of colleagues. He also urges the reader to learn vicariously through his personal anecdotes and observations — avoiding the pain of learning through personal experience. Furthermore, commentary from Dr. Edward Drawbaugh at the end of selected letters provides a second opinion from another esteemed physician with a different career path.

Such commitment to life-long learning is a hallmark of many professions. This concept took on a completely new meaning for me when I decided to pursue a career as a physician. When I completed graduate school in 2005, I never would have imagined the change in my life's course — just 10 years later. I would not have seen myself in my mid-30s sitting in an introductory physics course, in the beginning stages of my pre-med requirements. On the horizon was the hope of entering medical school. I had a relatively successful career in healthcare as a social worker. But I felt like a beginner in a classroom of 20-somethings and me with no math or science background and few related study skills. The two years it took to complete the program were tough and I learned many lessons including perseverance, humility and increased self-confidence.

With this experience, I look forward to the next chapter of my training — medical school. For me, the most challenging lesson from *Letters to an Aspiring Physician* is maintaining a beginner's mind. As we continually re-dedicate ourselves to developing into the competent physicians we want to be, I believe this principle holds true for each level of career progression — from pre-med to medical student, from medical student to resident and from resident to independent physician. However, Dr. White lays the challenge before us to treat every day and every encounter with patients and with colleagues as a beginner. This requires leaving assumptions behind to be fully present and able to listen to the message. Embracing this challenge will help us to learn and develop into the most effective professional possible.

I witnessed this approach when I first crossed paths with Dr. White. He was the Vice President for Value and Chief Medical Officer and I was a medical social worker at a medical center in Western Maryland. Dr. White presented on the fundamentals of quality to an interdisciplinary group of which I was a member. As a newly minted social worker, I had exposure to ideas of quality academically, but never the opportunity to apply the principles to resolve real-world issues. Through his presentation style and interpersonal communication, it was clear each member of the team was a valued contributor to the improvement process. The philosophy and vision resonated immediately with me. As a result, I looked for ways to learn more about quality improvement. I attended a statewide patient safety conference and completed online learning modules from the Institute for Healthcare Improvement. In subsequent positions my involvement in quality improvement progressed to improving health screening rates for female veterans, participating in root cause analysis and working to improve information system processes in public health. These experiences, among others, helped develop my vision of healthcare and what skills and abilities I could best contribute. This trajectory ultimately led me to where I am today – looking forward to starting medical school in the fall of 2017.

Undoubtedly, I will continue to find value in *Letters to an Aspiring Physician* as my career progresses. This is a book you may use in multiple ways. Read it through in its entirety. Then immediately connect your experiences, plans, motivation to become a physician, and fears for how or whether it will all work out to the wisdom shared by Dr. White. Plan to keep this volume close. Refer to it when grappling with an aspect of education, training, relationships or even wavering motivation. I anticipate more challenges on this road we have chosen and are blessed to be able pursue. I hope you will look to these letters as guidance to building a stable, satisfying and deeply meaningful career. I intend to do the same.

Best regards,
Amy E Theriault MA
Medical Student
University of Pikeville, Kentucky College of Osteopathic Medicine

Author's Note

Aspiring Physicians, allow me to both: 1) thank soon to be Dr. Amy for her thoughtful and kind perspectives and 2) work to ensure your investment in the letters that follow is "worth the squeeze." Therefore, before you embark, please fast forward to Dr. Brian Wong's afterword. He is one of the many heroes — it is good to have heroes — I will introduce to you. Up front, he will provide you the perspective of the senior national thought leader. Between soon to be Dr. Amy's ying and established Dr. Brian's yang, you will have enough information for you to determine if and how you personally may best proceed with Letters to an Aspiring Physician. Dr. Mike White

———

6

INTRODUCTION

"Simplicity does not precede complexity, but follows it."

ALAN PERLIS

The FountainHead WhiteHouse
Aspiring Physicians

1. *Hello.*
2. *Thank you for all you do daily so well for so many.*
3. *Let us begin...*

———•———

As I have matured in life and in medicine and as I have been forced to encounter and appreciate care as a patient, I have become a more complete physician. While still aspiring to motor forward, I observe my career has already been one heck of a ride. Therefore, if it is your inclination, I must give you every encouragement to give a career in medicine a go.

As a senior physician (aka old), I am often asked by the young or their parents and grandparents, "Should a young person pursue a career in medicine in 2017?" My instantaneous answer, "If you are gifted and called to the honor, privilege and responsibility of medicine, rush to it as few professions will provide the gratifying opportunities for important, meaningful work that makes a difference."

My considered answer is more complex. For the young to journey forward with eyes wide open, they require an understanding of the poet's, "What I know now that I wish I knew then." I have found a 90-minute meeting, often with parents present, at my kitchen table overlooking the 17th tee to be a very good but insufficient start. The main deficiency is an inability to efficiently and effectively convey that which needs to be said to ears that are unprepared to hear — a most inexact science.

An alternative technique has me share a series of thoughtful, personal letters for consideration by the individual aspiring to be a physician. In real-time, opinions may be appreciated or ignored. With experience, messages first found useless may blossom as the journey progresses and circumstances unfold. These personal letters have been assembled in this book.

I have requested that a trusted, insightful colleague, surgeon, physician executive and mentor, Dr. Ed Drawbaugh, consider each letter and, when appropriate, add his perspective — what I have right, wrong or omitted — through formal commentary. As intended, his observations reflect his experience, research and discussions with many and add balance and validity to my messages.

As a young physician executive, I had the honor and privilege to study and learn quality from a master — Dr. Phil Crosby. Influenced by his insights, my professional and personal endeavors became continuous quality improvement processes. So it is with this book. As you read, please share with me that which I have right, wrong or omitted so I, with attribution, may include your wisdom in subsequent undertakings. The best way to contact me is via email: drmikewhite@tmichaelwhitemd.com. I will be most pleased to hear from you.

———•———

4. *Other thoughts?*

Respectfully submitted,
Dr. Mike

———•———

7

Genesis and Formula

""The only gift is a portion of thyself.""

Ralph Waldo Emerson

The FountainHead Whitehouse
Aspiring Physicians

1. *Good morning.*
2. *Thank you for all you do daily so well for so many.*
3. *Where and why to begin…*

———◆———

I received a hand-written letter from a close colleague and dear friend. It came in a stamped envelope. It was written on his personal stationery. His cursive letters were artistically legible. With his having passed, his note survives among my few treasures.

He conveyed that he was stepping away from his academic, clinical and administrative internal medicine career. Although not retiring, he would "take time to step back and reassess."

He observed, "Upon initial review, I recognize it has been a great run. I have been blessed. And, the future too is most promising. It turns out options are plentiful even for an old-school physician like me. I anticipate I will return to my true love — to the bedside where I will guide the care of patients entrusted to our medical students, residents and fellows — and again see wonders unfold before their eyes."

But this note was not about him. His four children had each found personal and professional success — in the military, in law, in leadership and in finance. None had chosen to follow him into a career in medicine. Now, his oldest grandchild, Alex, was approaching her/his junior year in college and is seeking his counsel regarding a career in medicine. "At once, I find myself both extremely elated and yet too close to provide objective advice." So, he turned to me. "I am hopeful that you might find the energy and time to send a note outlining your positive and/or negative perspectives on a medical career. What thoughts will you share in 2017 with a brilliant young person who is aspiring towards a career in medicine? Where will introspection take you?"

I was delighted to hear from him. I was reminded of our warm, sometimes convoluted but always interesting career-long teaching/learning/teaching relationship. He had taught me the curse which together we addressed, "May you live in interesting times." As colleague and friend, he had been and remained one of my major professional and personal mentors. I was elated (and humbled) that he would ask my input on such an important issue — the career choice of his brilliant, charming, precious grandchild.

I was most inclined to provide my perspectives. For some time, I have felt compelled to write encouraging words to aspiring physicians; however, I could not arrive at a mechanism. How might I share my thoughts about a career in medicine? Of one thing I was certain, in conveying messages from my ancient perspective to the nascent, to be relevant my perceptions must be personal and conveyed from the heart. Remembering Emerson, *"Rings and jewels are not gifts, but apologies for gifts. The only gift is a portion of thyself. Thou must bleed for me. Therefore, the poet brings his poem; the shepherd, his lamb; the farmer, corn; the miner, a stone; the painter, his picture; the girl, a handkerchief of her own sewing."* So, without apology, I would share both what I observed and what I felt.

Emerson's words took me back to the impact that Sinclair Lewis (*Arrowsmith*) and A J Cronin (*The Citadel*) had on my pursuit of medicine. Ultimately, it was neither science nor rewards but complex human struggle that swayed me. Refusing the Pulitzer Prize for his novel, Lewis wrote, "All prizes, like all titles, are dangerous. The seekers for prizes tend to labor not for inherent excellence but for alien rewards." So, without apology, I share both struggle and prize.

I settled upon the elusive mechanism/vehicle. My format would be letters to his precious Alex. His timing was exquisite. My calendar was clear. To add perspective, clarity and validity, I would ask a trusted, insightful colleague, surgeon, physician executive and mentor, Dr. Ed Drawbaugh, to edit and, when inspired, to add commentary. Then thoughts would be forwarded to Alex — and perhaps beyond.

Frankly, I do not envision Alex taking this all in in real-time. Some thoughts may have immediate relevance. Others may immediately and forever be rejected. Still other thoughts, quickly perused and set aside to simmer may surface in circumstance-dictated reflective moments.

———

4. Other thoughts?

Respectfully submitted,
Dr. Mike White

———

8

LETTERS TO AN ASPIRING PHYSICIAN

*"When in doubt tell the truth. It will confound
your enemies and astound your friends."*

MARK TWAIN

The FountainHead WhiteHouse
Alex,

1. *Good morning.*
2. *Thank you for all you do daily so well for so many.*
3. *As an introduction…*

———

Your physician grandfather, who is among my professional and personal heroes, has asked that I share my thoughts with you, his most precious progeny, about a career in medicine. Honored, daunted and obliged, I shall comply.

Upon reflection, I believe I have something worthy of sharing. But what is the logical format? I have decided that as you consider your career path, I will send you a series of letters for your consideration. To keep me on track — I am easily distracted — I will format these as *Letters to an Aspiring Physician.*

To be entirely honest — I shall always endeavor to tell you all that I know — I envision these letters/thoughts/messages someday assembled as a book.

My musings will be most personal. My perspectives on career will be shared from the heart. At times, to find important truths, I will be forced to confront long-repressed, painful realities. Please understand my vulnerabilities and treat my ponderings with compassionate respect and kindness.

As you immerse yourself in the wondrous academic and social undertaking called college, please consider my letters to be a parallel course that you have chosen to audit. Although I do hope you will attend (i.e., read), there will be no assignments, tests or grades. However, as I write these letters to you, generations removed, I am on a steep learning curve. Therefore, occasional feedback (the right, the wrong or the omitted) from you to me will be appreciated and will surely improve my work.

Recognizing the importance of this undertaking, I have asked a respected trusted, insightful colleague, surgeon, physician executive and mentor, Dr. Ed Drawbaugh, to edit my work and add commentary before it is sent to you. We may be confident that you (the aspiring) and I (coach) will benefit greatly from his insights.

Some of my perceptions will be understandably beyond your station in life and beyond your ken. Rather than disregard, when perplexed, you may choose to explore their meaning with your mentors and/or with thoughtful peers. Sharing their reactions, revelations and insights with me will be invaluable to my work.

———

4. *Alex, tomorrow the journey begins.*
5. *Looking forward…*
6. *Other thoughts?*

Respectfully submitted,
Dr. Mike

———

9

Assembled Wisdom

"Passion is what gives meaning to our lives.
It's what allows us to achieve success
beyond our wildest imagination."

Henry Samueli

The FountainHead WhiteHouse
Alex,

1. *Good morning.*
2. *Thank you for all you do daily so well for so many.*
3. *To begin, I share the opinion of diverse currently practicing physicians with you. They, without knowledge of my perspectives, have answered my question, "In 2017 would you advise a career in medicine?" Despite their challenges in time and space — each certifiably busier than God — they have, on the behalf of you, the aspiring, found time to reply...*

———

Dr. Kalim Ahmed, Pulmonary and Critical Care Medicine, Hagerstown, Maryland

Although it's a very straightforward question and I have been asked it many times, the answer is not as simple as one might think. It all depends upon the person who is asking this question and her/his understanding of and motivation for choosing medicine as a career. The fact that one must spend enormous amounts of money and invest the prime time of one's life, motivation must be evaluated critically.

Although current healthcare professionals no longer enjoy the same autonomy, economic freedom and prestige of "the good old days" because of good or bad healthcare bureaucracy, regulatory burden and protocol driven medicine, they continue to be well respected by the broader society and in their work place. In general, they make a decent living, have job security and, most importantly, continue to make a palpable difference in the lives of patients and families.

Healthcare professionals will be challenged by the stubbornness of diseases and their complications, long and odd work hours, frustration of institutional politics and so on. At the same time, they will have the opportunity to embark on a journey to reach to the outer frontier of their intellectual boundaries. And each day, they will experience the eternal joy and happiness of thanks and prayers of gratified patients and families.

If this kind of diversity and drama excites your passion then medicine is definitely a good career choice as, for the hardworking, motivated and knowledgeable, nothing is impossible.

Dr. Jack J. Applefeld, Critical Care Medicine, Paradise Valley, Arizona

Without hesitation, I would recommend a career in medicine! Not because the road is easy or short, but for the priceless reward of a meaningful life able to help other human beings when they are vulnerable.

Medicine is unique among the professions. Some physicians are seen as "stars," while others have become fabulously wealthy. Yet most physicians labor in a system, although not very efficient, that still provides the potential for the best healthcare to any individual regardless of ability to pay. To be a part of this process is both humbling and rewarding beyond belief.

In my career as an intensive care physician and educator, I have had the privilege of taking care of patients who have life-threatening or life-ending conditions. On all occasions, I have tried to bring the best medical therapy to these patients. Some of the therapy was designed to ease the suffering of a painful death. Other therapies were utilized to prolong life and allow time for a full recovery. It is with the complete knowledge of the patient's illness that the physician has the opportunity, in conjunction with the consultants, to advise the patient and her or his family on the most appropriate course of care.

Medicine is fluid. Soon, many of the illnesses that we see today will have different modes of treatment as the advances in molecular biology, genetics and immunology are implemented.

As an educator, I tried to relay facts and wisdom to younger physicians. Many have gone on to careers in private practice, academics and administration. I am flattered when they remember their ICU rotation as a positive experience; thank me for spending time with them; express delight in their mastery of complex physiologic process and share their experiences trying to save patients' lives.

As I conclude these thoughts, my one admonishment would be for you, as you learn as much as you can, to never forget that when you apply your knowledge to your patients, they and their loved ones need your compassionate care.

Dr. William Bishop, VA Primary Care, Modesto, California

The question is: Would I recommend that a young person consider going into medicine given our current healthcare climate? Since I am a general internist, would I recommend going into primary care? The answers are yes, with a few caveats.

I am, of course, biased in thinking that primary care is the most difficult and challenging field of medicine. But I do not recommend arguing this point with our surgical or subspecialty colleagues.

From a practical standpoint, the solo practitioner is now a thing of the past. Medicine in America is now and for the foreseeable future dominated by big business and a handful of insurance companies. I am hopeful that with time America will come to understand that healthcare is a right of citizenship and not a commodity.

Although, quite challenging, being a doctor is noble:

- You help other people. What could be better than that?
- Every day is different.
- When you get right down to it, patients just want somebody to take care of them and to listen to them — and are most appreciative. Therefore,
- It is important, honorable and meaningful work.

But:

- The hours are long.
- The training is arduous and physically, intellectually and mentally challenging.
- Medicine, the jealous mistress, places significant stress on spouses and children.

One of the biggest problems, physicians face is burnout. One must try to guard against this. I have addressed this problem and have, to some degree, avoided it by changing what I do every 7-10 years. I started out in group practice, went to a hospital owned practice, did solo practice in a rural setting and then went to public sector (Veterans Administration). My current iteration has me enjoyably doing house calls/home care for the VA. Someday I will slow down, but hanging around the house and driving wife crazy will never be in the cards. Medicine will provide my outlet.

Providing relief in response to Hurricane Katrina was one of the most rewarding experiences I have had. Our team provided care to thousands of patients, kept minimal notes and did not charge a dime. It felt good to be a physician (I admire *Doctors without Borders* but lack the courage to do that). Who but a physician could have that experience?

As a primary care doctor, I have been adequately compensated, paid my bills and sent my kids to college. For me, this has been a fair deal. If your goal is to become independently wealthy, I suggest you investigate a more direct path — for example, commercial plumbing in San Francisco or a congressional seat.

Although healthcare in America is going through a difficult time, we will always need dedicated, compassionate people to join the ranks. Follow your heart. Go to medical school. Consider primary care. Be there to care for me and mine.

———

Dr. Brian Condit, Internal Medicine, Physical Medicine and Rehabilitation, Chief Medical Officer, Abingdon, Virginia

I suspect there are as many reasons that someone would choose to pursue medicine as there are physicians. The desire to help others, particularly those a person identifies with, is a strongly ingrained human trait. So, throughout history there are good-willed individuals who have sought to relieve the pain and suffering of others. They represent the heart and soul of medicine.

To become a physician is to embark on a challenging 4000-year-old journey. To be a physician, to help bring assurance and healing to the afflicted, is truly a great calling. It is the opportunity for an individual to do important fulfilling work that helps one's neighbors and community in a very personal way. Freud said that the two most important tasks in life are love and work. Medicine is where those two come together in the willful pursuit of the healing arts.

To be a physician in 2017 is to live in a complex, challenging and ever-changing world. Sometimes in the midst of the day to day, it is difficult to remember the idealism that undergirds the profession. Appointments, productivity, new evidence-based guidelines, patient satisfaction, electronic medical records, insurance queries and on and on intervene. For the modern physician working in the hospital or clinic, burnout is a real threat so work-life boundaries, personal growth and time off for renewal are key for professional survival.

Physician leadership is essential if we are to be successful in muddling forward from here. So that we can provide the excellent care we want to give and our patients deserve, we require:

- Leadership that builds the highly reliable care teams of the future and
- Leadership that promotes emotional intelligence in the design of our work and our organizations.

We physicians on the front lines know the true challenges and we physicians must advocate for how we care for our patients and for how we care for the future of the healing professions.

So, should you pursue a career in medicine? Absolutely yes — if you can answer:

- What is in your own heart?
- Is it truly what you want to do?
- Is there nothing else that will satisfy?
- Do you have the will, intelligence, perseverance and the grit to make the journey?
- Can you not lose sight of your own humanity and that of the patients you care for?
- Can you continue to learn and grow throughout your life?
- Are you willing to do the right thing, to make personal sacrifices for the greater good and perhaps to see that sacrifice unappreciated?

If the answers to these questions are yes, then by all means, join us.

Dr. Ibrahim Ghobrial, Internal Medicine Residency Program Director, Pittsburgh, Pennsylvania

Yes, I do advise you, my daughter, son or mentee, to pursue a career in medicine.

As I approach the final chapter in my medical career, I look back and remember what my peers wanted to pursue. Some cherished fulfillment, others prestige and many wanted missionary work — or so read their personal statements. In medicine, you don't have to choose between these goals.

Medical knowledge has exploded in ways that we have never imagined. Cure for many traditional "incurable diseases" is common place. Many opportunities for new discoveries exist.

At the same time, the amount of need in our communities has also grown. Many sick people cry out for help as they fall through numerous cracks in our convoluted and complicated healthcare system. Daily I experience joyful moments — among the most joyful moments of my life — ministering to the complex, vulnerable sick and needy.

After review, I must recommend my glorious life to you.

———————

Dr. David Lippman, Internist and Medical Director, Evansville, Indiana

I would not a recommend a career in medicine.

I am an internal medicine physician who has practiced primary care medicine for approximately 17 years. My daughter is doing very well in one of the top high schools in the country. She has no desire to study medicine and I am not encouraging her to go into the medical field.

Physician morale, particularly in primary care, is at historic lows. This, I believe, is related to multiple factors — overhead expenses of running a practice, regulatory and charting requirements, student loans, etc.

However, one fundamental negative change which has occurred in medicine is technical. In my opinion, the physician-patient relationship has transformed into one in which the provider is now viewed primarily as an interface to get patient data into an electronic medical record. Although, the electronic medical record has the potential to create a vast amount of benefits, it is occurring at the loss of the physician-patient relationship. This breakdown of the human relationship is creating a sense of loss for both the patient receiving care but also for the doctor providing care. It has become "providers" working for "the computer" rather than enhanced information serving the patient and healthcare team well.

The tragedy is that there could truly be a renaissance in primary care. We have never known as much as we do now to prevent disease and create a healthier, happier culture. In a reinvigorated primary care model, healthy communities such as the Okinawans could be studied and emulated. While bedrocks of prevention, such as immunizations, would be emphasized, education about disease states and healthy lifestyles would be a major focus. Individuals would be taught how to cook, eat, exercise and create strengthened social bonds. They would study their family tree, assess their own likely risk factors for certain disease states and take proactive action to prevent them.

Alas, I do not envision such an optimistic future in our current medical model.

Dr. Timothy Overlock FACP, General Internal Medicine, Texarkana, Texas

For me, to be a physician was my dream and its achievement was a gift of God. It is a privilege at any time to be a physician and this will continue in the future.

The profession itself teaches you caution, patience, science, thoroughness, diligence, precision, exactness, compassion, forgiveness and humility in ways unique to other professions. You have come into the world to save lives and reduce human suffering.

Disease and trauma are deadly enemies that stalk the innocent and against this enemy a physician offers resistance and protection. When one is strong and in good health, one takes these gifts for granted, but when one is stricken with disease one realizes one's own frailty.

Every physician has experienced entering a room wherein a family has gather around the bed of an afflicted loved one. The family feels powerless and in ignorance of what needs to be done to relieve distress or to save a life. While seconds tick away that can mean life or death, the physician asks questions, conducts an examination, makes a diagnosis, gives orders and a remedy is applied and before the very eyes of powerless witnesses a rescue or resuscitation occurs — an apparent miracle.

This is what a physician, by the grace of God, is positioned to do. It is one of the greatest things that anyone can do.

Dr. Emeric Palmer, Internal Medicine, Hospitalist, Consultant and Physician Executive, Chantilly, Virginia

Medicine remains a very viable career today because it offers reasonable income potential, significant job security and holds great promise for personal fulfillment.

The patient-doctor relationship is still one of the most revered professional relationships. It commands significant respect and reputation within communities.

Training in medicine is a very fulfilling experience that begins with the excitement of acceptance and entry into the experience of medical school. Based on one's personality and interests, there is a wide range of specialty options to satisfy any and all desires.

After training, comes the reality of practice. Discussions about such things as productivity, generating enough revenue, performance and quality ensue. Disruptive realities such as advanced practice professionals, telemedicine and technology appear. When these realities coalesce, it is possible for the young physician to feel like the huge world stage that he/she envisioned has become a small space.

Therefore, to succeed in today's world, as you embark on the journey of your medical career to serve your patients, you must: let growth, transformation and knowledge guide you; let population health, interdisciplinary collaboration and process improvement influence your professional interactions and seek wise mentorship — mentorship that anticipates the future. It can and will change your trajectory.

Depending on your desires, I encourage you to choose boldly to become anything from a primary care physician who interacts with her/his patients all day to a "nighthawk" radiologist who interprets images for patients a continent away who you will never directly see or touch. Your career in medicine will be a journey full of promise, opportunities for growth and entrance into a world of unbelievable experiences. There will be no shortage of surprises or affirmation.

Stepping back, the doctor-patient relationship is a two-dimensional construct. There is a third dimension — which I call the "Z axis" — the supportive elements around physicians that facilitate their care and mitigate the risks, challenges and threats to their effectiveness and impact. As you embark on the journey of your medical career, engage and lead the Z axis to find success and sustain a fulfilling career.

———

Dr. Jay Sterns, Internal Medicine and Hospitalist, Burlington, Vermont

The question of whether to advise the pursuit of a career in internal medicine brings to mind a college course whose text book included an article titled *The Sociologic Perspective.* The main point of the article was that the average man, throughout the course of his life may begin to feel that he is being driven by forces beyond his control unless he understands these forces to some degree and prepares accordingly. With this in mind, a career that requires years of study and results in useful skills possessed by few is advisable. An individual so prepared will always be able to provide for his family and himself in addition to having a degree of independence that is very rare in these days of diminished workers' rights and a shift in wealth away from the middle and lower classes.

My opinion cannot be taken as unbiased since everything that is held dear to me can be attributed to my having entered the medical profession. The initial 6 years of medical training in Mexico provided not only a good base of medical knowledge and a second language but a wife and family whose warmth has been beyond my previous comprehension. The privilege of having worked as a locum tenens hospitalist on an Indian reservation as well overseas for the past 17 years has provided my family and me with a unique view of the world and the human condition.

Since satisfaction, both professional and personal, depends on individual perspective and expectations, it must be stated that no particular career path is suited to all. One person's paradise can be the hell of another. Possession of some of the following characteristics might prove useful to those considering a medical career in the year 2017:

- Commitment to the lifelong pursuit of excellence while realizing that perfection is unobtainable.
- The realization that physical and mental health go together.
- The ability to bend rules and regulations for the patient's benefit, without destroying your career. Being able to say "NO" (especially when dealing with non-clinical hospital administrators).
- Acceptance that death is part of life and that doing too much can be just as harmful as doing too little.
- Being able to interact with the most pathetic, downtrodden individuals in our society with the realization that you are actually looking through the mirror into the what might have been had your circumstances been different.
- Acceptance that, while in the midst of apparent chaos, the universe is probably unfolding as it should.
- The ability to be objective in the saddest of situations.
- The realization that, when you are absolutely certain, you might be wrong.

- An ability to laugh when others would cry.
- Comfort in the inexplicable — long forgotten Japanese Gods loved apples and some little girls will always hate blueberries.

If you have some of the above qualities and a lot of determination, go for it. Above all, enjoy every moment of the journey.

———

Dr. Mark F Sullivan Sr, Cardio-Thoracic Surgery, Hagerstown, Maryland

I am pleased my son has chosen to follow me into a career in medicine.

As he does so, I advise him not to be distracted by the external influences impacting the field of medicine. There will always be changes affecting the field, and, in fact, the changes will also change.

What will always remain, and what in essence will never change, is the personal relationship between each patient and her/his physician. This is the most beautiful and by far the most rewarding aspect of the medical profession.

Every patient is unique in their personality, their specific medical problem and in their interaction with you as their physician. As physicians mature throughout their careers and gain knowledge and wisdom in their craft, they also improve their skills in the patient relationship.

The memories a physician will take with him at the end of his career are not the number of correct diagnoses that were made or the number of surgeries that were successful, but rather the special moments of personal encounter with the patients and their families throughout the process of caring for them. These moments are the single factor that makes a career in medicine a privilege that can never be altered.

———

4. *Alex, their reflections, from the heart and written so well, inspire me.*

5. *Through their diverse eyes, I so clearly see. If I were to be granted the opportunity to do it all over again, I would walk away from each yesterday and today start anew.*

6. *Other thoughts?*

Respectfully submitted,
Dr. Mike

Dr. Ed Drawbaugh Comments

These letters speak volumes for themselves. I will comment only on the one from Dr. Lippman. His concerns are quite valid and are echoed by many of my friends who are still actively practicing. Add in the increasing shortage of physicians, and the problems become even more daunting. Yet, having faith in mankind, I trust that current problems will be solved. Future generations of physicians, training in new delivery systems and not having experienced our perceived "good old days" will hopefully find satisfaction in their new world of medicine. It must be so, or we will all suffer terribly.

Baby Rhino, Botswana
EJDMD

II.Place

"A comfort zone is a beautiful place,
but nothing ever grows there."

APOCRYPHAL

10

PENULTIMATE FELLOWSHIP

"Victory is never final and defeat is never fatal."

WINSTON CHURCHILL

The FountainHead WhiteHouse
Alex,

1. *Good morning.*
2. *Thank you for all you do daily so well for so many.*
3. *As mentioned, I am both extremely honored and more than a tad daunted by my assignment to, at your doctor grandfather's request, share my humble wisdom with an aspiring physician. What if my wisdom is imperfect? What if I am uninspiring?*
4. *Honored and daunted, off to a good start and excited to proceed, I find myself stuck in an uncharacteristic tangle of writer's block. Generally, this means I have some serious conscious or unconscious unfinished business to tend to. Indeed, I do.*
5. *More to my anxious point, at this juncture, while encountering some editorial reservation, I feel compelled to relate that I cannot and must not be a salesman for a career in healthcare. Although I fully advocate that you find a career*

as infinitely wonderful and rewarding as mine, I cannot and must not por-
tray that all has been well in my career or will go well in yours. I have often
been on a steep (i.e., painful) learning curve. I have sometimes slipped and
regressed. Somehow though I have miraculously avoided fatal injury and am
here today encouragingly smiling at you.

6. *After review, my job is to share my travel through my tunnel with you. Your*
job is to decipher if and how my journey may apply to yours.

7. *At the end of our communications, I will enumerate some 20 chapters in my*
career — I call them fellowships. If writing Letters to an Aspiring Physician
and sharing these letters with you is to be my final fellowship, to assuage my
conscience, let me now share the pain of my penultimate fellowship. Towards
full disclosure…

It is true that life is what happens when we are making plans. Life has taken
me through some twenty-odd unique and important professional and personal growth opportunities/adventures. Some call them chapters. I refer to
them as fellowships.

Life had taken me to semi-retirement. I was writing my books, surveying
hospitals for a well-recognized firm part-time and playing golf (not necessarily in
that order). Except for the Peggy Lee thing, "Is that all there is?" life was good.

I was flattered when a second national firm recruited me to survey the status
of quality and safety in education of physicians-in-training. Having left my
career a bit early and needing health insurance for my younger wife — I was
Medicare eligible but she was not — I found myself cautiously attracted to the
benefits of full-time employment (and, yes, a full-time salary would be nice too).

It turns out that due to severe travel requirements, the firm was having
difficulty recruiting teams to conform to an aggressive survey schedule. In
contacting me, the recruiter offered me this deal:

- Salutary salary and benefits,
- Prepare (minor) for travel on Sunday,

- Travel and prepare for visit on Monday,
- Survey Tuesday (7 a.m. to 7 p.m.); meet with team and write draft report Tuesday evening,
- Survey Wednesday morning; finish report and present report to site leadership at noon,
- Communicate with next site while at airport and travel home Wednesday evening,
- Complete and submit report and expenses Thursday,
- Use Friday to prepare (major) for next visit and
- Enjoy Saturday off.

This seemed aggressive but I, bullet proof and invincible, was confident that the firm (before, still and always a favorite institution of mine) would not create something impossibly demanding.

I had several requirements:

- Since I lived 90 minutes from the airport, I would require a car and driver to and from as there was no way I could safely drive home exhausted from the airport after midnight on Wednesday,
- Experiencing a well-documented sleep disorder, I would not survey hospitals in distant time zones and
- Recognizing an important professional opportunity that would be physically and mentally demanding, I would remove all other considerations from my life (for, example golf) and concentrate only on making the outlined physical and intellectual challenges work.

Again, life is what happens while making plans. Here is what it actually looked like (for example):

- I was assigned a large program two-time zones away,
- Large programs required an extra day — return was to be late Thursday and everything was pushed back a day,
- Because of threatening weather, I had to leave on Sunday,

- Because of a weather delay, I could not return until Friday,
- Saturday was used to try and catch-up (backwards and forwards),
- Sunday and the new week came relentlessly exactly on time and
- Because of how the large site visit was designed by the firm, Tuesdays and Wednesdays were essentially sleepless for, telling myself the truth, a less than invincible me.

For the first time in my career — never a sick day in my life — I was forced to confront some physical realities and the reality that physical afflictions impact intellectual product. I learned:

- My version of age 66 is not the new 40,
- Quiescent cardiac, dermatologic, ENT, orthopedic, gastrointestinal and urologic conditions became manifest,
- Sleep deprivation was an insurmountable issue and
- Amid this, I had a fairly significant, inconvenient, non-life threatening, acute medical event.

As I was stepping forward to leadership to describe my circumstance and ask for accommodations, leadership stepped forward with an axe. With insincere admiration, I note it was expertly wielded. Severely wounded, I limped into my first career full retreat.

Saying I could not have tried harder, saying I might have been wiser (not taken the position) and saying that if I had been leadership I may have handled it differently, in defeat, I will just leave it at that and move forward.

———

8. *Alex, with this one fell swoop, I am placing my professional and personal inadequacies in plain view. Having done so, I feel I still may have acquired wisdom to impart and I feel my writer's block dissipating.*
9. *Defeated, I am remembering the wise coach's (John Wooden) 1979 wisdom to a defeated young coach (Bill Hodges) after his Larry Bird and Indiana State*

lost to Magic Johnson and Michigan State — *"I am sure you are disappointed, but you conducted yourself most admirably. Disappointment may be quite painful, but it is a temporary thing."* For the record, my disappointment was a temporary thing.

10. *Alex, in these thoughts I find peace of mind. After review, telling myself the truth (always), I am back — I do have some important perceptions for your consideration. Forewarned, you are forearmed. Stop here or read on.*

11. *Other thoughts?*

Respectfully submitted,
Dr. Mike

Dr. Ed Drawbaugh Comments

I perceive two important messages in this particular letter. First, Dr. White is being painfully open about a failure late in his career. By so doing, he cements his credentials as an honest source of information, not a cheerleader. Perhaps the more important point, though, is made in the Churchill quote at the beginning of the section. There will be problems along each and every career path. Expect them, learn from them and move on. As I give this advice, I am remembering William G. T. Shedd, "A ship is safe in harbor, but that's not what ships are for."

11

A Precious Natural Resource

"Privilege is here, and with privilege goes responsibility."

John F Kennedy

The FountainHead WhiteHouse
Alex,

1. *Good morning.*
2. *Thank you for all you do daily so well for so many.*
3. *From my perspective, a conversation regarding the pros and cons of a career in medicine must quickly turn, with admiration, to an appreciation of our most precious natural resource, you — a talented and courageous aspiring physician...*

———

As an aspiring physician, with professional and personal humility intact, please recognize that you are just that — among society's most precious natural resources. Of all the good people born to the world on the day of your birth — I calculate approximately 30,000,000 — you are among the very few who have been provided the gifts to be selected to the honor and privilege of considering a career in medicine. You are among the few, born with natural ability and nurtured in a safe, stimulating environment, who have taken full advantage to be positioned to have significant, salutary impact upon humanity.

Because of nature, nurture and your purposeful dedicated effort, you find yourself, against all odds in this envious position. Much of your circumstance is due to the bestowing of gifts beyond your control. Recognize your good fortune, rejoice in it, be thankful for it and then go forward with wisdom and parlay your privileged position into a long, productive, important, meaningful career that makes a difference.

As I advocate that you capitalize on your circumstance, I encourage you to find the energy and courage to seize every opportunity. I entreat you to take advantage of every advantage bestowed upon you. Recalling Kennedy's wisdom, *"Privilege is here, and with privilege goes responsibility,"* I anticipate you will step forward to responsibility and into a wondrous professional career and personal life.

————◆————

4. *Other thoughts?*

Respectfully submitted,
Dr. Mike

Dr. Edward Drawbaugh Comments

Dr. White makes an important point about privilege and opportunity in this letter. Yet, I believe that the emphasis should be on recognizing and congratulating you, the candidate, for the substantial academic effort required to have reached this point. Perhaps the "take away" thought should be, "With how fortunate you are and how hard you have worked, please carefully consider what wonderful opportunities you have."

————◆————

12

The First Time

"The good physician treats the disease;
The great physician treats the patient."

William Osler

The FountainHead WhiteHouse
Alex,

1. *Good morning.*
2. *Thank you for all you do daily so well for so many.*
3. *Let me share my recollection of the first time I understood the honor, privilege and responsibility of being "the" doctor...*

———————

Except for a few artificial clinical events — "Mike, go talk with this patient for an hour or so and come back and tell me what you observe and hear" — the first year of medical school concentrated on mind and butt-numbing basic science didactics. Although the second year continued with didactics, a classroom introduction to clinical medicine was included. Each week, master clinicians would, in their clinical white coats, step away from their hospital rounds to demonstrate the value of and application of our hard-won didactics. Magically, our dry basic science lexicon was translated into vibrant clinical relevance before our parched eyes and ears.

The conference room was special — an elevated amphitheater providing each of 100 classmates a front row seat. The clinicians were special — masters of advocacy, care, knowledge, interpersonal communications and professionalism. While speaking to the hundred, somehow each spoke only and intimately to me — entrusting and imprinting me with both the art and science of medicine.

I can see the patient as if she were before me now — a young (my age) sophisticated, elegant, beautiful, tall, thin lady. Her history was explored. From birth, she had experienced painful sickle cell anemia crises. An adept, modest exam by the master clinician assessed her general physical condition (heart, lungs, abdomen and extremities) to be normal. With the assistance of the patient, we came to understand how a painful crisis might affect her. She shared her disease's impact on her social, academic and athletic childhood. She was resigned to ultimate cardiac and liver complications of merciful, pain aborting transfusions. Having lost her spleen to repeated micro-infarcts, she spoke of her fear of pneumococcal sepsis. With sadness, she related a decision to remain childless. With love, she called her caring medical team "my family." Without resentment, she reported not infrequent unfeeling, unkind healthcare experiences in childhood, adolescence and adulthood. A pragmatist, she no longer traveled from the region for fear of a crisis in an unenlightened healthcare environment.

With the patient — our expert — remaining present, the lecture began. At its conclusion, a tapestry (advocacy, anatomy, ethics, genetics, hematology, immunology, microbiology, physiology, and psychology) had been expertly woven. For the first time, I appreciated how the application of my knowledge should, could and would miraculously come together.

As one of one hundred, I cared for my first patient that day. As one of one hundred, I became a doctor that day.

—◆—

4. *Alex, this shall always remain one of my most treasured memories.*
5. *Other thoughts?*

Respectfully submitted,
Dr. Mike

Dr. Ed Drawbaugh Comments

One of the most humbling experiences on the journey through medical education is when the student is viewed as part of the team, thereby being allowed to see, hear and touch the patient for the first time. It is at that exciting point that the drudgery of the classroom begins to fade and the wonder of clinical medicine begins. Simultaneously it is a point of awe and frightening responsibility. I remember it well. I wish it were just yesterday.

13

The Medicine Continuum

"When love and skill work together, expect a masterpiece."

John Ruskin

The FountainHead WhiteHouse
Alex,

1. *Good morning.*
2. *Thank you for all you do daily so well for so many.*
3. *Please appreciate an observation of mine that has proven useful in discussions with second year medical students beginning to consider their after-graduation career paths and choices of residency (for example, medicine, obstetrics/gynecology, pediatrics, psychiatry or surgery)…*

In observing the medical student, physicians-in-training and the physicians who trained them, I witnessed uniqueness — personalities, proclivities, learning styles, reactions to clinical experiences, approaches to provision of care and decisions about career choice. Early on, I invented a continuum in medicine that has held up pretty well. Although it shall always remain an inexact science, my continuum concept, for purposes of discussion, continues to show merit. It places psychiatry at one end and neurosurgery at the other. Fleshing it out, for me, the continuum approximates:

Psychiatry; Family Medicine, Internal Medicine, Neurology
Pathology, Radiology
Obstetrics/Gynecology, Ophthalmology, Otolaryngology
General Surgery, Urology, Orthopedics, Neurosurgery

It has been my experience that the ideal circumstance finds each individual physician in a career that most perfectly meets her/his unique and very personal personality and gifts (for example, motor skills) and academic, clinical and lifestyle preferences.

I am remembering countless stories of carefully chosen medicine careers enhancing lives — for example, the gifted athlete who channeled orthopedics into a sports medicine career and the long-distance runner who advanced exercise physiology. Consistent observations led me to the ridiculous, "If selling real estate is your medical passion, go for it. You will do it better with a medical degree." Then, of course, there is Dr. Frank Henry Netter:

- Highly successful commercial artist.
- Family pressure to study medicine.
- City College, New York University Medical School, Bellevue Hospital (surgical internship).
- Successful career as medical illustrator and educator (note: The Frank H. Netter M.D. School of Medicine at Quinnipiac University opened in 2013) combined graphic art with anatomy, physiology, pathology and treatment.
- His Clinical Symposia, subsidized by CIBA, taught thousands of physicians. I learned from them and used them regularly in discussions with students and residents.

- My prized Clinical Symposia collection was lost in a move. Today, I pine for those volumes. As Casey would say, "you could look it up." A good place to start — https://www.us.elsevierhealth.com.

---

4. *Alex, when I was a third-year medical student, CBS's 60 Minutes introduced me to the concept of (and misnomer), "idiot savant." Still inadequately referred to as "autistic savant," there are persons with developmental disabilities who demonstrate profound and prodigious abilities (calculation, art, memory, or musical) far in excess of what would be considered normal.*

5. *From this insight, I remembered: 1) a most normal high school acquaintance's ability to perfectly play seven instruments without lessons or capacity to read music and 2) my inability to master the piano (a musician parent's earnest wish) despite lessons, arduous study and practice. From there came my 60 Minute "aha moment" — each brain is programed with strengths and weaknesses. Recognize your inclinations and go with (and never against) the flow.*

6. *It has been my experience that carefully placing oneself ideally on the above invented medical continuum positions one for life and career-long joy and fulfillment.*

7. *On the other hand, it has been my experience that choosing the wrong discipline for the wrong reason (for example, the born psychiatrist goes into general surgery to appease his surgeon father) may lead to the eternal disharmony of a perpetual up-hill slog.*

8. *I will touch upon the continuum again when considering the struggling physician.*

9. *Should you make your way to medical school, please take care to carefully consider your uniqueness and where on the imperfect imaginary continuum you will find long-term career satisfaction.*

10. *Other thoughts?*

Respectfully submitted,
Dr. Mike

Dr. Edward Drawbaugh Comments

Choosing one's specialty is a very important point during the journey through medical education. There are a multitude of factors that likely influence the decision. Some are internal, some external. In my own case, I recognized that I had the physical ability to perform surgical tasks and that I found it rewarding to do so. Hence, I decided to look for a surgical specialty. At the same time, I was influenced by the residents and faculty of the services through which I rotated. I nearly abandoned my plan to accept a position in an Otolaryngology residency after a rotation in Urology with its very dynamic professor. Ultimately, I think I made the correct choice and stayed with my original plan. The best advice anyone could give the aspiring physician would be to take honest stock of one's abilities/gifts, keep one's eyes and ears open, consider all possibilities and choose a career path which will be both stimulating and satisfying.

14

'BETTER ANGELS' CALLED

"All God's angels come to us disguised."

JAMES RUSSELL LOWELL

The FountainHead WhiteHouse
Alex,

1. *Good morning.*
2. *Thank you for all you do daily so well for so many.*
3. *Dispensing messages one at a time, I struggle as to where to begin. Recognizing no certain answer, I feel compelled to get the concept of a vocation on the table.*
4. *As you consider a career in medicine, I am remembering a relatively recent formative experience that I wish to share with you...*

———————

I, a spouse-described 'LIOM' (legend in own mind), was reviewing a hospital system in New England for The Joint Commission. The facilities under review were geographically dispersed. A junior administrator, who had risen through the clinical ranks, was assigned to chauffeur me about. By necessity, there were long interludes in the car between stops. With my permission, she used the time to explore my perspectives on healthcare issues important to her.

Towards the end of a three-day visit, she asked, "Is our work in healthcare a calling — a vocation — or is it a job?" Although I was most prepared to answer, I took a moment to better understand the word vocation. We agreed upon an Oxford definition, "A person's employment or main occupation, especially regarded as particularly worthy and requiring great dedication."

I framed my answer by remembering a visit as a young faculty member to the Lincoln Memorial where I read his words, "We are not enemies, but friends. We must not be enemies. Though passion may have strained, it must not break our bonds of affection. The mystic chords of memory will swell when again touched, as surely they will be, by the better angels of our nature."

I was thunderstruck. At once I recognized the term, "better angels of our nature," describes my magnificently wonderful colleagues that I work with every day.

From my computer case, I took out a draft manuscript (please see now published *Safer Medical Care for You and Yours — Six Tools for Safe, Effective, Compassionate Care*) and turned to the chapter 'Better Angels' within. Although a tad out of context, the discussion held up well that day.

'BETTER ANGELS'

I have already alluded to our 'Better Angels' on several occasions. Let us step back and consider the wonderful healthcare teams that care for us so well and recognize our obligation to facilitate their complex work.

As we, the complex and vulnerable, present for scheduled or unanticipated emergent care, we fully expect — and are almost never disappointed — that our healthcare professionals (medical, nursing, pharmacy, support and therapy staffs) will be there to care for us. Who are these unfailingly reliable professionals? From my perspective, they are our 'Better Angels' who:

- Are among our best and brightest,

- Have dedicated their professional and personal lives to do meaningful, important work that makes a difference in the service of others,
- Have, through in-depth study and arduous training, achieved breathtaking expertise,
- Somehow have the energy to, on our behalf, step daily into our complex and vulnerable fray and
- Amazingly find the courage to each day strap on their gear, mount their horses and gallop again to our rescue.

5. *Alex, recognizing the investment of our 'Better Angels' in their devoted service to us, my text went on to say we, their patients, are obligated to partner with them in our care.*

Given their dedication and expertise, we may rest assured our 'Better Angels' will, in every case, strive to do their very best for us. In the interest of our safer medical care, I advocate:

- We consciously assist them to work smarter (not harder) on our behalf,
- We be involved in, informed about and responsible for our care,
- We provide them with our organized and accurate *My (Unique and Very) Personal Medical Record* and thereby
- We position our 'Better Angels' to provide us with safe, effective, compassionate care.

———

6. *Alex, surely these 'Better Angels' to whom I refer are addressing a vocation. Requisite expertise, energy, patience, passion and courage cannot be mustered daily if merely showing up for a job.*
7. *Other thoughts?*

Respectfully submitted,
Dr. Mike

Dr. Edward Drawbaugh Comments

The topic in this letter is "a" if not "the" foundational principle underpinning all of the healing arts. Those who are devoted to these endeavors find their work to truly be a vocation, and they derive great personal reward from the help that they give to others. Sadly, medical care today is increasingly encumbered by outside forces, leading to the disenchantment of many of our 'Better Angels' and the conversion of their once proud vocation to a simple job. Yet, those who remain foc*used on the vulnerable souls they serve need never surrender to these outside forces. These individuals are rewarded with a personally fulfilling lifetime vocation.

Calculating Evil Baboon, Botswana
EJDMD

15

SEE THE END

"He has achieved success
Who has lived well, laughed often and loved much;
Who has enjoyed the respect of intelligent men;
Who has filled his niche and accomplished his task;
Who has left the world better than he found it;
Who has always looked for the best in others
And given them the best he had."

BESSIE ANDERSON STANLEY

The FountainHead WhiteHouse
Alex,

1. *Good morning.*
2. *Thank you for all you do daily so well for so many.*
3. *When considering a career, I have found the aspiring physician benefits from appreciating the end result — what might their summative evaluation look like when all is said and done?*
4. *When I stood where you stand today at the entrance to the tunnel that represents a life-long career as a physician, I would have benefitted if someone had stepped forward and said, "Mike, as you begin, see the end."*

5. *Alex, when you are finished you will want your summative (final) evaluation —
   yes, to the end your work will be continuously evaluated — to approximate
   the following fiction. For emphasis, it is written with alternating gender pro-
   nouns. Please tolerate the intentional clumsiness...*

———

Summative Evaluation for Dr. Alex

*A*s *Dr. Alex leaves the profession of medicine and transitions to retirement, we
respectfully submit the following summative evaluation of her performance.
As we do so we address:*

SECTION I. PREREQUISITES

Dr. Alex came into the profession well prepared by her pre-medical college,
medical college, residency and fellowship training. Throughout her career, she
has advanced her education and maintained her certifications consistent with
the urgings of a medical school mentor, "Alex, your MD degree is your license
for the life-time study of medicine." Throughout her career, she has practiced
within the scope of her/his training.

SECTION II. THE SEVEN COMPETENCIES OF THE SUCCESSFUL PHYSICIAN

1. Compassionate Patient Care

Compassionate patient care is among Dr. Alex' strongest competencies. Once
he settled into comfort as a mature physician, teacher and administrator, he
role-modeled the ideal physician/patient relationship. Patients, families, colleagues, trainees and staff could always depend upon his calm, caring, mindful
attention. Coached by insightful mentors, his mission was consistently clear
to all, "create change that benefits all patients."

2. Knowledge

Dr. Alex would readily and comfortably state that, despite career-long study,
she is "not the sharpest tool in the shed." What she lacked in genius, she

made up in preparation and judgment. Each of her patients was provided the benefit of a meticulously assembled (case by case) healthcare team — ensuring that each patient and each patient's outcome were always in the best of hands.

3. Professionalism

Dr. Alex strove to be most professional. To the best of his ability, he would tell himself the truth and would strive to make decisions solely from the perspective of each patient's very personal and unique values, wishes and desires.

4. Interpersonal Communications

Dr. Alex was most articulate with the spoken and written word. She strove to be precise with verbal and non-verbal communications. Dr. Alex was adept in recognizing when her messages were not perceived and would patiently start the communication process over again. She was comfortable with and encouraged disagreement and discussion. As a result, patients, families, colleagues, nursing, pharmacy, trainees and support staff were always well-informed and working in harmony to advance patient care.

5. Practice-based Learning and Improvement (continuous quality improvement)

Dr. Alex was committed to the scrutiny of his work. He learned rapidly (painfully) from his mistakes and, with experience, became efficient in learning (less painfully) from the mistakes of others. As his career progressed, he dedicated himself to the enlightened study, design, implementation and maintenance of standardized hospital processes. His efforts were consistently committed to making the care of the next patient continuously safer.

6. Systems- based Practice (teamwork)

Dr. Alex parlayed her clinical, academic, professionalism and communication competencies and her formal training in quality and teaching into effective teamwork and team leadership.

7. Professional Vitality

While encouraging others to find vitality — a balance between their personal and professional lives — Dr. Alex struggled in this regard. To some extent, his vocation required sacrifice of family and person for the greater good. Without criticism, we recognize this as fact. With anticipation, we hope well-deserved retirement will allow him to explore incompletely addressed relationships and avocations.

Section III: Self-Assessment

As part of his summative evaluation process, Dr. Alex is required to provide a self-assessment. Dr. Alex has submitted:

"I shall be forever grateful to have had the honor, privilege and responsibility of serving as a physician. As I step away, I hope it is perceived that I have striven to be dedicated, committed and accountable to the compassionate care of my patients and to partnership with my colleagues. I hope it is perceived that I have been honest with others and with myself. I regret (minor) that I did not take more time to smell the roses. I regret (major) that my career has come and gone so fast — with so much left to do. I hope it is perceived that, each day:

- I recognized JFK's "privilege is here, and with privilege goes responsibility;"
- To the best of my ability, I respectfully addressed that honor, privilege and responsibility and
- I preserved the honor, privilege and responsibility of my profession for the next generation of physicians who will come forward to care for me and mine.

Section IV. Summative Evaluation

After review, it is our summative evaluation that, as Dr. Alex brings her/his career as a physician to a close, we recognize a superior performance that will serve as a model for the many. We congratulate her/him on her/his efforts. We wish her/him well in future endeavors.

Respectfully submitted,
Dr. Alex' Patients and Families
Dr. Alex' Students, Residents and Fellows
Dr. Alex' Administrative, Board, Nursing, Pharmacy and Physician Colleagues
Dr. Alex' Family and Friends

———

6. *Alex, the opportunity to envision the above impossibly unblemished summative evaluation fiction would have assisted me greatly way back when I was entering the tunnel which came to represent my professional and personal lives. Reading the above paradigm, I now recognize, if prescient, there were priorities I could have, should have and would have organized differently.*

7. *As you appreciate this summative evaluation process addressing the physician's seven competencies (after the ACGME's Dr. David Leach), please take this opportunity to ponder what you will desire your summative evaluation to look like a hundred years from today when your personal all has been given, said and done.*

8. *Other thoughts?*

Respectfully submitted,
Dr. Mike

Dr. Ed Drawbaugh Comments

A common tool in personal development programs is to have the students write a eulogy about how they would hope to be remembered after their passing. This reflection then provides insight about how to live what would be a meaningful life for the individual.

In the current vignette, Dr. White has gone through this exercise hoping to demonstrate to Alex two concepts:

- *The seven competencies Dr. White believes must be mastered by the physician and*
- *The language he would hope would describe his performance as perceived by others.*

Cheetah Brothers, Tanzania
EJDMD

16

Personal Mission Statement

"A relevant personal mission statement
informs leadership practice.
As a self-accountability tool, it is generally
thought of as a behavioral promise."

Dr. Brian D Wong

The FountainHead WhiteHouse
Alex,

1. *Good morning.*
2. *Thank you for all you do daily so well for so many.*
3. *Proudly, I knew and could articulate my institutions' visions and missions (please see: Know Your Business).*
4. *Then, mentor and coach Dr. Brian Wong's book, Heroes Need Not Apply — How to Build a Patient-Accountable Culture without Putting More on Your Plate, steepened my learning curve.*
5. *I readily came to understand that each day, as I saddled up to ride into my executive responsibilities, I needed my personal mission in focus.*

6. *As Chief Medical Officer, assisted by Dr. Wong's insights and input from my Chief Executive Officer, my mission statement evolved…*

———

Dr. Mike White's Personal Mission Statement

- I aspire to partner to create a culture that improves care;
- My chief objective is to facilitate the design, implementation and maintenance of change that benefits all patients;
- I will have most impact on care if I can help others see their role in improving care;
- I will have most impact on care if I empower others in their roles in improving care;
- My staff will be accountable to the patient (not to me);
- I will not have all the answers but I will consistently ask the questions that lead towards safe, timely, efficient, effective, equitable/just, patient-centered care (STEEEP);
- I will be dedicated to teamwork and team leadership;
- To ensure all have a voice to share personal perspectives and challenges and to advance trust, formal brainstorming and root cause analysis will be my primary tools;

Note 1: to best appreciate root cause analysis please review the letter: Root Cause Analysis. Note 2: A Brainstorming (Positive Deviance) Session is integral to the root cause analysis process. At the start of each brainstorming session, the ground rules are reviewed (from Unsafe to Safe — an Impatient Proposal for Safe Patient-centered Care):

1. *Brainstorming rules of engagement are reviewed and accepted: clock-wise rotation, one idea at a time, next idea need not follow-up upon last idea, no denigration of ideas, continue until all ideas are*

extinguished and ideas occurring post-meeting may be brought to attention of facilitator and added after the conclusion of the meeting.

2. *In addition, the root cause analysis team:*

   - *Reaffirms it functions in confidential peer review protected session,*
   - *Humbly appreciates the unfairness of applying the always infallible 'retrospectoscope' in the calm of the conference room to the scrutiny of complex 'chaordic' (i.e., both chaotic and organized) circumstances that evolved in real-time and*
   - *Remembers this continuous quality improvement root cause analysis process addresses "systems — not people." The evaluation of the individual proceeds through a just and equitable peer review process (please review the letter: Justice).*

- Our solutions will always come back to obvious and explained patient benefit;
- I will evaluate my staff and myself on seven competencies (care, knowledge, communications, professionalism, continuous improvement, teamwork/team leadership and vitality (balance between professional and personal lives) and
- As my staff strives for patient-centered care, I will assist their and my advancement from beginner to proficient and then ever onward towards mastery.

---

7. *Alex, today as author, consultant, mentor and self-acclaimed legend in own mind, my personal mission statement is much different.*
8. *As a college pre-med undergrad, what does yours look like?*
9. *As a medical student, what will it evolve to?*
10. *Other thoughts?*

Respectfully submitted,
Dr. Mike

Dr. Edward Drawbaugh Comments

I suspect that very few medical students, let alone undergraduates, have formal, written personal mission statements. Indeed, I doubt that many fully-trained physicians have gone through the process. Yet, one can easily see the utility of doing so. Everyone has a general idea of what they want to be and do, but a personal mission statement allows one to focus time and energy on only those things which help in the mission.

Curious Baby Elephant, Botswana

EJDMD

17

A Sample Contract

The FountainHead WhiteHouse
Alex,

1. *Good morning.*
2. *Thank you for all you do daily so well for so many.*
3. *As you have considered what a career summative evaluation and personal mission statement might approximate, at this very early, imperfect juncture, I want to introduce you to what a physician's contract might look like.*
4. *As a last dinosaur coming out of residency, I went into solo private practice. Thereafter, I held several corporate positions that required a contract between physician (me) and my institution. Ultimately, I was empowered to create the contract between the physician and institution. As an example...*

Institution's Logo

Date

Dear Doctor Example,

Physician and Institution will enter into a three-year agreement beginning xx/xx/xxxx with a renewal option after an annual evaluation. The agreement provides:

I. Physician's Professional Requirements:

1. The Physician will serve as general internal medicine faculty.
2. The Physician will report to the department chair.
3. The Physician will devote 100% of professional effort to this faculty position.
4. The Physician will work in support of the Institution's vision and mission.
5. The Physician will work in support of department chair and residency program director.
6. When carrying out his academic, clinical and research duties, the Physician will role-model seven competencies:
   a. Compassionate Care
   b. Medical Knowledge
   c. Interpersonal Communications
   d. Professionalism
   e. Continuous Quality Improvement
   f. Team (teamwork and leadership)
   g. Vitality (balance between professional and personal lives)
7. Physician will make a best-faith effort to provide Institution all required accurate and timely documentation needed to perform professional billing on behalf of the Physician.
8. Physician will maintain status as a member in good standing of the Institution's medical/dental staff for the entire duration of this agreement.
9. Physician will maintain board certification in internal medicine for the entire duration of this agreement.

II. Institution's Requirements

1. The Institution will provide the Physician with:
   a. An annual salary of $###,###.##. This will be paid in equal monthly installments according to the institution's payroll procedures.

b. Professional liability scope of services coverage for services pursuant to this agreement. If necessary, any tail coverage will be provided by the Institution.

c. $#,### per year towards CME and Leadership activities (materials, seminars, conferences) approved by the department chair. With the pre-approval of department chair, the Physician may have up to 10 days per year to attend CME and Leadership conferences.

d. Reimbursement of licenses and dues up to a maximum of $####.## for local state and national societies, medical staff dues, internal medicine boards and appropriate subscriptions and texts.

e. Medical/Vision/Dental insurance for Physician and family per the Institution's options.

f. Executive salary continuance and bonus opportunity in accordance with Institution's senior management benefit level.

g. Long-term disability providing for 70% of Physician's salary.

h. Life insurance per Institution's policy for non-union employees.

i. Eligibility to enroll in Institution's 401k plan.

j. Eligibility to enroll in flexible spending accounts.

k. Eligibility for seven paid holidays.

l. Eligibility for 31 days paid time off. Scheduled time-off requires pre-approval of department chair. A maximum of 10 unused days may be carried over to the next contract year.

III. Mutual understanding between Physician and Institution

1. All prior agreements are void.

2. Either party may cancel this policy with 365-day notice to the other party.

3. The Physician will participate in an annual evaluation process conducted by the department chair.

4. All services provided by the Physician and the Institution will conform to:

   a. All local, state and federal laws and regulations;

b. Standards of certifying agencies (for example, The Joint Commission);
c. Standards of third party payers (for example, Medicare):
d. Medical-Dental Staff rules and regulations and appointment/re-appointment requirements;
e. Institutional privacy requirements and
f. All Institutional quality, safety and utilization management requirements.

IV. AGREEMENT

If you agree with the above, please sign and date below.

Accepted:

_____   _____
Dr. Example   Date
General Internal Medicine

_____   _____
Dr. Osler   Date
Department Chair

———— ◆ ————

5. *Alex, at this time, this is probably as interesting as the science of paint drying.*
6. *Let me make it a tad more fascinating:*
   - *I have seen too many young doctors engage a lawyer to draft a contract. Many billable hours later, the doctor and institution remain at odds. Often, the process becomes unnecessarily confrontational,*
   - *A better approach is for physician to discuss requirements with the institution and then receive a draft contract from the institution. Thereafter, an hour's review by an attorney, will efficiently/affordably suggest desired changes and clarifications or*

- *With an institution's draft contract in one hand and the above example in the other, craft your own.*

7. *Finally, I have had too many young doctors proudly show me a contract that begins, "This is a ten-year contract" then goes on to include this language, "Either party may terminate with 90-day notice" — a 90-day contract.*

8. *Other thoughts?*

Respectfully submitted,
Dr. Mike

Dr. Ed Drawbaugh Comments

No one (I hope) would accept a new position without an employment contract. My suggestions to arrive at an agreement with the potential employer as easily and inexpensively as possible are similar to Dr. White's. Work out the details with your superior before the lawyers get involved. Let the institution or group you are joining pay its lawyers to put your verbal agreement in writing, understanding that they represent the employer and will be looking to protect them more than you. Next, have your attorney review the document and be certain that it is fair to you. NEVER, EVER, sign any legally binding document without having first had it reviewed by your own competent legal counsel.

A minor disagreement with Dr. White – perhaps a 90-day termination clause is too short, but I would not want to be bound by contract to stay in a position that I hated and could not change for an entire year. Perhaps something between the two?

———

18

THE MEDICAL SCHOOL INTERVIEW

"Prior preparation prevents poor performance."

JAMES BAKER

The FountainHead WhiteHouse
Alex,

1. *Good morning.*
2. *Thank you for all you do daily so well for so many.*
3. *A most influential mentor has told me to avoid being pedantic. Sound advice I share with you. Notwithstanding, an official approaching 'pedanticism' alert flag is raised.*
4. *From time to time, I find myself assisting young people with preparing for the medical school interview. I perceive a list of "what to do" comes across as (perish the thought) pedantic. So I turn to Einstein's most powerful force in the universe — the charismatic story.*
5. *If a bit boring on this halcyon day, please place in "parking lot" for a later date when anxiety provoking circumstance may assign value...*

———

Truth be told, the thought of the meeting was a bit of a bother. Having excelled in college and having already participated in several interviews, what could an ancient possibly teach her about strategically approaching her medical school interview? Nevertheless, mostly to appease her Dr. Dad, a colleague of the ancient, she kept the appointment.

At the ancient's request, she brought her mother along — protection for him from a millennial skeptic. The three met at his kitchen table with a bay window view of the 17th tee. After offering sweet tea, he got right to the bitter business at hand.

"Today I have the honor and privilege to share my humble perspectives on a career in medicine with a qualified candidate. Cutting to the chase: if medicine is for you, I give you every encouragement and if I were smarter, my message would be better.

As is so often the case, after today, impacted by you, I will be wiser. I feel very privileged to be provided with this opportunity to interface and learn from you. Always telling you the truth, in return, you will (a scary thought) be affected by me."

He mentioned, without prioritization or embellishments his credentials for their conversation, "blue-collar kid, pharmacy clerk, college student, medical student, intern and resident, practicing internist, faculty member, program director, department chair, chief medical officer, national consultant, author and patient = LIOM (legend in own mind)."

With too much to talk about, the conversation would be limited to approaching the medical school interview. Deservedly confident to a fault, the young lady was nonetheless all sixes and sevens about her upcoming interviews. Sadly, her college had offered no guidance. Left to her own devices, she was increasingly making the simple complex. Her senior coach sensed her unease, had her Google sangfroid and set out to make her preparations efficient and effective.

Confirming the millennial before him understood the concept of an index card (she, in fact, had seen one once), he placed four before her:

1. The face of the first index card read **KINDERGARTEN.** On the rear it stated:

Remember the respectful common sense that your family and your formative teachers instilled in you:

- Rested,
- On time,
- Coiffured,
- Pressed and polished,
- Controversies ameliorated (for example, tattoos covered),
- Attentive (smart phone off) and
- Assertively polite (handshake, eye contact, queries and responses).

2. The face of the second index card read **INTERVIEW SANDWICH.** On the rear it stated:

Believe[x] and convey:

- Bottom slice of bread: thank you for expending the time, energy and resources to grant me this interview. I am most grateful to have been provided this opportunity.
- Peanut butter and jelly middle: please be assured that if I am able to matriculate into your medical school class, I will strive each day to excel in my basic sciences and clinical rotations and then go on to excel in residency, fellowship training, practice and leadership. From the beginning, I shall endeavor to be a consummate professional and citizen.
- Top slice of bread: again, thank you for expending the time, energy and resources to grant me this interview. I am most grateful to have been provided this opportunity.

˟ *Note: if you do not believe these thoughts, do not attempt to convey. Cancel the interview and regroup.*

3. The face of the third index card read **BE PREPARED**. On the rear it stated:

Be prepared to provide accurate, interesting answers to anticipated and unanticipated obvious questions:

*   What was your first job?
*   What circumstances have you experienced that challenged you? How did you rise to the challenge?
*   What have you found most exciting about college? Why?
*   What individual(s) has/have most inspired you? How?
*   What is your greatest strength?
*   What is your greatest weakness?
*   Why do you desire a career in medicine will bring to you?
*   What do you desire your medical career to look like?

4. The face of the fourth index card read **BE PHILOSOPHICAL**. On the rear it stated:

Be prepared to wax philosophically about concepts that education and experience have made important to you. For example:

*   What are your life organizing principles?
*   How do the concepts quality and value pertain to your life?
*   Is medicine a vocation/calling or a job?
*   Why might a carefully selected medical student fail to have a satisfying professional career and personal life?
*   Tell me about a challenge/case that you addressed and how it impacted you?

- How will you prepare for your standardized exams?
- What do you want your summative evaluations from medical school, residency and fellowship to look like?

As the story goes, the medical school interview process took on new dimensions for the millennial. Common words — perspective, experience and wisdom — found new meaning.

———•———

6. *Alex, whenever coaching about the interview, I would recommend college admissions officer (Dartmouth) Rebecca Sabky's insightful New York Times Op-Ed: Check This Box if You're a Good Person.*
7. *I observe preparations for interview always provide applicants with a huge secondary gain — connection with and exploration of the serious implications of their career choice.*
8. *Other thoughts?*

Respectfully submitted,
Dr. Mike

Dr. Ed Drawbaugh Comments

In addition to the questions outlined above, I might ask, "Leaving out personal details, tell us about an episode of failure in your life, what you learned from it and how it has made you better."

———•———

19

DISTRACTION AND THE POST-BACCALAUREATE PRE-MED

"That's ten pounds of crazy in a five-pound bag."

APOCRYPHAL

The FountainHead WhiteHouse
Alex,

1. *Good morning.*
2. *Thank you for all you do daily so well for so many.*
3. *From time to time I receive a request to assist a deserving applicant connect with an elusive medical school interview. Although the requests are all different, at the same time they are much the same. Consider a story with two upfront messages:*
   - *Inefficient (distracted) pre-med and*
   - *The post-baccalaureate pre-med.*
4. *Note for clarification, this discussion does not apply to the mature first career individual who returns for pre-med prerequisites to pursue medicine as a second career. For an enlightened discussion of this, please refer to Cecilia*

Capuzzi Simon's thoughtful April 2012 New York Times': A Second Opinion: The Post-Baccalaureate...

———

The young lady was gifted. While her pre-med peers plodded, she floated like a god above.

As she matriculated into her collegiate pre-med studies at a fine university with a strong record for placing pre-med students into medical school, her agenda was robust. Her goals included (in four years): pre-med prerequisites (major); broadcast journalism (minor); and NCAA collegiate golf.

Her admirable goals were incompatible with achievable logistics. Golf, a two-semester sport, a daylight sport and a travel sport (at least 16 weeks away from campus each year) was an uncompromising master. Classes and labs were regularly missed. Requirements for summer media internships and competitive golf prevented concentrated summer scientific study.

When applying for medical school, her application reflected glorious recommendations, outstanding golf (All American), solid academic grades, sketchy science grades and middling MCATs. Shockingly, expected invitations to medical school interviews were not forthcoming.

A powerful friend of a powerful friend set her up with a powerful LIOM (legend in own mind) mentor (me) for the purpose of weaseling an interview. Instead, as a tonic, a dose of reality was administered. To wit (the bad news):

- Medical school positions are societal treasures,
- Medical schools may not be profligate,
- Given an over-qualified applicant pool, medical schools need not/ must not take chances and
- Your resume (performance in sciences; performance on standardized tests) reflects risk.

Then, the good news spin followed. She was encouraged to step back and proudly perceive that after four years:

- You have a pre-med major and a broadcast journalism minor,
- You have a "masters" degree in golf,
- You are leaving college debt free,
- Everyone thinks highly of you and most importantly
- Unlike many of your peers, you have seen the world and with a mature understanding of many alternatives recognize medicine is for you.

At once, she appreciated and treasured her accomplishments. Despite no invitations for medical school interview, her collegiate career had been a full-monty, a grand slam and a rare Pittsburgh's Myron Cope "double yoi." With perspective she recognized, as the kids say, "I have the goods." Proud, she stepped forward.

She entered a carefully chosen two-year post-baccalaureate pre-med program. In her first year, she aced her subjects, enhanced her MCATs, reported the weekend sports news on local TV and maintained her standing as a leading amateur golfer. With that, multiple medical schools had seen enough to know this was a serious aspiring physician, removed their reservations and admitted her that September.

Where has her journey taken her? There was pressure for her to pursue sports medicine. Others thought it logical for her to consult for network news. But life (that which happens while making plans) took her to family medicine in small town North Carolina. Today, living with a view of the 11th green, she serves as department chair, residency program director and perennial lady club champion.

———◆———

5. *Alex, from my perspective, this is all good. After review, there is no wasted effort here. Coordination of time and space may not be criticized. The young lady's aggressive, diverse, undergrad curriculum prepared her well.*

6. *Important to me (my bias) — when mounting educational debt is not an is-sue, a rush to the MD degree is not paramount.*
7. *Other thoughts?*

Respectfully submitted,
Dr. Mike

Golden Eagle, Tanzania
EJDMD

20

A Mid-Career Change

"Looking farther than you'll ever hope to see,
takes you places you don't know..."

Dan Fogelberg

The FountainHead WhiteHouse
Alex,

1. *Good morning.*
2. *Thank you for all you do daily so well for so many.*
3. *Some consider medicine as a second career. Here are the thoughts that one articulate individual, in the midst of a most successful career (social service) now heading for medicine, shared with me several years ago. Although, perhaps not relevant to you now, I anticipate you may find her thoughts and tone useful. Note: as she writes, you will note she has read ahead...*

———

Dr. Mike,

I tremendously appreciate you entrusting me with a draft of *Letters to an Aspiring Physician.* Your personal stories and reflections help me

93

better understand how a career in medicine is often a life-long walk on a tight rope, a continual balance of time, money, resources, relationships and expectations — albeit a balancing act with grand rewards if medicine is a true calling and you plan well and make good decisions.

I don't know if sharing personal stories is difficult for you. I think it takes a tremendous amount of courage. You do it gracefully with humor and obvious caring for the reader. Each letter offers principles (for example, quality and evaluation) that I intend to apply to my own work.

I do feel similarly to you regarding medicine as a spiritual calling and I do want to craft a career that reflects my personal philosophy.

Your wisdom on financing medical studies is particularly meaningful for me as an older (non-traditional) student. I am starting at the beginning of the path with taking GREs and trying to collect the required pre-med courses either on my own or through a pre-med/post-bac program. The programs are all, of course, expensive. I am trying to determine if completing a year-long intensive out of state program or taking the pay-for-it-as-you-go approach, and taking longer to complete is better.

Some post-baccalaureate pre-med programs "guarantee" "successful" graduates admission to their medical school. Understanding the tremendous investment of treasure and time required, this promise is very attractive to me. Then the rub — to realize the promise, one must meet imperfectly defined requirements of the "successful" graduate. Although providing only a whiff of security on a still terrifying foundation of a very big if, with confidence in myself, I will likely go down this path.

I am also grateful for your advice to determine if government or other programs will pay med school tuition. I have been considering military programs that provide tuition, reimbursement and a stipend during school in exchange for a specified number of years of service. For me, such a program is the only real option.

Needless to say, if I had a magic wand and could do it all over again — your golfer's Mulligan —I would find a straighter path: pre-med, medical school, the joys and tribulations of training and then onto my professional career and personal life. But, as Ben Hogan counsels, "The most important shot is your next shot."

Again, thank you so much for sharing your work (and your golf philosophy) with me.

Sincerely,

Amy

---

4. *Alex, although each of us is unique and specific, our journeys are often much the same. I anticipate there may be a phrase or two in the above letter that will, some place in time and space, resonate in a meaningful way with you.*

5. *Other thoughts?*

Respectfully submitted,
Dr. Mike

Dr. Ed Drawbaugh Comments

The road to a medical career need not be straight. There were several second-career students in my medical school class – one with a PhD in electrical engineering! Others had taken a year or two to complete pre-med requirements similar to the story above. My first-year roommate came back from a four-year stint in the Navy, including time in Vietnam. All went on to become fine physicians. I am privileged to have a close relative who entered medical school at the age of 30, graduated second in her class from a prestigious medical school and went on to enjoy a long and satisfying career.

21

RANK

"It's not who you are that holds you back,
It's who you think you're not."

DENIS WAITLEY

The FountainHead WhiteHouse
Alex,

1. *Good morning.*
2. *Thank you for all you do daily so well for so many.*
3. *I had written more than forty letters/thoughts to you for consideration. And then I found, I had neglected one — one so important it deserves early attention. So let me squeeze it in here…*

—◆—

The residency program had a fine academic and clinical reputation. In addition, it was located in an attractive city in a desirable region of the country. Therefore, it attracted many qualified applicants.

The program director had several hard and fast rules for the faculty regarding resident recruitment. Since the residency's academic, clinical and interpersonal culture would only be as strong as its weakest resident:

- Recruitment efforts would be tireless,
- All qualified applicants would be interviewed,
- Nothing/no one would be taken for granted and
- After completion of interviews, applicants would be ranked exactly as to their academic, clinical and interpersonal worthiness and would be matched accordingly.

Predictably, the top several applicants — on their way towards Nobel Prizes in Medicine — insightfully chose programs more compatible (academics, reputation, research, etc.) with their professional and personal goals.

Predictably, the residency program matched with a cadre of most talented aspiring physicians. Its academic, clinical and interpersonal culture was maintained.

Then the unpredictable — each year an "intern of the year" was democratically elected by peers, faculty and nursing. In retrospect, the winner was from the bottom of the match list. Two years running, it was the last applicant matched.

As junior faculty, I was intrigued. I went back and scrutinized the recruitment folders for process clues. A couple of factors stood out:

- Interviewers (me included) may have placed emphasis on the charming interview (appearance, agreeableness, etc.) and
- Medical school performance (grades, class rank, standardized scores and letters of reference) were imperfect predictors of who would have the energy, knowledge, interpersonal communication, professionalism, team building and continuous improvement skills to daily provide comprehensive, compassionate care.

As I moved on in my career, I brought this information with me. I continued to recruit the best and brightest. However, I took care to have unqualified robust expectations for each aspiring physician entrusted to my programs. And predictably, panning for gold, the unpredictable (those with the highest specific gravity — the truly gifted golden ones) remained in the pan.

———————

4. *Alex, the imperfection of the recruitment process may amuse you. Be entertained and enjoy.*
5. *However, please find my message to you. Mr. Waitley, above, has it right. Although many may want to read you by your cover, don't allow it. Your potential is not the sum of isolated encounters and arbitrary scores. You are the story of compassion, dedication, expertise and will told between the covers.*
6. *Other thoughts?*

Respectfully submitted,
Dr. Mike

Dr. Ed Drawbaugh Comments:

"You are the story of compassion, dedication, expertise and will told between the covers." To which I add, your life stands in front of you. Whether you choose medicine or some other path, give it everything you have and enjoy the journey.

———————

III. Core Curriculum

"They know enough who know how to learn."

Henry Brooks Adams

22

A Toltec Master

"Quiet the mind, and the soul will speak."

Ma Jaya Sati Bhagavati

The FountainHead WhiteHouse
Alex,

1. *Good morning.*
2. *Thank you for all you do daily so well for so many.*
3. *Having obsessed with my editorial staff about the order of these letters/messages, after due diligence, I recognize an irresolvable conundrum. After review, the order is best decided by the reader — again you have permission to/ are encouraged to explore.*
4. *Relieved and moving on, let me share an all too true fiction for your consideration. For the record, this kind intervention forever changed me...*

The senior physician was invited to accompany a master healthcare thought leader, consultant and author, Dr. Brian Wong, on a consultation in the

Northwest. Expecting technical assignments, he asked how he might prepare. His unanticipated task, "Familiarize yourself with the concept, Toltec Master." An internet search soon had him immersed in Don Miguel Ruiz's *The Four Agreements*. From that day, he has striven to follow six steps to personal freedom:

1. Tell yourself the truth,
2. Be meticulously faithful to your word,
3. Always do your best. Be unfailingly committed to quality — work done right the first time with zero defects (i.e., done right; on time; within budget),
4. Do not take things personally — do not be affected by the perspectives of others,
5. Do not make assumptions about the motives behind the behavior of others and
6. Remain eternally capable of transformation.

This unanticipated assignment provided the senior physician meaning, peace and tranquility in his professional career and his personal life. Wisely guided serendipity gloriously changed him forever. Life, he continually observes, works that way.

———

5. *Alex, of course this is all about me. Whenever lost without a compass, I unfailingly fall back to these six steps towards freedom and my way again becomes clear.*
6. *Other thoughts?*

Respectfully submitted,
Dr. Mike

Dr. Edward Drawbaugh Comments

This letter provides important guiding principles to achieve a personally satisfying and fulfilling life regardless of one's career path. I wish I had become acquainted with these teachings earlier in my life, as I learned many of them from the "school of hard knocks." I find conforming to #5 especially difficult and have to remind myself regularly to follow its directive. A parallel thought from Covey's "Seven Habits of Highly Effective People" states, "Seek first to understand, then be understood." I highly recommend that work as additional reading for any and all.

Grooming Lion Cub, Tanzania
EJDMD

23

KNOW YOUR BUSINESS

"To succeed in business, to reach the top,
an individual must know all it is possible
to know about that business."

J PAUL GETTY

The FountainHead WhiteHouse
Alex,

1. *Good morning.*
2. *Thank you for all you do daily so well for so many.*
3. *In life, we strive to advance from novice to beginner and on through competent and proficient and towards expert and master (from Hubert and Stuart Dreyfus).*
4. *Each summer, the family and I would get away to the Adirondacks (the importance of getting away (escape) is a topic for another letter, Avocation and Escape) and find our way to the Vermont farm where the master farmer, CEO and entrepreneur, Mr. Bill Gormly, would hold court. Among his sometimes humorous but always accurate, insightful, consistent messages, the requirement to "know your business" was paramount.*

5. *As you consider a career in healthcare it is critical that you explore and come to know your business. Provided my experience and training, I have come to "know" the business of healthcare and share the following thoughts with you...*

———

Your Business as a Patient and Family Member

As I have matured in life and in medicine, as I have increasingly become an advocate for my family seeking healthcare and as I myself have become a patient, I have become a more complete physician. That has come as a surprise to me. With wisdom, I recognize each complex and vulnerable patient has an obligation to be involved in, informed about and responsible for her/his own healthcare. Each must position her/himself to enable and receive safe, effective and compassionate care. Each is in the business of facilitating the work of the 'Better Angels' that assemble to care for us so well. In the process, each involved, informed and responsible patient, will nurture, promote and preserve our 'Better Angels" professional and personal vitality so they will have the energy and courage to carry on in our behalf.

Your Business as a Medical Student

When I was a second-year medical student at Albany Med, a senior physician and mentor, Dr. Eugene Furth, defined my business for me, "Mike, your MD degree is your license for the lifetime study of medicine." From that moment, his words of wisdom provided me with valuable and necessary career focus.

As a young practicing internist on vacation at the Vermont farm, exhausted by the honor, privilege and responsibility of practice and unencumbered by the work of running a farm, I suggested to my master mentor host, "Perhaps I should leave medicine and open a breakfast sandwich shop (by day) and a tavern (by night)." Saving me, he so rightly scoffed, "At least three businesses you know nothing about." And I would joyfully return to the wonders of my business — the lifetime study and application of medicine.

Your Business as a Physician-in Training

When you address your training, you are in the business of:

- Becoming expert in your chosen field,
- Becoming a proficient team member and
- Becoming a proficient team leader

so that you may effectively partner to care for the increasingly complex and vulnerable patients that will be entrusted to you.

Your HealthCare Institution's Business

It is imperative that you understand and support, and, when provided the opportunity, partner to lead the work of your institution's executive leadership. You must understand and be able to articulate your institution's mission (i.e., its business). With experience, I came to understand:

"**Whereas:** HealthCare Value equates to (=):

- Compassionate medical care +
- Quality outcomes +
- Patient and staff safety +
- Customer (patient, family and community) satisfaction +
- Patient advocacy +
- Professional (medical, nursing, pharmacy, support and therapy staff) vitality

Balanced by (÷)

- Resource utilization/cost and

Whereas: each individual patient is entitled to:

- Safe
- Timely
- Efficient
- Effective
- Equitable/Just
- Compassionate, Patient-Centered Care

Then: the institution's business/mission is to strive daily to deliver HealthCare Value to the increasingly complex and vulnerable individuals and communities it is privileged to serve through the daily provision of safe, timely, efficient, effective, equitable/just, compassionate patient-centered care to each individual patient.

Your Business: Self-Assessment

When all is said and done, you are in the business of satisfactorily — to your standards per your self-assessment — addressing seven competencies:

- Care
- Knowledge
- Professionalism
- Interpersonal Communications
- Continuous Improvement
- Teamwork and Team Leadership
- Vitality (balance between professional and personal lives)

6. *Alex, in my experience, this clarity of purpose — knowing your business — powerfully guides the executive decisions you will face. Know and stay true to your business and complexity will fall into place.*
7. *Other thoughts?*

Respectfully submitted,
Dr. Mike

Dr. Edward Drawbaugh Comments

There is great wisdom in this section. To know who you are, where you are and what you need to know and do is a primary requirement for success in any endeavor. Following that consciousness with the idea of "sticking to one's knitting" and not being distracted to pursue other things is valuable advice.

24

FEDORA

"A lot of people have gone further than they thought they could because someone else thought they could."

ANONYMOUS

The FountainHead WhiteHouse
Alex,

1. *Good morning.*
2. *Thank you for all you do daily so well for so many.*
3. *Today I wish to speak to the importance of mentors. Take care to find them. Once identified, treasure them and then emulate them. Mine are addressed in acknowledgments. Although not all are aware that I am a mentee, each touched and changed me in a personal way with a from the heart authentic message.*
4. *Speaking to David Feherty regarding her mentor, National Security Advisor Brent Skokroff, Condoleezza Rice said, "We have this conceit — I got there on my own. Nobody truly gets there on her/his own. There is always someone who advocates or cares for you as a truly important mentor." When speaking with sports psychologist and author Dr. Rob Bell about his new book, No One*

gets There Alone, he emphasizes a mentoring feedback cycle, "A better YOU makes a better US and a better US makes a better YOU."

5. *To begin to make my point, I will: 1) provide a definition of fedora: a soft felt or velvet medium-brimmed hat, usually with a band and 2) burden you with an opaque assignment — please ascertain the origin of the word fedora. Then consider...*

———◆———

Dr. Robert Cassidy, an eminent neurologist in Schenectady, now deceased, was among my most important mentors. The attributes that made him "mentor worthy" included his being: a brilliant clinician, a patient teacher, a compassionate doctor, a consummate professional and a humble individual who could/would slow down and, as if time had no meaning, connect with a nascent me.

Early on in my six-week third-year medical student neurology rotation with him, he ascertained I would latch on as a project. As a show of agreement, his first move was to assign me a task — the purchase of a fedora from a next-to-new shop.

With my two-dollar fedora in hand, he showed me to the office hat rack and instructed that, each day at quitting time I must check my hat band for "Dr. Bob notes" — terse, sometimes opaque, hints towards wisdom and growth.

We spent long days together. As he diagnosed and treated the unwell, he scrutinized and improved me. My deficiencies (cultural voids) were readily diagnosed. Insightful tonics (hat band missives) were expertly administered. Recalling examples:

- Detecting arrogance, I was assigned, without explanation, "*schadenfreude?*"
- Confused by marriage, "whither thou goest?"
- Pondering why so few (5/100) women were in my medical school class, "Rachel Carson?"

After a long day, instead of heading home, I went to the Union College library (no Google-connected smart phones then) to research and grow in the understanding of insensitive delight, Ruth's hymn and gender discrimination.

Of course, I was attracted to neurology and the promise of following his footsteps to a Chicago residency and the source of the fedora system — his neurology department chair. But, I came to understand that neurology's too much diagnosis, too little treatment and not enough hope — it is so much better in 2017 — was not for me. So, having, wrongly abandoned psychiatry, I left neurology behind and gravitated to medicine.

Thanks to Dr. Robert Cassidy's mentoring, as an internist I was exceptionally skilled in neurology; I was always in search of deeper meanings in life and I consulted encyclopedias as often as medical texts.

———

6. *Alex, years later (1988 and beyond), society became, if not entirely hatless, certainly fedora-less. Nevertheless, my office had a hat rack where students and residents hung (ever harder to find) used banded fedoras — so perfect for inserting a perceived necessary terse "Dr. Mike" missive, for example, "sang-froid?" — sending the so talented, unnecessarily anxious learner in search of calm.*

7. *Mentors possess the power of primers — caps that ignite the charge in an explosive. "Throw off the bowlines. Sail away from the safe harbor. Catch the trade winds in your sails. Explore. Dream. Discover," Mark Twain tells us. "A ship is safe in harbor but that is not what ships are for," counsels William G. T. Shedd.*

8. *As an aside and stating the obvious, note the power of relevant quotes. I encourage you to collect them, like priceless gems, and adroitly display them when the time feels right.*

9. *Other thoughts?*

Respectfully submitted,
Dr. Mike

Dr. Ed Drawbaugh Comments

A committed mentor is a priceless resource for students in all fields of endeavor. Sadly, they are not necessarily in great supply. Those who are fortunate enough to find one should cherish the relationship and take to heart the lessons offered.

Just Waking Up Leopard, Tanzania
EJDMD

25

QUALITY AND VALUE

*"It is the quality of our work which will
please God and not the quantity."*

MAHATMA GANDHI

*The FountainHead WhiteHouse
Alex,*

1. *Good morning.*
2. *Thank you for all you do daily so well for so many.*
3. *I sense we are somewhere in the leisurely middle of many (not entirely) discon-
nected concepts.*
4. *At this juncture, I feel compelled to expose you to: quality and value; the
concept 'charodic'; power grabs; root cause analysis; the just culture and the
struggling physician.*
5. *The next several letters, representing a bit of heavy lifting, flow together as
quality and justice primer.*
6. *For clarification, there will no written or oral exam.*
7. *Starting with quality and value — sometimes necessary change just comes to
you...*

My brilliant, caring, quite senior to me, hospital President/CEO Mr. Howard Jones, provided me, the too young and struggling physician executive, with the opportunity to spend time with a quality "guru" in Florida — Dr. Phil Crosby. All expenses were paid for an in-depth course at the Crosby Quality College.

Golf clubs were packed and transported but never used. An intense week was spent beside industrial engineering masters. Like my atomic energy engineer classmates, I was forever changed. With their mentoring, I came to understand:

1. All work is a process that can be studied and improved — including the complex work of physicians and staff providing patient care.
2. For quality to be realized both parties in a transaction, supplier and customer, must mutually agree upon the requirements of the transaction.
3. With #1 and #2 understood, quality has four absolutes:
   - *A Definition:* conformance to mutually agreed upon requirements,
   - *A Standard* (an attitude)*:* done right the first time with zero defects (done right; on time; within budget),
   - *A Measurement:* a transparent tally of the cost of errors/mistakes and
   - *A System:* prevention — the continuous recognition of opportunities for improvement and the continuous design, implementation and maintenance of ever improving processes.

Note: prevention is the arduous/hard part.

From that week on, I journeyed continuously forward towards quality in my professional and personal lives and my work and my relationships improved.

Sometime later, I came to understand the concept of Value — quality divided by cost. The gifts of expertise in quality and value bestowed upon me by Mr. Jones changed my career and changed my professional and my personal lives. With an understanding that value — safe, timely, efficient, effective, equitable/just, compassionate patient-centered care (STEEEP) at the best price — was the target for every administrative and personal decision, I became proficient in consistent executive decision making.

---

8. *Alex, as I share this epiphany with you, I encourage you to:*
   * *As an undergrad, master the concepts of quality and value and incorporate them into your professional and personal processes. With those in hand, you will sagely discriminate between choices and efficiently and effectively prioritize options and*
   * *Once a fully-trained, card-carrying, master-clinician, keep an eye on additional competencies that you may add to your quiver — for example, ethics, quality, safety, customer satisfaction and/or leadership.*
9. *Other thoughts?*

Respectfully submitted,
Dr. Mike

Dr. Edward Drawbaugh Comments

For an aspiring medical student, conscious thoughts about the concepts of quality and value are likely distant. Yet, they can have great impact in both one's personal and professional lives — including approach to, performance in and enjoyment of medical school. One would hope that young Alex will pay careful attention to this letter.

26

A 'Chaordic' Hospital

"Hospitals are not as safe as they can be;
Therefore, they are not as safe as they must be."

T Michael White

The FountainHead WhiteHouse
Alex,

1. *Good morning.*
2. *Thank you for all you do daily so well for so many.*
3. *I am often asked as to how I first became interested in quality and safety…*

———

As often stated, I advocate vicarious learning. However, unfortunately, I have learned most efficiently from my own painful mistakes. My quality career is rooted in my response to errors. Through unwise trial and error, I came to understand that hospitals are unsafe and to be painfully/brutally honest, despite my best intentions, I was part of the problem. After review, early on neither hospitals nor I understood quality. From this disturbing perspective emanated my career passion to partner to make care safer for the next patient.

A sentinel incident occurred when I was an intern in a city hospital back in prehistoric times. As I, with all rationalizations ramped up, recall events:

- A young thirty-something patient with a chronic condition (lupus) developed a pulmonary embolism and was appropriately diagnosed and treated with the blood thinner heparin.
- Heparin is a drug that deserves major respect.
- At this massive city hospital, there were too few resources. The patient's intern was responsible for drawing blood at a specific time *(note: the intern had no control of her/his schedule)*; doing an archaic unreliable bedside Lee White clotting time *(note: the intern had little training in performing clotting times);* and then administering a heparin dose *(note: calculated on a specious test often done at the wrong time).*
- Even to the inexpert (beginner/borderline competent) eye of the intern, this entire process was wrong:
  - Lab phlebotomist should draw the blood at the appointed time,
  - The lab should perform and report standardized and reproducible tests (for example, aPPTs — activated partial prothrombin times),
  - Heparin dosage should be scientifically based upon reproducible information and
  - Heparin administration should be a process with checks and balances (i.e., the physician orders, the pharmacy prepares and the nurse administers).

Where I had gone to medical school it was all done correctly and I was well acquainted with the state of the art. But, like a lemming, I just fell into and accepted the city hospital's "this is the way we have always done it" culture. Let me enumerate an incomplete list of the errors I was enabling (all within the context of daily dedication to excellence in patient care):

- No training in Lee White clotting times beyond, "see one; do one; teach one;"
- Dirty equipment (test tubes);
- Blood at the bedside (lots of blood) transmitting disease (lots of disease). Note: I remain amazed that I did not contract hepatitis. Several of my peers did;
- Tests done when intern was available instead of at designated time after the last dose of heparin;
- Intern pockets stuffed with hypodermic syringes, needles and test tubes at the ready for the next Lee White;
- Intern pockets stuffed with brown, green, and red labeled heparin vials at the ready for drug administration;
- Imperfect record keeping of times; test results and administered doses;
- No physician, pharmacy and/or nursing checks and balances of heparin administration;
- This heparin process (intern numerator) was done while intern was in the midst of simultaneously addressing another thousand or so important clinical issues (intern denominator) — i.e., heparin complexity was addressed in the midst of institutionalized organized chaos;
- Some interns (for example, me) had significant red/green/brown color blindness and
- Valuable physician intern time was used wrongly.

There were 60 straight medical interns in our huge program and early on I was provided feedback that I was "among the best." Looking back, I was "among the best" at making order out of chaos. Years later the ACGME's Dr. David Leach would teach me the Mr. Dee Hock portmanteau 'chaordic' — hospitals are 'chaordic' institutions that are always functioning at the interface between chaos and organized care. From that Leach/Hock enlightenment forward, I understood advancement towards quality as a challenge to make care safer for the next patient by designing, implementing and continuously improving order and diminishing chaos.

Today, my color-blind eyes and mind can see this as clearly as the moment it happened. The patient's room was flooded with late summer sunlight. With some difficulty (she had poor veins), I drew and tested the blood and came to my "guesstimate" of her heparin dose — 7 ccs = 7000 units. I then administered the dose intravenously. Just as I completed pushing the final cc into her vein, my eyes focused upon the two heparin vials I had placed on the sun-drenched windowsill where I had prepared the syringe. They were identical in size and shape. One (10,000 units per cc) had faint red lettering and the other (1000 units per cc) had faint green lettering. I was immediately panicked — which vial had I drawn the 7 ccs from? After review, I was confident that I had administered 7 ccs from the 10,000 units per cc red vial — 70,000 units — a seriously dangerous tenfold overdose.

My initial reaction was nausea and lightheadedness. Then I mustered shaking, tearful composure, sought out my supervising resident — sequestered in the on-call room studying for his internal medicine boards — and related my error. Together, we made sure the patient was safe, secure and closely monitored. I called and confessed to the attending physician. I explained my error to the patient.

Although her clotting studies were abnormal for five days — an unintended experiment in zero order kinetics — no specific harm came to the patient. Nevertheless, I was immediately scarred for life — and better for it I may add. The massively dear cost of nonconformance to requirements (error) has a way of changing you.

Looking into the 'retrospectoscope' — an always unfair, accurate, and painful device — I observe that it is fair to conclude:

- The system set me up for failure;
- Although I suspected the system was broken, I trusted that leaders wiser and more experienced than I knew better — they did not;
- Frankly, I was too overwhelmed with survival to recognize that I (yes, bottom of the totem lowly me) was obligated to step forward and modernize heparin treatment at this huge, prestigious medical center;

- If I were not "among the best" (i.e., an important and irreplaceable commodity to the program) and/or if the patient had been severely injured, I would have been (wrongly) immediately tossed out onto Spanish Harlem bricks in pursuit of an alternative career path;
- All hospitals now use standardized lab testing and
- All hospitals now have physician, pharmacy and nursing checks and balances ensuring appropriate ordering, preparation and administration.

Having dodged all bullets to include a fatal hemorrhagic stroke, harsh professional repercussions and Spanish Harlem bricks, I expertly moved back to innovative survival mode in my 'chaordic' institution. Not until 15 years later with the completion of my Crosby quality training (see letter: *Quality and Value*) would I understand what had happened and what I should have done — enhance safe, timely, efficient, effective, and equitable/just, compassionate, patient-centered care (STEEEP) by stepping forward with well-articulated concern and partnering with the "right people" to design, implement and continuously improve safe hospital-wide anticoagulation systems.

Soon thereafter, the program director called me in and stated that I would be among the "lucky few" who would move on as a senior resident in her/his steeply pyramided program. I ungracefully demurred (a story perhaps for another day) and moved on to an institution with both a culture for and the resources for clinical care, training and the continuous pursuit of safe patient-centered care.

———

4. *Alex, as I uncomfortably share how I came to a passion for quality and safety, I encourage you to train, practice and partner to lead in enlightened, ascendant institutions devoted to continuously making care safer for the next patient.*
5. *Other thoughts?*

Respectfully submitted,
Dr. Mike

Dr. Ed Drawbaugh Comments

Looking back to those times, in this vignette, Dr. White would have found himself to be a medical Don Quixote — comically pushing too loudly for change within a staid institution. As a lowly intern in a large program, he would have been quickly told the many reasons why newer, safer procedures could not have been adopted at the time. He likely would have gotten nowhere. Yet, it was his responsibility (and the responsibility of all who work in the medical arena) to speak up when systems and/or people threaten the vulnerable patients we serve. Ultimately, our first, last and only responsibility is to the patients.

Lunch on the Top Floor, Tanzania
EJDMD

27

Power Grab

*"Power tends to corrupt, and absolute
power corrupts absolutely."*

Lord Acton

*The FountainHead WhiteHouse
Alex,*

1. *Good morning.*
2. *Thank you for all you do daily so well for so many.*
3. *Uniformly, our healthcare 'Better Angels' assemble with pure hearts to care for us. As they assume powerful positions in our lives, we entrust them with our well-being.*
4. *Within that context, abuse of power in healthcare is always distressing and can be dangerous...*

———

Catherine met Rachel on the first day of her summer internship at the Washington DC corporate office. Rachel had been at the agency for three years and was assigned the responsibility of supervising young, eager and hopelessly incompetent (a Rachel look-alike four summers before) Catherine's summer internship.

From the beginning, there was great synergy between them. Although Rachel was several years the senior, they were taking steps on the same path in life. Their Western Pennsylvania/Pittsburgh upbringings were similar and they had mirror high school experiences. They attended sister colleges — a James Madison Duke and a Richmond Spider — where they realized their collegiate academic, athletic, leadership and social goals.

However, Rachel was and would always be four years in the lead. Both recognized that she would, in addition to roles of supervisor and good friend, forever serve as the "big sister" role-modeling:

- How to look like an adult at work (when you are still a kid),
- How to shoulder responsibility,
- Where to shop and dine,
- The trials and tribulations of large dog small apartment ownership,
- How to consider and respond to (i.e., say yes) to a marriage proposal from a cool, good-looking, rock solid, rocket scientist,
- What a great wedding looks like,
- What a strong young married couple looks like,
- The scary experience of home ownership,
- How to be in and party at a "little sister's" wedding,
- The joys and vicissitudes of pregnancy and
- Childbirth.

Then in a flash, a heart-beat, a blink, the equation changed. In the middle of the night when she was too alone and well beyond the end of her wits Rachel would call her for the moment "big little sister" Catherine.

The pregnancy had gone well. Her labor, which started as she prepared for bed, went quickly. Her obstetrician and the hospital's obstetrics team were professionally and interpersonally superb. Pre-partum testing suggested that the laboring mom should receive an antibiotic during labor and that was flawlessly addressed. Co-incident with a glorious dawn, baby Alice, a tiny six-pounds-something of perfection was in their lives.

The hospital stay would be brief. The family had prepared well to bring their first born home (as if two rookies can prepare for the complexity of bringing the first-born home). By design, "little sister" Catherine would be one of the few privileged hospital visitors so that she could get a full dose of Rachel's "big sister" childbirth message which went like this:

- It is a most beautiful and miraculous thing,
- You believe you understand it but you cannot until it happens to you,
- We have been blessed with the greatest gift, baby Alice, who is so perfectly fully equipped in a miraculous miniature way,
- She, frighteningly frail and vulnerable, is totally dependent upon us. I have never understood responsibility as I do now and
- She is growing and changing by the moment. In our short time together, she has already grown so much. I selfishly want her to slow down (especially when I am sleeping) so I may recognize her every subtle change.

Upon discharge, Rachel was told her perfect baby's bilirubin was elevated and that it was nothing to worry about. However, a repeat blood test would be necessary the next day. Despite all planning, the first day home proved a bit rough. Although all was under control, blessed sleep did not come gracefully to an uncomfortable Mom. a not-quite with the program Alice or to a more worried than useful Dad. With the sunrise, the adrenaline steroid-high associated with labor and hospital departed and exhaustion moved in.

As directed, they marshaled their energy, packed up and presented to the hospital for the follow-up bilirubin. Out-patient testing was a busy place. It felt much more rigidly bureaucratic than labor and delivery. Uncomfortable at home, Mom and baby were in distress with fewer options and less control in this impersonal setting. A very proficient lab tech took a blood sample from Alice's heel. There was some pain and some natural parental angst, "Are we doing what is best for our precious and defenseless Alice?"

They were discharged to home and told they would be called. By this time, the gridlock known as the DC Friday afternoon commute was in play.

They were only home for moments, when a covering pediatrician called and impatiently — perhaps a bit too officiously — told them they must immediately return to the hospital so baby Alice would be admitted for photo-therapy. Because of the bilirubin level and Mom and Alice's blood groups, home therapy would not suffice. At the same time, NASA regrettably called the Dad with a problem that required his expertise. Soon Dad, Mom, Alice, Discomfort, Fatigue and Guilt were again back on the road. After several hours of waiting for a bed, Alice was admitted to the pediatric service where Mom would stay at her side.

Rachel and Dad immediately independently perceived that, unlike the kind and gentle staff in obstetrics that had adopted them as family, the admitting pediatric nurse had an attitude. They perceived strong antipathy. Something was palpably amiss: a nurse having a bad day, staffing overload, an inappropriate admission, intolerance for their parental naïveté, intolerance for generational weakness, something ethnic, something political (military), the cut of their jibs or something they said?

When the time came, Rachel tearfully broke down and stated that she was beyond exhaustion with significant discomfort, was struggling and was most hopeful for some merciful advice, analgesia and rest. Both Dad and she perceived the nurse's response to be less than empathetic. In her absence, they questioned if they should ask for another nurse but, having no understanding of how a hospital works and dealing with a perceived stiff covering pediatrician, they were fearful of unknown and unintended consequences and decided to make the most of their present circumstance.

Mother and baby were soon in a well-appointed pediatric room. It was immediately determined Dad was an official supernumerary and it would be his job to go home and sleep like a dead man. Then, in the morning, he would energetically swoop in like cavalry and serve as doctor, husband, father and mother until Rachel found some rest and GrandMother — official battle-tested and field-decorated cavalry — mercifully arrived. Rachel and Alice (under the lights) settled in. Just at the point when the happy ending should begin, Alice became inconsolable.

Rachel went through her newborn ABC drill and then went through it again. Beyond the time to call for help, she hesitantly called "Nurse Mildred Ratched" for assistance. After an interminable delay, the pediatric nurse arrived, did a dispassionate assessment and came to a palpably annoyed, perfunctory conclusion that there was "nothing to be done." Rachel observed that she was freezing and questioned the temperature of the room. Without investigation, she was told, "The room is fine."

So with husband in coma, mother on an airplane and covering-physician asleep, Rachel had a cell phone and two 2:45 a.m. options: 911 or "big little sister" Catherine. Called, Catherine awoke from a deep sleep and collected the information to the best of her ability to understand. Then, as Rachel had hopefully anticipated, Catherine called her father — a physician executive back in Pennsylvania. Within minutes Rachel was speaking with Catherine's — and by proxy her — Dr. Dad. Testing a few facts and clarifying that she was inviting him into her family as an external personal professional patient advocate — a doctor in the family — he sprang into action:

1. He called the hospital switchboard; identified himself as "Dr. Smith," asked to be connected with the Nursing Supervisor in charge of the pediatric unit and stated he would stay on hold until connected.

2. An apologetic hospital operator came back on and said the Nursing Supervisor was "too busy" to accept an external call.

3. He thanked the operator saying he understood how busy Nursing Supervisors can be, gave her his cell phone number and asked to be immediately connected to:
   - The Administrator on Call,
   - The Chief Medical Officer,
   - The Vice President for Nursing and
   - The Hospital's President/Chief Executive Officer.

He stated he expected immediate call backs. He stated that he was leaving for the hospital and would be there by sunrise.

4. As he headed for a quick shower, he put a call in to the covering pediatrician's answering service. He explained that he needed an immediate return call regarding in-patient Alice. He detected the operator seemed reluctant to put the call through and lacked confidence in call turnaround time.

5. Immediately, the "too busy" Nursing Supervisor called. She explained she was assisting with a pediatric trauma. He stated he fully understood and thanked her for "having the expertise and courage to run a city pediatric hospital at night." Immediately, the good-old doctor and the good-old nurse began to get on famously. They agreed that something was out of sorts on the pediatric unit, that the Nursing Supervisor would immediately roller-skate by and the doctor/family member would soon get a call back. They also agreed that she would measure and report Alice's "seven vital signs" — the usual six (temperature, blood pressure, pulse, respirations, pain control, and oxygen saturation) and a unique seventh — room temperature.

6. Within a very short time he received a conference call from the Nurse Supervisor and a sobbing, relived Rachel. "Mom and baby are well. The room, with pedi-lights blazing is a frigid 64. Inexplicably, all HVAC vents in room have been closed off? Space heating is arriving as we speak. Vents will soon be opened. A new nurse is already assigned to the case. Mom is being medicated and we will ensure that she gets some rest." Dr. Dad expressed his gratitude and spoke briefly and privately to Rachel, "I think we are now OK. I am not going to come to the hospital. If you have any concern call me directly and I will be at my proxy daughter's bedside before you can hang-up the phone." Rachel agreed and observed Alice and she were now being ministered to by "Florence Nightingale."

7. He then (5 a.m.) called Catherine and said he was confident that the ship had righted itself. All were well. So as not to violate privacy,

details would have to come from Rachel. Catherine and her husband should cancel all Saturday plans and provide unobtrusive energy and support (for example, PF Chang hospital room delivery) to Rachel and bedside nurses.

8. Prior to going back to sleep, he wrote a note of highest esteem and most sincere personal and professional gratitude to the Nurse Supervisor, copied the President/Chief Executive Officer and gently requested follow-up to ensure that "the hospital will be better prepared to serve the next mother and newborn."

9. At 10:15 a.m., as he was teeing off on the third hole in the senior club championship — a reverential, almost religious undertaking — the Saturday covering pediatrician, who was now covering the unresponsive Friday covering pediatrician, called. Dr. Dad gave a brief report, expressed confidence in progress made and gratitude for response all around, mentioned "alarm" at a colleague's failure to call and was provided a direct number by a chagrined covering pediatrician should additional weekend communications prove necessary.

From there on in, it was all happy ending. By Monday, baby's hue was normal, home was organized, troops were on the ground and combatants were well rested. While provisions were stocked, plans were being made for Alice's pre-school, prep school, and higher educations. And, Dr. Dad had the perfect excuse — critical late-night life-saving interventions — for his poor showing in the senior club championship.

———

5. *Alex, as hospitals examine care and safety processes, a phenomenon is identified: sometimes our good healthcare workers (often unconsciously) grab a position of power over an already complex and vulnerable patient who does not have the clinical or organizational wherewithal to resist. The root of this power grab behavior is multifactorial. My inexact, incomplete list includes:*

flawed mentoring, paternalism, antipathy, transference, bias, workload, bad-hair day, bad-hair life (so sad), etc.

6. *Most importantly, having recognized that this phenomenon exists and recognizing that it represents the antithesis of patient advocacy (our core business) we must be committed to extinguishing the power grab by identifying such behavior as a significant breach of professionalism, investigating it and adjudicating it through a leadership-directed just culture/accountability process (see letter: Justice).*

7. *Yes, the medicine profession is complex. That is why it is so rewarding. Who would want it any other way?*

8. *Other thoughts?*

Respectfully submitted,
Dr. Mike

Dr. Ed Drawbaugh Comments
Please see commentary after next letter.

————

28

ROOT CAUSE ANALYSIS

*"Challenges can be stepping stones or stumbling blocks.
It's just a matter of how you view them."*

APOCRYPHAL

The FountainHead WhiteHouse
Alex,

1. *Good morning.*
2. *Thank you for all you do daily so well for so many.*
3. *Please look back for a moment to letter: See the End. One of the competencies your performance will be judged upon is practice-based learning and improvement which I refer to as continuous quality improvement.*
4. *When things go awry in clinical care, they must be scrutinized, understood and opportunities for improvement must be addressed. The tool is root cause analysis.*
5. *Continuing the above Power Grab story...*

———

Ten weeks elapsed and found everyone in a better place. At that time, Dr. Dad received a written report from the hospital's President/Chief Executive Officer which stated, "With the permission of the patient and family, I wish to express my regret that you had to get involved, express our gratitude that you did and provide you with the following feedback. After our internal root cause analysis directed by our patient safety team, our **fishbone analysis** recognized that infant and mother were inexplicably left uncomfortable and cold because of:

I.   A failure to **professionally communicate**? — Yes.
II. A failure to have and/or appropriately utilize **equipment** (human factors engineering)? — Yes
III. **External factors** beyond our control? — No
IV. **Human error?** — Perhaps (this has been referred to our departmental just culture/accountability process)
V.   **Human resources/staffing/supervision**? — No
VI. A **Leadership/culture** failure — Yes
VII. **Patient physiology**? — No
VIII. Absent **policies and procedures**? — Yes
IX. Inadequate **training; education; and orientation**? — Yes

6. *Alex, in fishbone analysis, failure to professionally communicate is almost always an issue. As part of my quality training, Dr. Phil Crosby taught me two concepts that enhance an institutions communication culture:*
    *   *There is a hierarchy for decision making: edict (easy), majority vote, near unanimous majority and consensus (hard). Note: avoid voting. For buy in, always strive towards general agreement/consensus and*
    *   *Humans (and healthcare professionals are humans too) share by degrees: facts and information, feelings and values, ideas and, finally, trust. Trust is developed through open and honest work, recognition and willingness to work together. Strive towards trust.*

After review, we have taken the following actions:

- Upon admission, each patient and family is given a business card that encourages them to, without prejudice, call 1-800-We-Listen if they ever feel that their care is moving in the wrong direction and they want the second opinion and expertise of management. Our promised response time is "immediate."
- We are taking each of our 2252 employees (including me) through a process to remind each of us as to why we chose to take on the privilege and responsibility of a healthcare profession.
- We are taking each of our 2252 employees (including me) through a process to remind each of us that, in final analysis, we are the advocate for each of our complex and vulnerable patients and their families. Therefore, we must ensure they receive the care we would demand for our own loved-ones.
- We recognize that we must better recognize and celebrate our high performers, nurture, mentor and grow our mid performers and hold our low performers accountable (coach, discipline and when necessary terminate).
- Having investigated your 'bona fides', we will formally invite you (under separate cover) to participate as an external advocate (a newly created position) on our Hospital Board Care/Quality/Safety Committee."

Dr. Dad answered. "Thank you for sharing your analysis, synthesis and plan with me. I commend you on your timely and thorough review and action processes.

I will be pleased to join your Hospital Board Care/Quality/Safety Committee. I am hopeful that an appropriate member of your committee will cross-pollinate the Hospital Board Care/Quality/Safety Committee at my hospital.

Although I am confident you have addressed it, I observe you failed to list one action — recognition and celebration of the immediate, courageous actions taken by your most talented, professional and compassionate Nurse Supervisor to whom our dear Rachel and Alice shall always be indebted.

Provided my career experience and after detailed thoughts about this case, I wish to clearly put forward my own understanding of the root cause:

hospitals have provided our good bedside professionals with too much power (i.e., created an immense power gap) over our complex and vulnerable patients who find themselves in a system they do not know how to navigate. I observe that the spirit (we do want you to call and when you call we will listen to you) of your 1-800-We-Listen is "just what the doctor ordered" to balance the power gap. In addition, I believe that patient and family should be able to, without prejudice, bring in an external personal professional patient advocate (such as myself) whenever patient and family perceive there is a break down in communications with and/or a lack of trust in the healthcare team."

———

7. *Alex, with these two stories, much is addressed. Among the issues:*
   * *Advocacy,*
   * *Continuous quality improvement through root cause analysis,*
   * *Power (grab and cure),*
   * *Mitigation of poor performance and*
   * *Celebration of expected performance.*
8. *How should the concern for the index bedside nurse be investigated? Please see letter: Justice.*
9. *Again, the medicine profession is complex. That is why it is so rewarding. Who would want it any other way?*
10. *Other thoughts?*

Respectfully submitted,
Dr. Mike

Dr. Ed Drawbaugh Comments

Physician as healer, physician as patient advocate — two sides of the coin, both of equal importance. Is this left brain vs. right brain? Perhaps, but the salient point is that physicians are expected and empowered to perform both functions. Those seeking to enter the field should envision what a powerful role they can play in the lives of others.

These last two stories (Power Grab and Root Cause Analysis) illustrate how quickly anyone can be thrust into a position of vulnerability in the medical care arena and how a misguided caregiver can quickly worsen the situation. They show a reality-based need for continuous quality improvement and peer review processes as we strive to constantly do better for the patients we all serve. The enlightened CEO "got it right" after the incident. Our next goal is to always "get it right" and prevent the incident.

Aspiring physicians should also take note of the powerful role Dr. Dad was able to play as a professional advocate for the mother and child. Your medical degree and training open many doors through which you can be of tremendous help to others.

———

29

JUSTICE

*"Justice consists not in being neutral
between right and wrong, but in
finding out the right and upholding it,
wherever found, against the wrong."*

THEODORE ROOSEVELT

The FountainHead WhiteHouse
Alex,

1. *Good morning.*
2. *Thank you for all you do daily so well for so many.*
3. *In the above story (A 'Chaordic' Hospital) about my heparin misadventure, I, miraculously, did not find myself on the Spanish Harlem bricks in search of a new career.*
4. *The reasons for my good fortune: wisdom, empathy, pity, track record, service requirements, ennui or a sense that stuff like my mistake just happens? After review, probably all came into play.*

5. *Today, the enlightened ascendant institution — let's call it 'Our Hospital' — would make a judgement through a just and equitable peer review process...*

———————

Time passed. I transformed from beginner (intern) to leader (vice president for medical affairs) and I found myself in a leadership role at 'Our Hospital.' From time to time, errors would occur. At first, I had no process to address them. I am sure I fell back on wisdom, empathy, pity, track record, service requirements, ennui or a sense that stuff just happens. Then three events changed me...

- Early on, I came to understand the concept of quality from an industrial engineering perspective (see letter: *Quality and Value*). The fact that all work could be studied and improved through Dr. Phil Crosby's four absolutes (definition, standard, measurement, and system) became apparent. A formal approach to the design, implementation, maintenance and continuous improvement of processes became second nature to me.
- A bit later, I came to understand how (transparently) and when (often) to utilize root cause analysis (please see letter: *Root Cause Analysis*). Analysis allowed for an investigation of the nine weak points that might have contributed to error (communications, equipment, facilities, human factors, external factors, human error, human resources/staffing, leadership/culture, patient physiology, policies/procedures/protocols and training/orientation/education). Synthesis allowed for identification of root causes and design and implementation of logical efficient and effective cures.

For a long time, my tool box consisted of these two elegant tools plus a clunker — the blame free environment, which, to enhance reporting, provided that professionals reporting errors would not be punished (i.e., would not be shown the Spanish Harlem bricks). This logic would make our hospital safer by enhancing the identification, understanding and prevention of error. Uncomfortably, this would allow the professional guilty of unconscionable, egregious professional error to skate free.

- Then I attended an intense seminar presented by David Marx JD that demonstrated how to design and implement a uniform, just and equitable accountability (peer review) process for all healthcare professionals — how to design and implement an institutional just culture. From that moment, I proceeded with these 'Our Hospital' operational take-aways:
  - Our attitude is zero defects,
  - If and when error occurs, the professionals involved are professionally obligated/required to report it and
  - Significant error is subjected to root cause analysis.
  - If/when human error is a suspected root cause, the concern is referred to the 'Our Hospital' standardized equitable and just accountability (peer review) process where appropriate peer leadership (medical staff, nursing or pharmacy, etc.) would explore four uniform questions:
    1. Did the individual act deliberately?
    2. Was the individual impaired?
    3. Should the individual have known how to proceed correctly within our system?
    4. Would a peer in our system have acted just as the individual did?

By following this standardized equitable and just peer review process, 'Our Hospital' was positioned to justly and equitably adjudicate accountability for all.

Suddenly the Institute of Medicine's STEEEP goal (safe, timely, efficient, effective, equitable/just, compassionate, patient-centered care) made perfect complete and attainable sense.

———

6. *Alex, a wise master nurse colleague (Patient Safety Officer Joie Rotz) eloquent-ly taught me, "Personal accountability is the healthcare professional's sine qua non. Aspire to be a hospital that makes patient safety a sustained value which is never subject to compromise and is always driven by the ongoing quest to identify the system-based causes of errors and the at-risk behaviors that con-tribute to them — a hospital in which each professional understands that her/his primary responsibility is personal accountability for the safe, timely, efficient, effective, equitable/just, compassionate, patient-centered care of the unique, complex and vulnerable patient before her/him."*
7. *Other thoughts?*

Respectfully submitted,
Dr. Mike

Dr. Ed Drawbaugh Comments

In the medical world, as in the aviation industry and other industrial endeavors, "stuff" cannot be allowed to "just happen." Every negative occurrence demands investigation and an understanding of how that problem came about. The appli-cation of industrial engineering quality/safety measures such as root cause analysis gave medical leaders the tools to understand system problems. Institutional just culture programs have now added an appropriate way to address human errors. Both must be employed continuously if we are to have any hope of achieving the Institute of Medicine's STEEEP goals outlined above.

30

THE STRUGGLING PHYSICIAN

*"Your attitude towards failure determines
your altitude after failure."*

JOHN C MAXWELL

The FountainHead WhiteHouse
Alex,

1. *Good morning.*
2. *Thank you for all you do daily so well for so many.*
3. *In my youth, uninitiated to the complexities of life, I was befuddled to observe
   celebrities and others in society who "had it made" struggling with success —
   the "snatching defeat from the jaws of victory" thing. Then, as a young, con-
   tent physician, I was confused to find fellow physicians unfulfilled. Later as a
   residency program director and physician executive, I had to deal with what I
   came to call "the struggling physician."*
4. *My responsibilities have taken me to this understanding...*

———◆———

From time to time, the individual who had been so carefully selected into medical school and then so carefully selected into residency would struggle. Struggling would manifest as failure to satisfactorily address one or more of the seven competencies (after Dr. David Leach and the ACGME — care, knowledge, professionalism, interpersonal communications, continuous improvement, team (teamwork and team leadership) and/or vitality (balance between professional and personal lives). Most often, after initial success, there would be a slip sliding into failure. Initially perplexed, through training and experience, I came to assemble an imperfect list of usual suspects. The struggle at hand invariably related to one or several of the usual suspects.

On rare occasions root cause analysis would determine that human error by a physician may be the root cause. The question then must be asked and answered, why would a well-trained most precious natural resource (for example, a physician) err? Or alternatively, why would a physician struggle? In my experience, the answer is facilitated by rounding-up the usual suspects. Experience demonstrates professionals struggle because:

1. After investigation, there was no issue (that is, the conclusion of human error was prematurely assigned),
2. Inadequate academic and/or intellectual prerequisites (for example, an aspiring professional paid someone to sit for standardized exams),
3. Failure to match with uniquely and personally logical residency — her/his place on the medical continuum — for example, not competitive for or not discovered by fourth year of medical school,
4. Confused priorities (finances, geography, relationships, etc.) placed ahead of career inclinations,
5. Disappointment with a medical career (for example, a born pathologist is trapped into providing compassionate primary care),
6. Disappointment with chosen discipline (for example, a born surgeon is trapped in internal medicine),
7. Disappointment with specialty (for example, a born cardiologist is trapped as a generalist),

8. Affairs of the heart (for example, soul mates matched to residencies on opposite coasts),

9. Affairs of the pocket book (for example, family physician's income and plastic surgeon's tastes),

10. Behavioral health issues (for example, depression, psychosis or personality disorder),

11. Illness (for example, fatigue, sleep apnea or dementia),

12. Substance abuse (for example, alcohol),

13. Failure to find balance between personal and professional lives and/or

14. Something else?

With experience, my leadership teams and I became increasingly adept at efficiently identifying issues and addressing interventions. With experience, we came to find relief in uncovering some usual suspects (for example, physicians do very well confronting substance abuse and recidivism is low) and abhor uncovering others (for example, the onset of schizophrenia in the young physician is tragically devastating).

———

5. *Alex, this sorely incomplete list ascertains why the individual is failing to sync with the system. Looking to the other side, at times there must be concern for the medical school admissions process — does it accept the right individuals? I recall a touching and enlightening New York Times Op-Ed, "Check This Box if You're a Good Person", by college admissions officer (Dartmouth) Rebecca Sabky who described a unique letter of reference form a high school custodian. She wrote, "The custodian wrote that he was compelled to support this student's candidacy because of his thoughtfulness. This young man was the only person in the school who knew the names of every member of the janitorial staff. He turned off lights in empty rooms, consistently thanked the hallway monitor each morning and tidied up after his peers even if nobody was watching. This student, the custodian wrote, had a refreshing respect for every person at the school, regardless of position,*

popularity or clout." As the story goes, the applicant was admitted. I am hoping he was pre-med.

6. *One more thought: with these insights in hand, customer/employee satisfaction/experience guru Mr. Quint Studer (another hero) emphasizes that we must daily recognize our all-stars, coach- up our middle performers and usher recalcitrant low performers out of our organizations. As mentioned, in my experience, happily, coaching-up the rare struggling physician professional is generally successful. Sadly, spending precious energies on problems, we too often fail to celebrate our stars. Take this moment to create a short list of heroes in your life and then communicate to them their value to you before the sun goes down. It will change them. It will change you. Note: I am writing Mr. Studer (and his colleague, Ms. Jeanne Martin) today.*

7. *Please recognize this pessimistic/optimistic message both: 1) addresses a small minority and 2) optimistically positions you to vicariously appreciate potential struggles — always the preferred efficient, effective, less painful way to learn.*

8. *Other thoughts?*

Respectfully submitted,
Dr. Mike

Dr. Edward Drawbaugh Comments

To the aspiring physician, the message here is clear. Be aware of potentially dysfunctional behavior on the part of others or yourself. Seek guidance, counseling, advice from a mentor, etc. for yourself if necessary or compassionately steer others in that direction.

31

WHO RUNS THE HOSPITAL?

Dear Alex,

1. *Hello.*
2. *Thank you for all you do daily so well for so many.*
3. *Early on, I need to ask you a question and then provide my answer. Q: Who runs the hospital? A: Nursing.*
4. *With that addressed, I asked an especially insightful senior nurse executive to review and, if appropriate, contribute thoughts for your consideration. Without delay, she got right back in this format...*

———

Hagerstown Community College
Dear Alex,

I find it interesting, but not surprising, that Dr. White has asked a nurse to interject. He is wise on two accounts:

- He knows I know there are somethings that professionals like me have to say that may be important for aspiring physicians like you to hear and

- I recognize that this text will also find its way to aspiring nurses. It is important for me to say and for them to hear...

Congratulations on considering a medical career. You will enter a profession that calls the spirit to serve others through science and art. Committed physicians have given you sage advice and wisdom gleaned from their own rich experiences, successes and failures. As you practice, keep their wise words in your heart.

I am speaking to you with the voice of an experienced registered nurse. I have been privileged to work with Drs. White and Drawbaugh and know them to be principled, highly skilled physicians. Their collective wisdom will serve you well as you begin and continue through your medical career.

My expertise is professional nursing, healthcare leadership and teamwork. I was privileged to serve my "home" hospital as a graduate nurse in clinical nursing; in medical-surgical nursing; in intensive care, trauma, post anesthesia care and emergency services and in home-health. My leadership positions included managing neurosurgical, trauma and orthopedics; directing nursing operations and serving as vice president/chief nursing officer.

In all of my experiences, physician/nurse relationships played a key role in the health and well-being of the patient and her/his clinical outcome. To some, these relationships seemed to have a "soft" impact on the patient — a "nice to have." I can assure you this is not the case. Teamwork is critical to patient outcomes. As this becomes accepted, fewer and fewer, unenlightened physicians and nurses engage in one-upmanship — placing emphasis on individual ego instead of the value added to the patient and family by collaboration.

As scientists, physicians love data. Studies by the Robert Woods Johnson Foundation and in numerous replications by Magnet organizations have demonstrated that good physician/nurse relationships reduce patient mortality and morbidity. This must be so as the professional registered nurse spends more time with the patient and family and has a clear understanding of medical, social, psychosocial and emotional dynamics to share with attending and consulting physicians.

As you go about your medical education and practice, pay close attention to how individual physicians interact with nurses. You will quickly recognize and admire the physicians who get the most important information from nurses, take the time to ask nurses' opinion, listen carefully to nursing's feedback and act on that feedback. Emulate them — nurses are your eyes and ears!

There are physicians who avoid nurses. They try to enter and leave the nursing unit as quickly as possible. They argue that, as physicians, they are pressed for time and believe their work requires only "getting the facts and just the facts." They fail to engage the patient's professional registered nurse. This is folly. The time spent in listening to the nurses feedback adds to the quality of history and physical, prepares for patient and family questions and saves time by reducing the inevitable phone calls that result when nursing's clarifications and concerns have not been addressed.

Nurses are human. Strong professional relationships make them your best professional friends. Nurses talk. They know which physicians can readily be approached to discuss patient care. They know which ones cannot be approached. They know which ones must be worked around and avoided at all costs. They know who they may entrust (or not) with care of family and friends

A culture of a healthcare power hierarchy still exists in this time of enlightenment and advanced education. The timid nurse, or even the experienced nurse, can be intimidated by a brash, impatient, and yes, sometimes rude physician. How will the nurse communicate with that physician? In person encounters are avoided. This frequently results in incomplete communications by phone so that the nurse can escape from the conversation if it becomes abusive.

I remember as a critical care nurse, our team protected the physicians with whom we had good relationships. We knew that 24/7 physicians need sleep. If there were questions that needed the physician's attention, we worked diligently to place phone calls prior to 10 at night and/or save them for dawn. That courtesy was less likely extended to the few physicians who were non-responsive, short tempered or belittling of the nurses. 3:00 a.m. calls for an overlooked laxative or ambulation order might be anticipated.

Remember, nurses are also asked for opinions about physicians from patients and families. While I have never heard a nurse bash a physician to a patient or family, it is not uncommon for a nurse to respond, "You can always seek a second opinion." In nurse speak this often means "look for a different physician". When asked to recommend a physician, many of my colleagues and I will answer, "While I can't recommend a specific physician, if I needed a physician for my mother, I would engage Dr. Smith-Jones." Never underestimate nursing's insights into referrals and the power patients and families assign to those insights.

At the end of the day, my comments are all about your career and how it will impact your patients and families. Remember, as you strive to "first, do no harm," we have all made mistakes and we will all make future mistakes. Your positive, collaborative relationships with other members of the healthcare team, including professional registered nurses, pharmacist, physical and occupational therapists and support staff will reduce the chance of mistakes, will reduce harms to your patients and will insulate you from the anguish and pain of becoming a "second victim."
Mary Towe BSN RN MBA
Hagerstown, Maryland

———————

5. *Alex, I know CNO Towe well. She gets to the point. As you step forward towards a career in medicine, I observe she feels it necessary to give her team-work — for patients' sake, don't be a jerk — lecture. Contemplating her remarks, I recognize we physicians resemble them and therefore, I, again, heed them and recommend them to you.*

6. *Other thoughts?*

Respectfully submitted,
Dr. Mike

Dr. Ed Drawbaugh Comments:

Wise physicians have always respected and benefited from the insights of their partners in patient care, nurses. Those who have failed to do so have placed themselves and their patients in peril. Today's healthcare team has been expanded to include many others— mid-level practitioners, pharmacists, PT's, OT's. Each brings different training, skill sets and observations into the dynamic process of patient care. Yet, the bedside nurse still is the patient and physician's first, best and last line of defense.

Mr. Cape Buffalo, Tanzania
EJDMD

IV. Reflections

*"Failure is a great teacher; but never
insist on hiring one for yourself.
Learn vicariously from others' teachers."*

ASHOK KALLARAKKAL

32

LaGuardia — A Clinical Epiphany

*"The magic of the street is the mingling
of the errand and the epiphany."*

REBECCA SOLNIT

The FountainHead WhiteHouse
Alex,

1. *Good morning.*
2. *Thank you for all you do daily so well for so many. Keep on keeping on.*
3. *At this point, I hope to assist you to try on the mantel of being a physician.*
4. *The next three letters will address a late career clinical epiphany, a very early career emotional epiphany and then a happy ending...*

———

As I have matured in life, I have matured as a physician. It happens to the best of us. As I have begun to advocate for my family (for example, for my living large in Florida well-past age 90 mother) and as I have begun to grudgingly address my own infirmities as a patient, I have become a more complete physician.

After surveying a fine hospital in Queens for The Joint Commission, I was delayed in a surprisingly civilized La Guardia restaurant. I was making the most of a tolerable dinner happily paid for with OPM (other people's money). Without provocation, a lesion on a prominent part of my face began to profusely bleed. A major farrago — a true debacle ensued. As I set out in search of a bandage, many became flummoxed. It turns out it is not socially acceptable to hemorrhage in public. Who knew? Thirty muddled minutes later my snout was inartistically bandaged. Too tired to be humiliated, I limped onto a much-delayed flight towards home.

On the tarmac, awaiting take-off and anticipating nod-off, reality came to me. I had just experienced a life changing near-miss. If my mortifying but inconsequential airport restaurant bleed had been in my brain rather than on my nose, I would have been brought, without my wits about me, by kind strangers to a strange Queens' emergency department. There, wonderful, well-intentioned strange 'Better Angels', knowing nothing about me, would assemble to care for me. This panicked me.

Unable to sleep, with purpose I strolled the airplane aisle to scrutinize my fellow travelers. The picture was not a pretty one. Unlike the bullet-proof and invincible travelers they (and I) envision ourselves to be, they were in truth, like me, a weary, vulnerable lot.

This clinical epiphany started me on a mission — to assist you and yours and me and mine to enable safe, effective compassionate care. Disraeli states, "The best way to become acquainted with a subject is to write about it" — so, with a colleague, Dr. Steve Hightower, I wrote a book *Safer Medical Care for You and Yours —Six Tools for Safe, Effective Compassionate Care.* Let me share the cliff notes with you. We designed and implemented what now have become seven tools and I applied them to my life circumstance:

1. *My (Unique and Very) Personal Medical Record;*
2. *Ready Access to My Hospital's Healthcare Information Portal;*
3. *My Chief Complaint (my story — why I am here today);*

4. *My (Unique and Very) Personal HealthCare Values, Wishes and Desires;*
5. *My HealthCare Power of Attorney (and My Advanced Directives);*
6. *My Personal Professional Patient Advocate (My P3A) and*
7. *My Safer Medical Care Emergency Alert System*

Then we set out on a mission. In the interest of *Safer Medical Care for You and Yours,* we shared my actual examples with any and all who would listen and assisted them to emulate them.

Quickly, with Dr. Hightower's insights and encouragement, I was personally in a better place. And then the unexpected happened — our readers and seminar attendees provided us with feedback that made me a more complete physician.

They explained that the sharing of very personal examples — instead of hectoring them to get moving in some foggy, complex direction — was just what they needed to move from talking to walking. So now I, the more complete physician, am much more facile at demonstrating how I (with the privilege of professional wisdom) personally go about it.

————————

5. *Other thoughts?*

Respectfully submitted,
Dr. Mike

Dr. Ed Drawbaugh Comments

This story is an example of Dr. White employing his avocation (writing) to share his knowledge and experience as an advocate for others. Anyone can assist in the process, but one with medical training can be of greater help. Since Dr. White has found the power of sharing personal experiences, I will add my story. A few months ago, while preparing to return from an East African country at the end of a wonderful photo safari (my avocation), I became ill with bacterial gastroenteritis.

I was transported to a local hospital by ambulance, treated, and admitted over-night. I produced my Personal Medical Record on my iPad, and my ER physician was thrilled, especially with my list of medications and allergies. Her command of English was fairly good, but having things in writing seemed to make our com-munication much easier. I cannot know if having my Personal Medical Record prevented a complication, but I was certainly glad that I had it that night.

Mr. Zebra, Tanzania
EJDMD

33

TEST DRIVE — A TRAGIC MISSED OPPORTUNITY

"Allow opportunities so they won't
become missed opportunities."

FRANKLIN GILLETTE

The FountainHead WhiteHouse
Alex,

1. *Good morning.*
2. *Thank you for all you do daily so well for so many.*
3. *Stepping up to a career in medicine and into the responsibility of lives en-trusted to you is a formidable undertaking.*
4. *You may perceive today's letter to be a bit daunting. Don't be put off. If medi-cine's responsibility is for you, start getting used to it.*
5. *Take a test drive of the honor, privilege and responsibility of being a physician. Try it on for size...*

———

As a physician executive responsible for healthcare quality and safety, I have come to understand the key to safer, timely, efficient, effective, equitable/just patient-centered medical care — we, the patients, are each obligated to be involved in, informed about and responsible for our healthcare. At the same time, we are each responsible to nurture, promote and preserve the professional and personal vitality of our 'Better Angels' that care for us so well. In meeting our obligations, we each will be positioned to enable and receive robust safer medical care.

All well and good, but I am not just a casual physician executive participant. I am on a mission. I fervently and passionately desire to assist you and yours (and me mine) to position ourselves to enable and receive safe, effective, compassionate medical care.

When and where did my mission start? I observe my fervent passion to advance safer medical care emanates from a tragic missed opportunity early on in my professional and personal lives. Looking back, this was my emotional epiphany. I have already shared my late career clinical epiphany (please refer to *LaGuardia*).

———◆———

As a medical resident (age 28), I lived life in survival mode at the speed of light. My sad formula for survival: practice and study (too much), family (too little), play (too little) and sleep (too little). The pace of my existence was compounded (for example, working nights in the chemistry lab) by the stresses accompanying a prolonged state of abject poverty called college, medical school, internship and residency. However, with life moving at the speed of light, there was no time for assessment, analysis, synthesis or regret — life just was.

If I had stepped back (an impossibility) and contemplated my father's life (age 53 at the time), I would have seen an honorable man of great integrity role modeling rectitude in support of his family. Although no longer a young man (someday I too would begin to understand what his 53 years felt like), he worked three jobs: at 4 a.m. he delivered a mobile newspaper route, from seven to four he served as a letter carrier (a job he detested) and evenings and weekends he masterfully played trombone and bass — his true love and calling.

Let me expand on my Dad and his trombone. He was among the best musicians in the Tri-City (Albany/Schenectady/Troy) area. When a Frank Sinatra came to town, my Dad would be recruited for the back-up orchestra. I remember being at a 1960s Bee Gee concert (music that was far from his artistic sweet spot) in Saratoga with him in their tuxedoed 40-piece orchestra. Wow! Double Wow!! He was just that good.

Getting to the tragic point, as a distracted, over-matched and unmindful medical resident, the status of my father's healthcare never came onto my radar screen. If I ever considered his care at all, I would have, convenient to my survival, assumed that he was bullet-proof and invincible and/or in the good care of our fine long-term family physician (Dr. Henry Damn). I would have been wrong on both accounts. In retrospect, I should have found a quiet Sunday morning, sat with him at the kitchen table as his *My Personal Professional Patient Advocate (My P3A)* and partnered with him to create his own organized and accurate *My (Unique and Very) Personal Medical Record* and placed it at his fingertips (for details, refer to Dr. Steve Hightower's and my book, *Safer Medical Care for You and Yours —Six Tools for Safe, Effective Compassionate Care*). Had I done so, he and I would have immediately understood:

- Invincible, bullet-proof and too busy — also living his life in survival mode at the speed of light — he saw no reason to see a doctor and had not done so for several years,
- Silent to him, his blood pressure was significantly out of control,
- Commensurate with his schedule and age, he was tired and worn out. He was no longer able to make the cramming of 10 pounds into a 5-pound bag look like a walk in the park and
- A change in life style was in order and long overdue.

Instead, I went blindly about my business without so much of a thought about the healthcare of those nearest and dearest to me. In the January of my second year of residency, while rotating at Yale, I took a call from my Albany

Medical School professor of neurology, Dr. Bob Cassidy. My Dad, he said, was hospitalized under his care with a "mild" brainstem stroke. It appeared to be secondary to uncontrolled hypertension. He was stable with only some double vision and some minor incoordination of his tongue and lips (drooling). Stability and significant recovery were anticipated.

There was some recovery but thereafter my Dad's life was never the same. Imperfect vision made it difficult for him to read music — a minor inconvenience as he could play everything backwards and inside out by ear. Tragically, his "minor" stroke changed forever the coordination of his lips and tongue — his embouchure was altered. From that point forward, his all-important "chops" were never the same —better perhaps than most, but not good enough for him. He observed his clinically "mild/minor" neurological syndrome was artistically "severe/major." Fate had demoted him from the musician major leagues to utility play in the minor leagues. Avoiding humiliation, he benched himself — "to give the more talented their chance."

Although always a gentleman about it, he was habitually crushed. Over the years (he would live until age 89), there would be additional minor strokes. Sadly, intolerant of his imperfect sound, he would only assemble his trombone and play when he was confident all had departed and he and his music were alone at home. Robbed of his *raison d'etre* — his music — he was chronically troubled by and struggled with anxiety and depression.

——◆——

6. *Alex, diligently trying not to be too hard on myself (I was just a kid in survival mode living at the speed of light), I regularly painfully confront my tragic missed opportunity to contribute to a full life well lived. Therefore, committed to never again, I am fervently and passionately compelled (my mission) to ensure that I and those near and dear to me have our organized and accurate My (Unique and Very) Personal Medical Records and our My (Unique and Very) Personal HealthCare Values, Wishes and Desires, in order and at our fingertips. And I feel professionally duty-bound (my mission) to fervently and passionately*

advocate that you to do the same — *first for your bullet-proof, invincible self and then for those near and dear to you.*

7. *OK, enough about my mission and its genesis. Now, back to you — with the benefit of the above context, I encourage you to become a physician/advocate for someone near and dear to you for two purposes: first to position that individual for safe, effective, compassionate care and second to force you to experience (test drive) the honor, privilege and responsibility of the physician advocate. To accomplish both: 1) please flip to* **Tool 1: My (Unique and Very) Personal Medical Record — a gift example** *in this book's appendix and then 2) please sit at the kitchen table with someone near and dear and use the example gift tool (which was previously published in Safer Medical Care for You and Yours — Six Tools for Safe, Effective Compassionate Care to create her/his document. I anticipate the experience will change you.*

8. *Alex, if/when you have assisted someone near and dear with this task you have given them several gifts:*
   - *An organized and accurate medical record at her/his fingertips,*
   - *An involved, informed and responsible understanding of her/his care,*
   - *Facilitated safe, efficient, effective care and*
   - *Peace of mind.*

9. *You have organized, educated and provided peace — you have been the doctor.*
10. *Other thoughts?*

Respectfully submitted,
Dr. Mike

Dr. Ed Drawbaugh Comments

This is another illustration of how the physician may serve in the role of advocate for another. However, in this example, the advocacy is pre-emptive and may help the patient to avoid problems and/or complications at a future date.

34

A Lady's Story

*"The glimpses of human strength and frailty
that a physician sees are with me still."*

Daniel Nathans

The FountainHead WhiteHouse
Alex,

1. *Good morning.*
2. *Thank you for all you do daily so well for so many.*
3. *The previous tragic missed opportunity is a bit harsh. Let's investigate what success feels like.*
4. *As you consider becoming a physician, you must be cognizant that you will each day deal with mortality (including your own), aging (you too) and death. The burden is significant. Let me share one lady's story...*

———

She was the matriarch. She was living large in Florida. She was proudly spending her children's inheritance.

She had been the care giver for her husband until his passing seven years before. Since that time, she had found her way to a physical, emotional and social plateau. At age 93, each day she awoke to a pleasing equilibrium:

- She had successfully transplanted from the Adirondacks to the Gulf Coast of Florida 35 years ago. She had never looked back,
- Her condo, pool and beach were a family destination. Polite and respectful children, grandchildren and great-grandchildren were either visiting or were going to be visiting. The cycle kept her going,
- Her habits were regular. Nutrition, stretching, exercise and sleep were well addressed,
- Weather permitting, she "walked and talked" for an hour in the heated out-door pool,
- Several days a week, she played cards in the afternoon. At least one evening a week she was called to "fill in" a bridge table,
- Several evenings each week, she ate out with friends. Leftovers made for ideal, convenient lunches,
- A daily slowly sipped Brandy Manhattan was *de rigueur,*
- On her big screen high definition TV, she followed her football and baseball teams. Although she vowed to never forgive Joe Madden for his move to the Chicago Cubs, she still adored Mr. Madden and
- Lamenting a constant attrition of familiar faces, she nevertheless closely followed the PGA tour and found new favorites with young faces and modern (Dustin, Jason, Jordan, and Justin) names.

Since breast cancer surgery a decade before, she had not been in the hospital. Her fine geriatrician had her and her 10 plus medications in equilibrium. Then one morning, she was not herself. Grandchildren and great-grandchildren had just left after an energetic visit. She called her physician son, "my son the doctor," back in the Adirondacks and said she was "blue" — missing the family. A good listener, he soon understood:

- It started suddenly the day before,
- Her spirits were indeed low,

- She was weak as a kitten,
- She was a bit short of breath,
- Her chest felt congested,
- Her appetite was off and
- Her blood pressure and pulse were uncharacteristically hard to self-measure.

He instructed her to put on her Sunday best and, with her organized and accurate *My Unique and Very Personal Medical Record* at her fingertips (please see previous letter regarding a tragic missed opportunity for an example) — that she had been sure she "would never need" — have a trusted friend provide a ride to her preferred hospital emergency department. She was scripted to say (and only say), "I am weak, short of breath and nauseated. I think it is my heart."

She played her role perfectly. The assembled 'Better Angels' immediately placed her in a cardiac bay. With her history and medications crystal clear, within minutes her brilliant team understood she had an irregular heart beat (atrial fibrillation) and she was in heart failure. They efficiently and effectively stabilized her and admitted her to the coronary care unit.

Within three days, her cardiologist and her geriatrician had her tuned-up. Provided a perfect understanding of her prior meds and her going forward medications and a bit of oversight by her physician son and nurse daughter-in-law, she was safely discharged to home — instead of to the complexity, potential dangers and expense of a skilled nursing facility — two days early.

Within a few days, she was again on a plateau. But the plateau's altitude was not quite as high. Her energy, confidence and independence had slipped. Her physician did not want her to drive for a while. The family insisted that a driver and a housekeeper enter the picture. She acquiesced as she understood she had to give up some independence to continue to live independently. Her "son the doctor" updated her *My Unique and Very Personal Medical Record* — now with the patient's confidence that going forward "it just might come in handy." A trusted neighbor organized her medications weekly. Pool, cards, dinner and sports slowly came back into the picture. One month in, children, grandchildren (with great grandchildren in tow) renewed the cycle of visits to her "resort accommodations."

Grateful, she, her physicians, her family and her peers were cognizant that her meticulous involved, informed and responsible on-going attention to her healthcare had minimized the impact of her cardiac event, shortened her hospitalization and contributed significantly to her return to an independent plateau.

———

5. *Alex, three messages:*
   - *Life begins complex and proceeds from there. With age it becomes increasingly frail and then slides towards fragile,*
   - *If you want to understand the difference a physician makes, ask her/his family and*
   - *Take that above mentioned test drive (see Test Drive) today.*
6. *Other thoughts?*

Respectfully submitted,
Dr. Mike

Dr. Ed Drawbaugh Comments

As a physician, who will be your patients? Only the people that you see in the office or hospital? Family members, friends, acquaintances? Your medical training will equip you to help in many situations beyond direct patient care. A desire to help, an attentive ear and a phone call can often be of invaluable assistance to someone. A casual acquaintance once approached me, apologized for bothering me (which he most certainly was not) and asked for advice. He described symptoms which suggested to me that he had an esophageal problem, possibly cancer. He had decided on his own to wait a month or two to see of the situation would resolve on its own. I urged him not to do that and to seek medical attention immediately. Unfortunately, my fears were correct, and he did eventually succumb to the cancer.

However, he contacted me again while under treatment and profusely thanked me for having steered him to treatment earlier, thereby prolonging his useful life — a very small thing on my part, but a major benefit to him and his family.

Ms. Leopard, Tanzania
EJDMD

35

ANNE AND DUSTY

"The darkest night is often the bridge to the brightest tomorrow"

JONATHAN LOCKWOOD HUIE

The FountainHead WhiteHouse
Alex,

1. *Good morning.*
2. *Thank you for all you do daily so well for so many.*
3. *Events surrounding the unexpected death of a mentor and friend may assist me in conveying the importance of a spiritual outlook for maintaining requisite professional strength and vitality...*

—•—

By all accounts, he was a true Renaissance Man: a model father and husband; a kind, sincere and loyal friend; an elegant gentleman; a brilliant clinician; an adored personal physician; an accomplished teacher; a strategic leader; a bridge, blackjack, and poker master; an oenophile and a competitive golfer.

When he was found lifeless at home in the prime of life, his many friends (me among them), patients (me among them) and family (like many, I felt like family) were inconsolable. None could begin to fathom this random, inexplicable loss. Personally, I was angry with him for robbing me of so much promised, yet unrealized, too long delayed adventure and joy.

Through my selfish personal angst, I began to understand the enormity of his loving wife's loss — and I desired to somehow reach out and lessen her pain. While listening to a duet of favorite artists, a lucid message of certain immortality and life in the hereafter — we will all be together again — came to me. Yes, he had departed but he was not gone. I prepared the message for his wife and family just as it came to me...

———◆———

I think there is something important for you to experience. I sense it is a message my dear friend has sent to me to both lessen my pain and share with you. Seek out a duet — Anne Murray and Dusty Springfield (now deceased) singing 'I Just Fall in Love Again' [Anne Murray — *Duets: Friends and Legends*, EMI 2007]. With quality headphones adjusted, play it through a time or two. Then, start it over and hear the bass come in and follow it through. Next, start it over again and hear the rim shots. Again, start it over and concentrate on Anne's so perfect voice and be startled to detect a straining vocal cord — does this not represent our mortality?

As you start it over (bass, rim shots, Anne), appreciate the change of key (death freeing us from this earth to immortality?) that introduces Dusty's heavenly, angelic voice. Perhaps the words have special meaning too, "It is easy for you to take me to the stars. Heaven's in the moment when I look into your eyes."

Sharing my understanding — such beauty and perfection cannot die. There must be a hereafter. There just has to be. With me find the solace and joy to see through our enigmatically sad moment. With confidence, we shall all be together again.

———◆———

4. *Alex, I consistently contend that a career in medicine is not a job — it is a spiritual undertaking. Find your own spiritual connection. From there will flow the strength and vitality that will maintain you daily in your important, meaningful work.*

5. *Other thoughts?*

Respectfully submitted,
Dr. Mike

Dr. Ed Drawbaugh Comments

As a committed Christian, I certainly believe in life after death. My faith has sustained me throughout my medical career and has carried me through many difficult situations, preventing the cynicism which might otherwise have captured me.

———

36

FRED, WILLIE AND PROFESSIONAL VITALITY

*"Vitality shows not only in the ability to
persist but in the ability to start over."*

F SCOTT FITZGERALD

The Bolton Landing WhiteHouse
Alex,

1. *Good morning.*
2. *Thank you for all you do daily so well for so many.*
3. *I have often mentioned professional vitality — the vitality that enables our courageous, challenged 'Better Angels' to get back on their horses each day.*
4. *As a physician executive, I found my non-clinical administrative colleagues — having not journeyed through the physician's tunnel — sometimes had difficulty understanding that our 'Better Angels' had a special need — a need to boost their professional vitality.*
5. *To shed light, I shared a story...*

———

I am always at my best when complex issues come together for me. I was struggling with my family life. I was struggling with my professional life. I was struggling.

I attended a Fred Lee workshop about how I should approach my professional life as if I worked at Disney — how I should really get into my role as a major player in the life of each patient and her/his family. His thoughtful, energetic, perfectly delivered, light-hearted, accurate, important message left me flat.

Then a very special patient and family tragically entered my life. On a steamy summer afternoon, a beautiful two-year-old fell through a second-story screened window to the pavement below. Angel had sustained a major closed-head injury and ended up in my ICU with her devastated parents and siblings at her side.

This event shocked me even deeper into my struggles. After a physically and emotionally grueling first day, on my way home Willie was inexplicably, totally out of genre, singing *Angel Flying Too Close to the Ground* on my jazz/blues station. He sang as if only to me:

> *If you had not have fallen, then I would not have found you*
> *Angel flying too close to the ground*
> *And I patched up your broken wing and hung around awhile*
> *Trying to keep your spirits up and your fever down*

The next day, the toddler was in a coma. The neurosurgeons were hopeful. The family was indefatigably at the bedside. A cute as can be 10-year old big sister, Abby, who felt somehow responsible, was constantly present. She asked me "do you believe in angels?" After reflection, remembering that my guardian angel had awakened me daily at 6 AM in 5th grade for church before school, I said I did. In response, she proceeded to demonstrate in the ICU corridor how angels fly — a bit like a porpoise rhythmically rolling through the sea.

At this point, I dedicated myself to this patient and her family and meaning immediately returned to my life and to my work. I took daily assignments for a month without a break. Angel's recovery was slow, steady and quite miraculous. I became part of the family and we, the family, were joyous. And, I jealously began to understand that this gift would soon be taken from me. My angel would fly to home and away from my life:

> *I knew some day that you would fly away, for*
> *love's the greatest healer to be found*
> *So, leave me if you need to. I will still remember*
> *Angel flying too close to the ground.*

Then, as sudden as her fall, there was a dramatic change for the worse. Despite all efforts, one evening she lay dying before the family and me. With new meaning, I quietly sang my sweet young friend these words and gave her up freely as she slipped away:

> *Fly on; fly on past the speed of sound*
> *I'd rather see you up than see you down.*
> *So, leave me if you need to. I will still remember*
> *Angel flying too close to the ground.*

Minutes, hours, days, weeks, months, and now years have passed. But my Angel's influence on me and mine continues:

- Each day, I recognize the honor and privilege bestowed upon me — to provide care and comfort to my patients and their families,
- Each day, I again remember why I chose this calling,
- Each day, my family recognizes the important work I do, supports me in my work and consciously lightens my load. Each day, I thank them for that,
- I think of Fred Lee and wonder if he knows how right he and his message are,
- I think of Willie and wonder if he ever hits a rough patch and finds strength in knowing how much he has done for me, mine and the many and

- I recognize that each day, as I give, I harvest so much more in return — so that I may pass forward and later receive in the perpetuation of an amazing, miraculous, inexhaustible, circular motion.

Big sister Abby is now an accomplished graphic artist. Of course, for me, she will always remain the cute as a button 10-year old flying angel. Each holiday season she sends me a card depicting an angel flying (her corporate logo) which, to my eye, may be just a bit too close to the ground. Inside, crafted in perfect, simple, caring calligraphy, is always the same message, *"for love's the greatest healer to be found…"*

———————

6. *Alex, for me this story has a moral — although the work we have chosen is arduous, it is packed daily with gifts of joy that sustain us. As you labor, recognize these gifts. Let them touch you. Rejoice in them. Recharge.*
7. *For the record, my executive colleagues didn't see much in this story. On the other hand, our clinicians valued it. When a fine never perplexed senior executive admitted, "I don't get it," our nurse executive gently quoted the poet (Sawyer Brown), "some folks do."*
8. *Other thoughts?*

Respectfully submitted,
Dr. Mike

Dr. Edward Drawbaugh Comments

The thoughts in this letter bring us back to the realization that medicine is a vocation, a true profession, not a job. At times, it can sap our vitality and emotions, yet at other times, it can have the opposite effect. Practitioners at all levels derive much from their patients, just as they give much in return. Although I have now been out of direct patient care for greater than ten years, I still deeply miss the doctor-patient interactions of my days in practice.   Each day they lifted, sustained and changed me.

Pale Chanting Goshawk, Tanzania
EJDMD

37

Jaguar

"A man is rich in proportion to the number
of things he can afford to let alone."

Thoreau

The FountainHead WhiteHouse
Alex,

1. *Good morning.*
2. *Thank you for all you do daily so well for so many.*
3. *As I write (pontificate), it might be easy for you (or me) to misconstrue that my personal and professional lives have traversed the shortest distance between two points. Au contraire.*
4. *As residency program director, I would encourage my physicians-in-training to become fiscally astute and responsible. I would counsel, "Stanley and Danko's The Millionaire Next Door: The Surprising Secrets of America's Wealthy might be a very good positive place to start."*
5. *My interest in advancing their financial well-being stemmed from my own fiscal incompetency...*

———

At age 30, leaving a dozen years of abject poverty behind — it had never occurred to me I was in abject poverty — I came out of residency. With the favorable winds of circumstance in my sails, I created/fell into a most successful private practice of internal medicine in an underserved Connecticut small town. Important to and framing my fiscal psyche, I carried massive educational loans forward — loans I came to rationalize as my first mortgage.

Einstein's logic — "the most powerful force in the universe is compound interest" — had yet to be shared with me. In my ignorance, I was determined:

- To (wrongly) search for happiness in material things and
- To enable that misguided search, not save a penny until age 40.

My mistakenly structured brain envisioned happiness as me behind the wheel of the perfect car (Jaguar) with the perfect sound system (Jansen) gently blasting idyllic contemporary jazz (Herb Alpert's *"Rise"*).

All was on track the day I purchased my Richelieu Red XJ6 Series III Jaguar. My joy began to fade when my engineer patient explained my curse in one word, "electrical." My very next patient, a spiritual type, wished me happiness "on the two best days of your life — the day you bought your Jaguar and the day you will get rid of it."

Within one year, I told my accountant that because of incessant, irresolvable electrical problems — the only way to turn the wipers off was to turn the car off — I had to get rid of the Jaguar as "it is killing me." He counseled that it was not killing me. It was merely driving me insane. He then went on to patiently explain that, for sound tax reasons, I could not divorce the Jaguar. My response was to grab him by the shoulders, look him straight in the eye and with a firm shake scream, "It is killing me."

The next day it was gone. In round figures, the Jaguar cost $25,000 and after one year I lost a very round $10,000. Running the numbers, as an alternative to the Jaguar, I had an opportunity to:

- Put $12,500 (with tax savings $10,000 = $12,500) into a 401k at a modest 6% per year;
- Per the financial planning rule of 72 (72 ÷ 6% = 12), it would double every 12 years;
- Today, some 40 years later, it would have grown to about $125,000 and
- Although $125,000 is not what it used to be, $125,000 is still a nice sum — I want that $125,000.

When I would give clinical lectures, the residents often would often nod off. For this message, they were riveted. I occasionally get notes from my former residents. Many recall and thank me for my "Jaguar" lecture. Not one mentions my lectures on venous thromboembolic disease.

———

6. *Alex, this story has a happy ending. It turns out that $10,000 was a small price for me to pay to learn the best things in life are indeed free. Care that I have taken over the years in purchasing cars has alone saved me countless thousands. For example, today (2017), I happily drive an immaculate, low-mileage, almost Richelieu Red, 2007 Pacifica with a bumper sticker that reads "my Jaguar is in the shop."*

7. Later in life, Thoreau would teach me, *"A man is rich in proportion to the number of things he can afford to let alone."* Then a dear senior pulmonary/critical care/sleep physician, Dr. Sukhdev Grover, would teach students, residents, faculty and me), *"the physician should have but four financial goals:*
    - *Her/his education,*
    - *Her/his family's educations,*
    - *Her/his home and*
    - *Her/his retirement."*

8. *As I read and re-read Dr. Grover's list, I cannot rationalize Jaguar. A life mentor and good friend, Dr. Wm James Howard, would explain to me, "There are wants and there are needs." Eyeing my Jaguar — an obvious want — Dr. Howard would go on to say, "The unaware can quickly find themselves one want short of bankruptcy."*

9. *Indeed, Thoreau had it right. Today, Thoreau's quote — "A man is rich in proportion to the number of things he can afford to let alone" — sits prominently before me on my desk. I recommend his wisdom to you.*

10. *Other thoughts?*

Respectfully submitted,
Dr. Mike

Dr. Edward Drawbaugh Comments

Unfortunately for me and my physician contemporaries (including Dr. White), financial education was completely ignored during our training years. I do not know to what extent that omission has been corrected. If it is not part of one's formal training process, each aspiring physician should seek such education independently. Yet, even with education, one must arrive at a personal decision as to where to place the fulcrum on the teeter-totter which balances instant versus delayed gratification. A wizened mentor — "Never go out and buy the Jaguar until you have talked to someone else who already did" — can be of tremendous help in these matters.

38

Compassion

"Sic transit gloria mundi"

Latin Phrase

The FountainHead WhiteHouse
Alex,

1. *Good morning.*
2. *Thank you for all you do daily so well for so many.*
3. *I left residency training as a board-certified internist — a doctor for adults. Truth be told, I was (some would argue I remain) a bit full of myself.*
4. *However, after two years of practice, I came to understand that I was not taught all I needed to know in medical school or in training. With experience, I developed and/or refined many necessary skills. After two years of practice, I became much closer to being a complete physician. After almost forty years, the journey continues. But, as I entered practice, I was the master of my domain. I knew it all — except that which I did not know I did not know. As a medical student, my senior resident, Dr. Sal Pipito, would counsel, "Mike, one's eyes cannot see what one's brain does not know."*
5. *Wisdom aside, one thing I did possess was an innate sense of compassion — as I approached the care of each patient, I did so with sympathy, empathy,*

concern, kindness and patience. Others noticed. At graduation from medical school, I was recognized as "the student who most approximated the ideal physician/patient relationship." While basking in that glow, let me share one instance when compassion abandoned me...

O n a routine day in my private-practice office, I went about the routine of caring for a new patient. After these many years, I see her exactly as she, with her husband beside her, stood before me. She was an elegant, sophisticated, middle-aged, bank middle-manager. She was heavy with concern. She had been to see another physician who told her she "was fine." She lost confidence in that physician and her nurse friends recommended that she see me. I am confident their referrals fed my omniscience.

Her history revealed that, although she was quite athletic (tennis and skiing), she had become clumsy. She ane her family were most concerned because of an inexplicable fall down the stairs at home. After a very comprehensive physical exam, I knew the answer. Subtle fasciculations and atrophy were consistent with amyotrophic lateral sclerosis (ALS) — Lou Gehrig's Disease.

As a medical student, I had a keen interest in psychiatry and neurology. Extensive electives in neurology taught me well. Truth be told, my proficiency in neurology proudly exceeded that of the average internist *(note: in medicine and life, vainglory is never a good thing)*.

The practice of internal medicine swings between much mundane (another case of the flu — cough, cough) and abject terror (cardiogenic shock). To have a complex, rare diagnosis before me in a controlled situation — patient's suffering aside — was intellectually rewarding.

After the exam, I brought the patient and husband into my consultation office and we discussed my findings and next steps:

- A neurological syndrome. I am not sure I specifically mentioned ALS. Sadly, I am not sure, I did not,

- Admission to the local hospital — the only way to get a neurologist involved within less than a month and
- Consultation with a brilliant big city neurologist.

Later that evening, as I admitted her to the hospital, we met again. She could not/would not look at me. Unmistakably, she hated me. My mere presence was anathema. On my steep learning curve, I rounded up the usual suspects:

- She was immersed in anger and denial,
- She could not separate the bearer of the news from the news (the shooting the messenger thing),
- In our conversation in the office, I had been too definitive — I had not left enough room for doubt,
- For admission, I had to suggest a diagnosis and perhaps I had written rule-out ALS. Admitting nurses and staff may have innocently confronted her with this diagnosis as a *fate accompli* and/or
- In our inchoate relationship, she detected how pleased I was with my diagnostic acumen (in the face of her tragedy) and that I had been intellectually rewarded (at her expense).

Striving to tell myself the truth, to my mortified chagrin, I recognize all the above, and especially the latter, to be in play.

The neurologist consulted and all was confirmed. In her devastation, the patient never again made eye contact with me. Throughout her brief hospitalization, her anger remained palpable. After discharge, I never saw her again.

———

6. *Alex, let me move away from conjecture and towards truth:*
    - *I had performed shamefully,*
    - *To my discredit, she had seen glee and self-approbation in my non-verbal communications,*

- *In my excellent rheumatology training (Dr. Richard Danehower), I had been cautioned, "do not jump to definitive diagnoses (for example, rheumatoid arthritis). Use a dose of tincture-of-time to both bring clarity to the diagnosis and provide space for the patient to begin to ponder the enormity of its significance,"*
- *I had been provided all the information and tools necessary to get this right:*
  - *Initial consultation,*
  - *Internal/silent hypothesis (working diagnosis),*
  - *Neurology specialist opinion and*
  - *Patiently advanced short and long-term denouements.*

7. *This is a story that. As program director, I would tell new interns on their first day. What do I hope they (and you) take away? As you care for each patient, recognize the privilege granted to you. First be a sentient being. Always, always, place compassion above all. As you place the patient's inner-self first, touch the truth of your inner-self. Ensure pride has no place.*

8. *Other thoughts?*

Respectfully submitted,
Dr. Mike

Dr. Ed Drawbaugh Comments

Medical school is primarily about learning the science of medicine. That learning never stops throughout a physician's life. As training progresses, however, learning the art of medical care becomes equally important. The good physician will understand that "it is always about the patient, not you." Everything that is said and done with a patient should be tempered through the lens of how the physician would feel if the positions were changed. In this scenario, the science of the patient's care was handled perfectly, but the art was forgotten.

39

CADAVERS

"I will keep pure and holy both my life and my art."

FROM THE ORIGINAL HIPPOCRATIC OATH

The FountainHead WhiteHouse
Alex,

1. *Good morning.*
2. *Thank you for all you do daily so well for so many.*
3. *As I thought of messages to send you for your consideration, this one was lost in the pea soup of a foggy past. Suddenly, it has come back to me.*
4. *This message has me confused. Is my position shocked high dudgeon or the kid's gleeful LOL (laugh out loud)?*
5. *Let me play it straight...*

My medical college was founded in 1839. When I matriculated in the autumn of 1969, my very first experience was gross anatomy — the studied dissection of a corpse. The lab was on the top floor of the oldest building on campus. The elevator was vintage 1838.

I remember 100 students on their first Monday making their way up the rickety elevator six at a time. I remember ascending in my full-length white lab coat and wondering if I was "man enough" to be introduced to my cadaver — my first patient — and to successfully navigate a full semester.

My patient was an emaciated, elderly gentleman. To my inexperienced eyes, his soulless remains suggested a very hard life. A military tattoo on his upper arm was his only identifier. I took a moment to formally thank him for his gift — be it thoughtful or fortuitous — for his contribution to my education and for his influence on the well-being of my future patients. Then, with great respect, I proceeded into the wonderments he would share with me.

In the lab, there were 25 cadavers with four students (2/side) assigned to each. Our cadaver was on a bier in the middle of the lab. Amid these quiet, almost religious proceedings, a commotion stirred in the front of the room. It was discovered that cadavers had been moved from their assigned positions. Between the Friday faculty set-up and this Monday morning, positions had been exchanged.

Facts surfaced. Some students, familiar with the workings of the anatomy lab, determined student assignments, including their own, to specific tables. With that information, over the weekend they had entered the locked lab and moved preferred thin bodies to and obese bodies from their assigned tables. The professors were irate. I was doubly aghast at the unimaginable deed and the unconscionable disrespect for cadavers and peers.

Having just seriously considered and proudly taken the modern Hippocratic Oath (please refer to Dr. Wong's Afterword), I ascertained these actions represented egregious professional offense. I awaited the requisite professional hammer — suspension or expulsion. The hammer never came. By the afternoon, business proceeded as usual.

Within minutes, events had juxtaposed the revered sacred profession I had sacrificed for and dedicated myself to with a cruel, harsh competitive pragmatic business — an uncomfortable juxtaposition that would surface regularly throughout my career.

6. *Alex, twenty years later as a too young department chair on a very steep learning curve, still looking to make sense of it, I presented this circumstance to Mr. Howard Jones, my wise chief executive officer and mentor. For him, it was a mere business deal...*

7. *He explained, if there had been merely one culprit, leadership may have made an example and hurried a happy someone in from the long applicant wait list. However, if there were several, it would all become unmanageably complex. Tuition (small) and grants (large) would have been placed at risk. "In the end," he would say, "dollars trump culture. Whenever logic is defied, follow the dollar."*

8. *Other thoughts?*

Respectfully submitted,
Dr. Mike

Dr. Ed Drawbaugh Comments

I have to diverge with Dr. Mike on this story. I actually found humor in the attempt of some of the students to get ahead by switching cadavers. In truth, having a cadaver with some extra adipose tissue would not have been a significant disadvantage to the other teams. As a fellow student, I would certainly not have been affronted. As the Dean of the school, I would have chuckled inwardly while reminding the class of the severe penalty for true cheating.

Another good lesson from this story is that the field of medicine is very competitive. While competition in and of itself is healthy, it must be done on one's own merits and not at the expense of others.

40

PROFESSIONAL COURAGE

"Courage is resistance to fear, mastery
of fear, not absence of fear."

MARK TWAIN

The FountainHead WhiteHouse
Alex,

1. *Good morning.*
2. *Thank you for all you do daily so well for so many.*
3. *I am imperfectly remembering six stories regarding professional courage —*
   three where it was arguably present and three where, to my lasting chagrin, it
   was absent.
4. *Calvin Coolidge observes, "Heroism is not only in the man, but in the oc-*
   casion." An important truth — it takes professional courage to step up
   to a career as a physician. It takes professional courage to, each day, be a
   physician...

———

41. Acute Epidural Hematoma

It was the third-year medical student's first surgical rotation. He had been arbitrarily assigned to neurosurgery.

To that point, his medical career had been a panoply of mixed experiences:

- When he came home from first grade with a straight A report card, his letter-carrier father announced, "you are going to medical school."
- As the oldest of all the sibs and cousins, he was often left in charge at family functions (a scary thought) and his Aunt Marie declared "you will be a pediatrician."
- When anxious regarding the prospects of confronting "blood and gore," his mother invented "they make you wash your hands in blood and you get used to it."
- He worked evenings and weekends at the local pharmacy and toyed with going to pharmacy school rather than medical school until his horrified pharmacist boss and mentor disabused him of such folly.
- In college, the thought that he might not be accepted to medical school made him determined to succeed (whether he actually wanted to or not).
- In his arduous first two years of medical school, he came to enjoy and appreciate both the science and the glimpse of the art of medicine he was exposed to.
- Having rotated through pediatrics, he understood that caring for seriously ill precious little ones who had no understanding that his well-intentioned painful interventions were in their best interest was not for him. Along the way, he observed that surgeons are born (not made) and he had not been born to be among them. Therefore, his career would fall to the cognitive adult side of the profession — medicine, neurology or psychiatry.

Already he recognized a sine-wave pattern to his career. Having been accepted into pre-med, he was among the elite in high school but as a freshman in college, he was relegated to the basement. Having been accepted into medical school, he was again among the elite in his college class but his first day of medical school returned him to the basement. Two years of success in the basic sciences had separated him from the pack; however, each third-year clinical rotation started him back in the basement. And the roller coaster rides the future would hold were becoming clear to him: medical school graduate, intern, junior resident, senior resident, junior attending, attending, chair, dean — a relentless series of hard won peaks immediately reverted to basements.

His ego was nonetheless sound. He had no trouble with this sine-wave. He appreciated that, as a an supernumerary third year medical student, he had been granted a position of great privilege — to each day join senior physicians in their complex work attempting to advance the circumstances and lives of their complex and vulnerable patients and, with this granted privilege, he understood his responsibility — to take it all in and use it to find his unique place in medicine--- to find the career that would have him be his most productive, do his most meaningful work and make the greatest difference for those he was privileged to serve.

His neurosurgery team's rounds started in 5:30 a.m. darkness. The chief resident and his senior residents were finished with 'oversight rounds' and in the OR by 7:00 a.m. where they would be sequestered until 4:00 p.m. The work of 'grunt' rounds, orders and notes was left to the intern (not yet OR worthy) and the novice third-year student (never OR worthy).

Neurosurgery was the most competitive surgical field and attracted only the best, the brightest and the most dedicated. It also attracted those with the most stamina as their seven years of training required every other night on call in the hospital. With sardonic sadness, they would lament "so we must miss half the good cases." Unsurprisingly, his intern was brilliant. As he supervised and taught on meticulous rounds, the student learned exponentially — basic post-op care, complex neurosurgery concepts and major organizational skills.

Unbelievable as it will sound, the day before the intern had had significant surgery (pilonidal cyst). By all accounts, he should have been home medicated and recuperating. But, as was clearly implicitly expected, he was there taking one for the team. Nevertheless, he did have to excuse himself to go to his call room and change his dressing and, as he did so, he left his intern beeper (covering all neurosurgery outside of the OR) with his paralyzed-by-fright student.

Unbelievably, the beeper immediately went off. When the student called the number, he was (unbelievably) speaking with the chief resident in the OR via speaker phone who said, "A painter fell off his ladder, had a concussion, is now alert and has been admitted to the floor to our service by ED assholes who don't know chicken shit from chicken salad. Run down and make sure he is OK."

This first day on neurosurgery third year medical student found his way for the first time to the neurosurgical floor and found the patient in his room being admitted by a third year, soon to graduate, nursing student. He was stunned to find a head injury patient who was unconscious and demonstrating deep sonorous respirations. From his meager classroom clinical medicine conferences, he recognized a syndrome (head injury, unconscious, alert and again unconscious) consistent with an acute epidural bleed and understood that only immediate acute neurosurgical intervention could save this patient.

Unbelievably, this lowest figure on the totem pole told the 'powerful' nursing student to find the head nurse, send her in and then set up for an IV. As he placed the IV, he told the 'more powerful than God' head nurse to call the OR and inform the neurosurgical 'thinks he is God' chief resident that his patient is on his way with a likely acute epidural hematoma. Within moments an unconscious patient, a head nurse in a state of shock, an impressed nursing student and a determined first-day-on neurosurgery third-year medical student had the patient in the OR elevator.

As the doors opened an angry OR head nurse, an angrier anesthesiologist and a frankly bewildered neurosurgical chief resident confronted the inexplicable scene: bed, patient, head nurse, student nurse and medical student. After only a moment with the patient, the chief resident flew into action. Within minutes the patient was undergoing emergent craniotomy.

At about this time, the intern found his beeper and his student in the OR men's locker room. The student was shaking and weeping. He was all apologies, "I am so sorry but I thought it was my responsibility to do what was best for my patient." He was convinced of impending doom, "Surely the Chief of Surgery will demand my ass and the Dean will bounce my ass." A flummoxed intern listened and consoled without understanding. Then, a beaming chief resident appeared with good news, "A most fortunate patient will likely survive an assuredly fatal, brilliantly diagnosed and courageously managed acute epidural hematoma."

Within minutes, the service was back to normal. Rounds were completed and the pecking order was appropriately re-established. As predicted, there was regression to the third-year medical student neurosurgical mean — for every right answer proffered by the medical student there would be two wrong. And, soon all would be forgotten until almost two years later at awards day when the head nurse would retell the story and the painter would hand the graduating medical student the Patient Advocate Award — presented to the student who most nearly approximates the ideal doctor/patient relationship.

---

42. City Hospital Intern

I am clearly remembering an evening on call as an intern in a city hospital. It was about 7:00 p.m. and there was break in the action on the general medicine unit. For this small-town lad, our patients were an extremely sick and very rough bunch. Yet, each, in her/his own dignified way, was respectful and appreciative of our efforts.

My fellow intern was in the middle of the hall and was publicly berating a young male patient — a drug addict with endocarditis who was seeking analgesia. The doctor announced for all to hear, "you are a low-life, scum of the earth dirt ball and you will get no hospital hooch from me."

All 5' 10", 155 pounds of my small-town (Schenectady) self leapt from the nursing station into the hall. I was immediately in the intern's face — a big city, street-savvy face attached to a formidable 6' 2" 220-pound Bronx frame. I blurted, "Doctor you may not speak to this patient in this way."

199

Then the street fight began (my first, his hundredth). My recollection is I got the worst of it — OK, striving for truth, he got none of it. Mercifully, the cavalry arrived and separated us. Duty called and we were quickly back to business as usual.

The next day, there was a touching thank you note and small (proportionally large) gift waiting for me from the patient — a treat from his breakfast tray. And, as important, the nurses and support staff who always addressed me as "doctor" said it in a new way — a way that seemed like they meant it. With just barely perceptible winks and nods, the patients on my rounds gave me knowing, affectionate smiles. It had me choked up and near tears. It remains the best morning of my professional career.

---

43. The Punch

With less clarity (it is amazing what denial, rationalization and repression can do to memory), I recall being a too young department chair and residency program director with a harassed (I am not sure the term existed then) intern seated before me. The intern was rotating through surgery and the night before, in response to a perceived mistake, was punched in the arm by the supervising surgical resident. "I was punched hard. It really hurt."

Much time has passed and much salve has been layered on this wound. I recall no leap to rescue this fine professional soul entrusted to me. I cannot point to high dudgeon or indignation on my part. My primary reaction was fear — fear of being required to take on the firmly entrenched, politically powerful, more savvy and better armed academic colleagues.

I am sure I did something. I am sure it was not enough. I am sure I learned from my inaction and I (and those entrusted to me) were later better for it. Nevertheless, despite repressed recollections and expert rationalizations, I recognize a lack of professional courage.

---

44. De-Termination

If the above is forgivable, this is not. An executive was planning an institutional celebration at a country club. The event would include golf, tennis and pool for participants. I was invited to play a practice round of golf — a most desirable invitation — with three other executives as "part of the deal." We had a most enjoyable Friday afternoon documenting the obvious — the fine golf course was 'golfable'. Truth told, it very much beat working. After intense review, event arrangements were declared meticulously investigated and sound.

Suddenly the executive was on the carpet for inappropriate use of funds. The issue was the four rounds round of golf, which I had naively understood to be part of the event package. The executive was being terminated. I was blindsided by and stunned by the pace and depth and breadth of events, allegations and conclusions. Making some sense of it, there were whispers of other sub-rosa concerns. However, it was guilt about being too casually complicit that contributed to my weak acceptance of the dismissal.

Using the always unfair too accurate 'retrospectoscope':

- I should have stridently stated that this executive is good people and represents an irreplaceable asset to the organization,
- I should have stated that although I was unaware of details, having failed to ask adequate questions, I too share responsibility and therefore, I too require like punishment,
- I should have offered to use my personal funds to cover all expenses and make the institution whole and
- I should have vociferously argued against punishment that does not match the crime.

If I had stepped up, perhaps I would have been informed that there was more to the story. I did not and was not. In fact, as time has passed, there has never been a whisper of other allegations.

I must conclude, based upon available information, I failed to muster the professional courage to protect a colleague. When the dust settled, I, too late, recognized my leadership short-coming — failure to step up and rightfully address wrong. To the best of my knowledge, I, determinedly, never again did.

All well and good. However, I still live with the weight of having failed to step up and protect a deserving colleague — remembering, as hard as it may seem at the moment, in the long run, it is always easier to have the courage to do the right professional thing rightly. These years later an elegant, successful, kind executive colleague, mentor and friend continues to compassionately counsel, "That injustice did me a favor. It changed my career and life for the better. It freed me to go where I would not have gone. Life is like that. It is long past time for you to move on." Listening (not my strong suit), I have begun to.

---

45. Malingering

A valued, clinical colleague came to me (a hallway consult — aka curbside consult) with new physical complaints. I referred him to the clinic. His complaints were multiple and protean. His findings and studies were normal. Senior colleagues, with great confidence, declared he was malingering. Despite his dramatically direct pleas to me for redress, I allowed their powerful opinions to prevail.

Months and years later (and now again), I revisit this circumstance. With each review, I must again conclude — there just was nothing about that fine professional, about his approach to life or his life circumstance that could explain erosion to malingering. A medical or behavioral health diagnosis was being incompletely investigated and was being missed on my watch because, Dr. Pipito again, "eyes cannot see what brains do not know."

In time, conditions such as chronic fatigue syndrome and fibromyalgia became better understood. This fine man was troubled by something. As his hallway physician advocate (I had accepted that role), I should have assisted him pursue a diagnostic work-up at a major medical center (for example, the Mayo Clinic) where keen specialists could begin anew.

With this painful missed opportunity behind ne, I would never again allow external forces to intervene in and derail my advocacy for a patient.

---

46. Safe, Respectful Workplaces

Years later, I came to understand the leadership requirements entrusted to me.

On several occasions, healthcare professionals came to me to report being subjected daily to withering disruptive behavior. They felt professionally and personally bullied, humiliated and belittled. They came to dread coming to work. Despite unquestioned expertise and deft execution of duties, they did not perceive safe and respectful workplaces — workplaces their enlightened, ascendant institutions so proudly espoused.

I used the human resources and medical staff systems that were available to me to address the circumstances. Investigations revealed unsafe work environments. Others, too timid to step forward, were similarly concerned.

When low-level collegial interventions (conversations over cups of coffee) were unproductive, medical staff leaders — like me with the battered intern — were flummoxed and beyond their ken. After consulting those much wiser than me, I would take the concerns to administrative and board leadership. In every circumstance, they clarified their institutions' unyielding requirements for safe, respectful workplaces. In every circumstance, the workplaces immediately improved for many (and generally, the offending parties were elevated to better places).

After review, those treks to administrations and boards were among the most difficult journeys of my career. All bunched up in their support were surprising, uncomfortable, implied/*sub rosa* questions: were the workplaces, in fact, unsafe? Couldn't all this, in fact, be resolved at a lower level (for example, under the rug)? Was too much (relationships, legal exposure) being risked for too little? Were the risk/benefit ratios, in fact, right? Was this a reflection of (my) administrative incompetency?

For me the answers were and are clear. Afterwards, I lost not a moment's sleep over trekking those arduous, anxiety-provoking, sleepless journeys. Like Yogi, coming to forks in the road, I took them. After institutions walked their talk, the professionals and institutions better positioned to provide safe, effective care (note: in the midst of these machinations, disruptive behavior came to be recognized as a serious patient safety concern.

Most of what I did in my leadership roles, I would have done for free. It was this hard stuff institutions paid me for. It was this hard stuff, staff counted on me for.

With *A Safe, Respectful Workplace* and *The Punch* so closely juxtaposed, I again ponder the battered intern — was there a loss of faith in the system? Was a career negatively impacted? And I wonder, what became of the surgical resident? Did a talented physician slide further down a slippery slope because of my failure to intervene and attempt an early career rescue?

———

5. *Alex, this has been a tough row for me to hoe. My message — be prepared to be courageous, understand the systems and use them, act immediately, always resolve issues at the lowest possible level and, when you are the last resort and your professionalism is on the line, do the right thing.*

6. *As I was writing this, an obituary (Larry Colburn) helped me understand what courage looks like. At Mai Lai, Chief Warrant Officer Hugh Thompson Jr confronted the officer in command of a rampaging platoon but was rebuffed. He then positioned his helicopter between the troops and the surviving villagers and faced off against another lieutenant. Mr. Thompson ordered Mr. Colburn to fire his M-60 machine gun at any soldiers who tried to inflict further harm on the villagers. Thirty years later when being awarded the Soldier's Medal, he quoted General MacArthur, "The soldier, be he friend or foe, is charged with*

the protection of the weak and the unarmed. It is his very existence for being." So too with doctors.

7.   *Other thoughts?*

Respectfully submitted,
Dr. Mike

Dr. Ed Drawbaugh Comments
In all aspects of life, doing the right thing is always the right thing to do. This is especially true when one has responsibility for the well-being of others, whether they be subordinates, peers or patients.

47

LEARN VICARIOUSLY

"There, but for the grace of God, go I."

REVEREND JOHN BRADFORD

The FountainHead WhiteHouse
Alex,

1. *Good morning.*
2. *Thank you for all you do daily so well for so many.*
3. *Here is my personal scale for effective learning:*
   - *Painful error (powerful);*
   - *Observation of painful error of peers (powerful and much preferred);*
   - *Guidance of consultant in case specific circumstance (strong);*
   - *Lecture (average) and*
   - *Text (below average).*
4. *As my career as a physician executive advanced, I assembled a tool box. Among my most powerful tools: learn vicariously. Observe peers' mistakes. Appreciate and learn from their endured painful consequences. For clarification and*

emphasis: although efficient and effective, avoid lessons learned through pain-
ful personal ineptitude.

5. *Let me share a clinical story…*

———————

Sickle Cell Anemia

Graduate Medical Education (GME) is a wondrous process. Civilians become medical students who, on merit, advance from classrooms and closely supervised clinical observations to the increasingly independent clinical responsibilities of the intern, resident and fellow under the supervision of expert and master senior physicians.

As residents and interns, at a large city hospital, the care of our cases was largely left to the wisdom and judgment of the most senior resident. Expert, master attending physician supervision was confined to the conference room (versus the bedside). Their expert opinion and guidance was largely dependent upon their perceptions of the observations of the physicians-in-training. Since "eyes cannot see what brains do not know," interns and residents would present that which they perceived and masters would wax expertly relevantly or irrelevantly on accurate or inaccurate observations — a very scary thought.

When supervision was provided by an accomplished third-year resident who was approaching graduation (i.e., almost a board eligible internist), care was generally appropriate. When supervision was provided by a "brandy new" second year resident (who was an intern the day before), care was randomly and unpredictably inconsistent — reflecting the supervising resident's education and experience. If the patient was smart/lucky enough to present with a condition in the senior resident's comfort zone, all was well. However, when the patient's complaints failed to line up with the resident's educational and experiential sweet spots, an element of chance was introduced into the pursuit of correct diagnosis and treatment.

Primarily because of the lack of supervision and teaching, after internship I transferred to a hospital where the residents and interns were closely supervised at the bedside by brilliant, talented and compassionate attending physicians. I soon recognized that many conditions that the city housestaff (including me) were assigning to anxiety (when we chose to be kind) or to malingering (when the unaccepting patient confronted our diagnostic acumen and irritated us) actually were genuine syndromes with specific treatments — ouch, that truth still really hurts.

Sickle cell anemia crisis was a case in point. We, the inexperienced and unsupervised, understood this was a genetic condition, it primarily impacts people of African ancestry and we must avoid creating drug addicts. With this limited set of information, too often, when a vulnerable patient would present with subjective excruciatingly painful crisis (and with few objective signs and symptoms), we (the partially informed) would get our stethoscopes into an unnecessary tangle — is this patient really having pain or is he/she trying to work the system (i.e., work us) with drug seeking behavior?

As I began residency in my new (supervised) setting, an experienced hematologist and master consultant gently taught me:

- The patient with sickle cell disease understands her/his condition far better than we ever will,
- The patient with sickle cell disease can be in crisis without objective findings. We must trust her/his perceptions,
- The patient with sickle cell disease has, through no fault of her/his own, been assigned an unsolicited genetic burden,
- He (the master physician) would much prefer to be "beat out of a dose of narcotics, then to ever withhold analgesia from a patient in pain,"
- To evaluate the pattern and not the incident. The majority present upon rare occasions and can be trusted. Rare patients, who have frequent crises, may or may not have drug seeking behavior. This circumstance can be calmly and professionally investigated and addressed by consulted trained behavioral health specialists and
- Perfect is the enemy of good — in the complex business of caring for patients, we must find the middle. The unreasonable quest to get

each case "perfect" will invariably bring in irresolvable complexities of values and bias and often diminish the greater clinical good.

---

6. *Alex, my editors are enamored with this letter. They find it chock full of messages as important as a plea for vicarious learning. I anticipate those messages are apparent to you. With this as background, I especially look forward to Dr. Drawbaugh's perceptions.*
7. *Other thoughts?*

Respectfully submitted,
Dr. Mike

Dr. Ed Drawbaugh Comments

I suppose that a portion of the message here is about vicarious learning. Dr. White was able to see the mistakes made by his not-fully-trained and not-yet-ready-to teach fellow residents at the large city hospital — but only after he had moved on to more fertile teaching/learning ground. There, he found a better milieu for direct education from fully trained experts.

However, I find the more powerful message to be that of the need for humility. The mature physician will never assume that he/she knows everything and that a patient with a problem which eludes diagnosis must be malingering. Rather, that individual will assume that every patient has a real problem and that the failure to diagnose is the physician's issue. Only after all efforts have been exhausted will the master physician assign befuddling physical complaints to nefarious motives by the patient.

48

*"I say, you work eight hours, and you sleep eight hours.
Be sure they're not the same eight hours."*

T. BOONE PICKENS

The FountainHead WhiteHouse
Alex,

1. *Good morning.*
2. *Thank you for all you do daily so well for so many.*
3. *Sleep is important.   At times, sleep is a precious commodity in short sup-ply for the physician.   As you consider medicine, let me share a few soporific thoughts...*

———

49. Standard Operating Procedure
Currently, residency and fellowship training programs are required to take steps to ensure that physicians caring for patients do not become overly fatigued.

Techniques include duty hour restrictions and support services (for example, lab phlebotomy teams). Targets include enhanced patient outcomes, patient safety and physician wellness. I welcome these efforts to mitigate physician fatigue. So that the importance of this is not lost on you, taken for granted by you or negotiated away from an inattentive you, let me share several remembrances from prehistoric times:

- As a third-year medical student, we put in long days (for example, 5:00 a.m. to 7 p.m. on neurosurgery); however, we were permitted to go home at night — leaving our sleep-deprived supervising interns and residents in the hospital to keep the ship afloat. This provided some painless, vicarious insight for what was to come.
- Fourth year students sometimes were assigned to "acting internships" and took on the responsibilities of the intern day and night. "Acting internships" were fabulous for preparing one to believe he/she could, in fact, clinically, physically and psychologically "man- up/woman-up" to the daunting clinical, academic, administrative, physical and psychic aspects of training.
- When I was entering internship and residency, every third night call was the norm. Let us clarify what every third night looked like:
  - Monday arrive at 7:00 a.m. and leave the hospital Tuesday at 6:00 p.m. — about a 35-hour shift. Sleep if/when able. Sleep like a dead man Tuesday night.
  - Wednesday work 7:00 a.m. to 6:00 p.m. Sleep like a dead man Wednesday night.
  - Thursday arrive at 7:00 a.m. and leave the hospital Friday at 6:00 p.m. — another 35-hour shift. Sleep if/when able. Attempt socialization until sleep like a dead man intervenes on Friday night.
  - Brief Saturday rounds from 7:00 a.m. to noon. Enjoy social day and evening. Force sleep like a dead man in preparation for and fear of Sunday to Monday call (or suffer the consequences).
  - Sunday arrive at 7:00 a.m. and leave the hospital Monday at 6:00 p.m. about a 35-hour shift. Sleep if/when able.

Note1: if you were not on call on Sunday, you did not come to the hospital — a full day off. If you were on call Saturday night, you left Sunday as soon as your work was done.

Note2: if the month started on a Monday with you on call, your first and only Sunday off would occur on the third Sunday — the 22nd of the month.

Note3: adept interns calculated on call schedules with the passion and expertise of autistic adolescents addressing train timetables.

- Sometimes (for example, Intensive Care Unit rotations) when the rotation was really important (read especially academically, clinically, physically and psychically challenging), you were asked to step up to the honor of every-other-night call. Yes, we are talking 35 hours on (sleep if/when able) and 13 off (sleep like a dead man) for the month.

Note: ICU gallows humor: Q: What is the problem with being on call every-other-night? A: You miss half the good cases.

---

50. Rationalization

One might reasonably ask: how could the powers that be for running hospitals and training programs design, implement and maintain such pernicious schedules? We (yes, I was to join their leadership ranks) were adept at perverse rationalizations:

- "We did it,"
- "It is a necessary and honorable initiation into the club designed to separate wheat from chaff and strong from weak,"
- "A young physician needs this hyper-compressed effort and experience to master his specialty in only three to five years,"

- "Our complex and vulnerable patients require our presence. It is all about patient care" and
- "It makes a 'man/woman' of you and prepares you for a lifetime of rigorous practice."

---

51. Near Tragedy

Later in my career as a program director trying to balance resident education with the quality and safety of the hospital's patient care, I fell too comfortably into the above rationalizations. Two incidents separated by twenty years changed me...

A fellow intern, normal in every way but perhaps just a tad less physically resilient than most, was addressing "the honor and privilege" of every-other-night Intensive Care Unit call (despite the residents' union every fourth night contract, ICU call was every other night). Leaving the hospital parking lot at 7:00 p.m., he/she merged onto a Manhattan street into the path of an unseen transit authority bus. Death by bus was only narrowly avoided. Serious injuries required her/him to step away from training for six months and threw her/his training off cycle. Again, now, painfully telling myself the truth, my peers and I attributed her/his accident to her/his personal weakness.

Twenty years hence I was recruited away from my residency program to take on more complex leadership circumstances. A few months later, I contacted one of my favorite (yes, we all have favorites) former residents to check on his progress with his career choices. I was stunned as he casually mentioned that he had "fully recovered from the accident." Driving home one summer afternoon after 30 hours of call (in a residency designed and signed-off on by me), he ran off the highway. Many hours later (he was always getting home later than anticipated), his wife reported him missing. A search of his likely way home found him and his car in a ditch. Airbags and safety belts prevented irreversible harm. Mild ambient temperatures prevented an exposure death. Lessons (I should have learned 20 years before) were immediately learned and policies, procedures, attitudes and behaviors were immediately changed.

---

52. Bees

I was a fourth-year medical student assigned as an acting intern. Proudly on my way to physician manhood, I had had another sleepless night. I was enthusiastically attending a noon-hour endocrine conference on pheochromo-cytoma and attentively sat in the second row. Lunch was served. Beautiful spring sunlight brightened and warmed the room.

I was soon asleep and immediately dreaming — a sign of sleep depriva-tion. I dreamt I was, cloaked in my medical garb, on the perfect Oakmont Country Club practice green on the perfect summer day. Peculiarly, in the middle of the green a four-foot pipe stood with an elegant fine china platter on top. I walked over and removed the ornate dish to study it when angry bees swarmed out of the pipe and attacked me. In painful panic, I screamed and ran.

My resident, sitting next to me in the second row, woke me up. As the story goes, I went from seated quiet sleep to the animated standing screaming of bloody murder. Brief pandemonium ensued. Already a bit of a lightning rod — never a good thing for a lowly medical student — my celebrity was immortalized when a new syndrome was named for me — The White Acting Intern REM Sleep Syndrome.

---

53. Choice of Residency

As I communicate these thoughts, I find I am confronting a previously un-confronted truth. In choosing my straight medical residency train-ing, I weighed academics, clinical experience, reputation, opportunity for fellowship, family requirements, salary and geography. Logically, this small-town lad would have chosen the prestigious University of Rochester Strong Memorial program. Instead, I chose a New York City program where the residents and fellows had a union that had negotiated both every fourth night call and relatively robust salaries. Judiciously considering all requirements (academics, clinical experience, reputation, opportunity for fellowship, family requirements, salary and geography), I chose a Manhattan program. Telling myself the truth, my decision was based on one factor: every fourth night call = 30 fewer calls per year.

54. Beef Burgundy

As a senior resident coming off 35-hour call Friday at 5: 00 p.m., I looked forward to a beef burgundy dinner that my favorite nurse — we would later marry and live happily ever after — was, with great care, proudly preparing. In concert with the festive mood, I, a notoriously non-big drinker, crafted a crude Manhattan. My recollections from here on in are as reported to me: acute vertigo (dizziness) alleviated only by bed rest with one foot on the floor and a dinner never served.

My Saturday noon awakening found remnants of scorched beef burgundy in the trash. To my relief, my kind and compassionate chef recognized I was more victim of sleep deprivation than guilty of over-indulgence and after quite tardy Saturday rounds, we had a lovely day.

Note: I am observing that in all our years, beef burgundy has not once made it back onto a WhiteHouse dinner menu.

55. Two Graduate Medical Education Sleep Syndromes

A near final thought describes two personally discovered graduate medical education sleep syndromes:

- **"4:00 a.m. Transient Addison's Disease"** (as an aspiring physician, please take a moment to Google and comprehend primary adrenal insufficiency, aka Addison's Disease). The symptom complex:
  - Every third night call,
  - Sleepless,
  - Pre-dawn weakness, nausea and vomiting and
  - Resolution with sunrise, the merciful arrival of help (the colleague cavalry) and coffee, eggs and bacon.
- **Valium Equivalent Resident Syndrome** — the symptom complex:
  - Every third night call,
  - Sleepless,
  - 4:00 a.m. Transient Addison's Disease diagnosis, treatment and recovery,
  - Immediate and lasting post-recovery state:
    - Awake
    - Seemingly alert
    - Trance-like state
    - Slow-motion (we are talking slow, slow-motion)
    - Unperturbed by nuclear blasts and
    - Unaware that complex decisions thought infallible were often muddled.
  - Resolution with eleven hours dead man sleep.

———

56. Short Term Memory Loss

Finally, just this year, I was playing golf with a good friend, a good golfer and a great psychiatrist. Our conversation wandered from discussion of our magnificent games to speaking about physicians' career sleep deprivation. It started with his description of an early-that-morning call from the hospital's psychiatric ward. I brought up sleep deprivation. He mused, "My wife has fond memories of significant events — such as the daughter's wedding rehearsal dinner — that she and I participated in over the years for which I have, at best, only vague recollections. I attribute my failure to make memories to professional preoccupations and sleep deprivation." Having the same vague memories for important events — for example, despite lovingly gifted orchestra seats, zero recollection of the lively Broadway show, Barnum — I concurred.

---

4. *Alex, as you move forward with your medical career:*
   - *Understand sleep deprivation, fatigue and actions to mitigate,*
   - *Choose your training and practice circumstances accordingly and*
   - *Carry this knowledge forward and apply it to your entire career. For example, don't be the cardiologist who takes sleepless call all night and then sees patients in the office the entire next day. Put a governor in place.*
5. *Other thoughts?*

Respectfully submitted,
Dr. White (Mike)

Dr. Edward Drawbaugh Comments

As Dr. White has noted in this letter, "in the old days" interns and residents were subjected to inappropriate work schedules. I, myself, endured almost 18 months of 36 on, 12 off rotations. In that milieu, learning is sacrificed for surviving. Fortunately, most of this has now been regulated out of existence. Yet, individuals must guard against voluntarily returning to the old ways for whatever reason. Especially for the practicing physician, where there are no protective rules, the tendency to overwork must be recognized and avoided.

———

57

Keep Your Own Counsel

"What we got here is failure to communicate."

From Cool Hand Luke

The FountainHead WhiteHouse
Alex,

1. *Good morning.*
2. *Thank you for all you do daily so well for so many.*
3. *This message regarding critical communications is very important. If you are not already familiar, please learn and implement today. As you do so, I shall strive to do better in my communications. For now, please, do as I say.*
4. *The message has three components:*
   - *As a physician, you will have a very important and powerful role in your community and in society. You will be part leader and part celebrity. Many will be interested in knowing your business. Therefore, it is important for you to be protective of your public persona. You must keep the workings of your business and your social lives private. Provided your position in your community, it will be wise to consciously and expertly keep your own counsel. Indeed, attention-grabbing words are like toothpaste — once out impossible to put back in. Take care.*

- *When transmitting important, sensitive, communications, less is more. In this regard, a wink is in fact better than a nod; a nod is better than a word; a word is better than a phrase, a phrase is better than a sentence and a sentence is better than paragraph.*
- *Each Important, sensitive communication requires thoughtful preparation. It must be scripted, rehearsed and re-rehearsed. Then, it must be expertly delivered. After delivery, you must, using the broken record technique, stay on point.*

5. *A story may prove illustrative...*

S he was the beautiful scion of the industrial family. As heiress, she was stylishly sophisticated, cultured and traveled. As a blue-collar medical student, full of potential, he was none of those things.

An elegant black-tie university affair brought them in proximity. Opposites do attract. They became inseparable. Her family was aghast. Despite her family's threatening protestations, they moved in together. Her family cut her off.

They pooled their resources. Coming from much, she brought little. He had little. With love keeping them together, they scraped through the hardscrabble existence of the wait staff (her) and senior medical student (him). Knowing no different status, he flourished. Despite devoted effort, the circumstances proved unacceptably confining for her.

Their parting was a blow to both. She was sad. He was crushed. Thoughtless harsh unmeant words were exchanged. She returned to a relieved family who removed her to Tuscany. He soldiered on. Then the letter arrived:

Aspiring Doctor,

I represent the interests of the industrial family. They have become aware that you have taken financial advantage of their daughter. Therefore, to make amends, please submit a check to me for $10,000.

As you are aware, the family is a major benefactor of the university and medical school. As you are aware, the family is professionally and personally connected with university leadership. Receipt of your check will preclude the necessity of complicated revelations.
Sincerely,
Senior Counsel

The stones came down on him. Ten thousand, blood from a stone, might as well be a million. His career and life were at an end.

Truth surfaced. They had pooled their funds. She came with almost nothing. His emergency $1,000 had been dissipated. As the missive arrived, he, tapped out, was negotiating another "absolutely last survival emergency student loan" with an again annoyed dean.

Although sick with worry, he spoke with no one. Finally, he thoughtfully showed the letter to his trusted, invested and very wise medical school advisor, Dr. Smith. Concerned, the professor said, "I do my best thinking when not thinking. Let me let this percolate in my brain for a while." He came back with this plan/script:

- I will call the "senior counsel" as "Doctor/Professor of Psychiatry Smith" (true),
- I will sound important to the inner workings of the university (bluster),
- I will say, "the kids had an affair of the heart" (true),
- I will say "the kids pooled their meager funds and the aspiring doctor contributed more than his share" (true),
- I will say, "there was no $10,000" (true) and then
- I will, from an unwavering script, read, "your letter has been reviewed (bluster). Concern is expressed that there are elements of unvarnished extortion (true) which you may anticipate the university board will not abide (unvarnished bluster)." Click.

———◆———

6. *Alex, the call was perfectly executed. The dramatic hang up occurred only after an anticipated speechless pause on the other end. The phone call was the end of the story.*

7. *A senior attorney, Atty. Jessica Collins White, previewed this chapter and commented, "Implied in the advice is to use preparation to control the emotional part of communications but also to leverage communications to strategically impact another's emotions in addition to his or her thought."*

8. *Back to the message: protect your brand, keep your own counsel and, when imperative, script and execute exact, concise communications.*

9. *Other thoughts?*

Respectfully submitted,
Dr. Mike

Dr. Ed Drawbaugh Comments

The important information in this letter is contained in the three bullet points of paragraph #4. Although the story is illustrative of the third point, I think that the most valuable advice is contained in the first two.

58

AUNT MARIE

"He determines to try this case, by god,
and to prove that the doctors
who took her mind away from her were guilty
of incompetence and dishonesty."

ROGER EBERT RE *THE VERDICT*

The FountainHead WhiteHouse
Alex,

1. *Good morning.*
2. *Thank you for all you do daily so well for so many.*
3. *Let me reluctantly share a life-event as I remember it. I am reluctant because
   of unresolved pain. I am reluctant because I am acutely aware that, if I knew
   then what I know now, there was so much more, I the advocate, should have
   done.*

———•———

When I was just starting out as faculty in Arizona, my mother called with a request from my ancient and revered grandmother — would I please fly back East and look in on my dear Aunt Marie who had been hospitalized with complications of chemotherapy? She, with devoted family at her side, was frightened and asked that I — her favorite (and only) physician nephew — come to her bedside. With travel partially funded by senior family (a necessary consideration in those days), I was soon aloft.

Aunt Marie was the youngest of my grandmother's three children and my mother's younger sister. She was the mother of seven ranging in ages from 24 to 12. For four years after World War II, I was the only nephew or niece to come along and she doted on me. In many ways, she felt like my kind and loving older sister. I was the unwilling four-year-old ring bearer at her wedding. Over the years, she and her husband, Uncle Al, served as vast resources of life's wisdom: driver's license, summer employment, career choice and affairs of the heart. There can be no mistaking that she was my favorite aunt.

I arrived at 5:00 p.m. on a summer Saturday. My uncle took me directly to the bedside. Aunt Marie was tearfully fearful and tearfully relieved to see me. She had been unexpectedly severely ravaged by her out-patient chemotherapy, was dramatically losing her hair, had lost her oral mucosa and her bone marrow (white cells, red cells and platelets). She was febrile. Antibiotics and transfusions were being administered. She rightly feared for her life.

The hospital was nationally recognized as a leading tertiary care, community teaching hospital. Her bedside nurses (a student nurse precepted by an RN), were competent, kind and compassionate. They were immediately very appreciative of and comfortable with my presence. The medical intern caring for Aunt Marie stopped by and provided me with a comprehensive update on her status. Since I was in the business of recruiting and training of medical residents, I came to understand that this fine young man had done his undergrad work at a fine New England college and had graduated from a Caribbean medical school (given the hospital's reputation, this surprised me a bit). He informed me that he and his senior resident (who I was never to meet) were "in charge" of the case. I assured him that I was sure that, with the supervision of the attending oncologist, she was in the best of hands and clarified that my role was that of informed advocate for my aunt and uncle.

At my request, a call went out to the attending oncologist. I wanted to say hello, tell him I had arrived and coordinate times to ensure I would be present when he made Sunday rounds. Shortly thereafter, he returned the call, told me that I was interrupting his preparations for a dinner party, seemed to not be tightly connected to my aunt's case, was at best impolite, was uninformative and stated he could not clarify if/when rounds would be made. I was stunned.

At about 9:00 p.m. the intern returned. He desired consent for placement of a central line. When we asked who would place the line, he said he would under the supervision of his senior resident. After discussion, we called him back and with nursing present we said, "Since the patient is high risk (e.g., bleeding, infection), we consent to the safest central line as advised by and placed by a consulted most experienced surgeon." Specifically we stated, "We do not consent to the placement of a central line by medical housestaff in this high-risk patient." The intern stated he would convey our requirements to the senior resident for his consideration.

At 11:00 p.m. we went to Al and Marie's comfortable home where I was put up in the guest room. At 4:00 a.m. my uncle was called to return to the hospital for a medical emergency. We were directed to ICU waiting. After many hours of exhausting confusion, we eventually pieced together that while the intern and resident were inexplicably placing a subclavian central line my aunt suffered a pneumothorax and a hemothorax and shock. She was transferred to ICU. Not until noon were we permitted to see her by a most officious (mean really) ICU nurse. Aunt Marie was on a ventilator, had a chest tube and was unconscious. Sleepless, exhausted and confused, we were devastated. How could this happen?

Physicians were nowhere to be found. Because the ICU nurse was so un-accommodating (rude actually), my uncle and I asked to speak to a hospital administrator. The nursing director and nurse supervisor met with us. We tearfully explained what had happened. They listened attentively and compassionately. They removed the offensive nurse from the case. From that point forward, the nursing care and physician care of my aunt was exemplary.

Within a few days, we began to understand she had sustained irreversible brain damage. I returned to Arizona — forever changed. Eventually, she would be discharged to a rehabilitation hospital. Without recovery, she was discharged to home where her dining room was converted to a hospital room. After several years of bed-bound family care (falling primarily to the tender-aged youngest siblings), she would pass without finding a lucid moment from that fateful night on.

From a pragmatic point of view, the hospital voluntarily covered all un-insured expenses. My uncle hired an attorney who I understand negotiated a settlement of less than $100.000. And, these many decades later as I write to you, I contemplate:

- The devastating loss sustained by aunt's family with incalculable spou-sal, maternal/child, educational and social implications for those in their formative stages.
- What I might have done:
  - As a physician member of the family and advocate, manned up — been less professionally polite?
  - Legally pursued an invasive procedure done without consent as assault and battery. Should not I have called the sheriff that Sunday?
  - Guided my uncle in his malpractice proceedings. Should I have recognized an incompetent, ambivalent or otherwise distracted (perhaps complicit) attorney and fired him?
  - Personally demanded court proceedings. Should I not have pro-vided my uncle and his children the opportunity to demonstrate their devastation to the physicians and their institution?

Art and life often come together. For a better understanding of that which I am trying to convey please view a classic Paul Newman movie: *The Verdict (1982)*

4. *Alex, years later a similar case in a Boston oncology hospital was discovered to be due to an error in the calculation and administration of chemotherapy dose. With sadness, I shall forever sadly wonder.*

5. *Alex, years later in my book Safer Medical Care for You and Yours — Six Tools for Safe, Effective Compassionate Care, I create and discuss the concept of The Personal Professional Patient Advocate (P3A). All families should have one. With you, Doctor, in the family, your family will.*

6. *Other thoughts?*

Respectfully submitted,
Dr. Mike

Dr. Ed Drawbaugh Comments

What is the message in this story? The family called for help. The young physician came and recognized the danger of central line insertion in a high-risk patient by not-fully-trained housestaff. Family intention that the procedure was to be done only by a well-trained surgical consultant was conveyed. That the housestaff would choose to ignore the family's directive could not have been anticipated. What more could the advocate have done to prevent this tragic outcome? Perhaps nothing, for the intern and resident proved that they were not going to abide by the wishes of the family. But, (pure speculation on my part), one wonders if the advocate and family had been more aggressive in their interactions with the intern, would he have been less headstrong and gotten the consultant involved? No one can know, but I think a possible message is that whenever one is in the role of advocate for another, be it physician-patient or physician-family or friend, there is no place for passivity. One must be as vigilant and aggressive as the situation requires.

59

AVOCATION AND ESCAPE

*"Whatever career you may choose for yourself - doctor,
lawyer, teacher - let me propose an avocation to be pursued
along with it. Become a dedicated fighter for civil rights.
Make it a central part of your life. It will make you a
better doctor, a better lawyer, a better teacher. It will enrich
your spirit as nothing else possibly can. It will give you
that rare sense of nobility that can only spring from love
and selflessly helping your fellow man. Make a career of
humanity. Commit yourself to the noble struggle for human
rights. You will make a greater person of yourself, a greater
nation of your country and a finer world to live in."*

MARTIN LUTHER KING JR

The FountainHead Whitehouse
January 26th
Alex,

1. *Good morning.*
2. *Thank you for all you do daily so well for so many.*

3. *From the beginning, I found it difficult to be "off" when I was not working. I found it necessary to immerse myself in an avocation/hobby. Initially I chose distractions in line with my career — for example, clinical research — that, like Velcro, glued me to my work. Later I found two diversions (golf and writing) that took my mind away from medicine.*

4. *To emphasize the power and productivity of escape, commentator Dr. Drawbaugh's avocations (exotic travel and animal portraiture) are prominently illustrated throughout Letters to an Aspiring Physician.*

5. *In our community, the design of a major intersection poses significant danger for pedestrians. The following letter to the editor took me, in search of concise, perfectly worded phrases — clearly a challenge for me — towards that issue, and, for a time, mercifully away from my professional responsibilities...*

A Dark Route 40 Tale

Although things had not worked out as planned, he was committed to make sense of life. Increasingly, despite best efforts, he can't win for losing.

Not that long ago, he, like your child and mine, was a golden boy — a great student, a superb athlete and everybody's (teachers, co-workers, peers and family) favorite. In college, he continued to excel. But upon graduation, he found himself, like our many, underemployed and overly in educational debt. Half for survival and half to do the right thing, he joined the military. A year later an explosion took his lower legs.

He was having trouble with his prostheses. The rural VA arranged for him to be seen by a specialist in DC. With funds, spirit and energy at low ebb but with the moral and financial support of his humble family, driving his dicey prehistoric vehicle, he made his way from the mountains of Western Maryland to the specialist. The process (traffic, parking, meals, housing) was complex for the wobbly small-town boy but his care was excellent. Problems were identified. Solutions were planned. Hope was restored for ambulation without pain. Employment seemed feasible. Optimism had an important life-making difference on the horizon.

Elated, he had just enough energy and funds to limp home by midnight. On a chilly, dark and rainy night, his vehicle balked at climbing Braddock Mountain. Ascending South Mountain, it became insubordinate. Recognizing a mechanical crisis, he pulled off on 40 West and made his way to a motel parking lot near where 40 and a major boulevard intersect. There his vehicle died.

A motel room was beyond his pay grade. Despite the cold and damp, he would sleep in the car. He was confident cavalry (steely ancient grandmother) would ride to the rescue in the morning and he and she would sort things out from there.

He judged his few remaining coins would best be spent on food at the grocery store. In pain and moving slowly, he set out for a quarter mile walk to the market. Among the bravest of the brave, he was truly frightened crossing Antietam Creek on a busy (spraying vehicles flying by), dark, wet bridge with no designated space for a pedestrian. Having survived that, he found there was no lighting or crosswalk assistance at the major intersection. Motorists' abuse of right-on-red caused uninterrupted traffic flow. In pain, unable to move faster than a snail, he considered retreat. Cold, hunger and thirst drove him on.

In the morning, the news reported another pedestrian fatality on route 40. The grocery staff vividly recalled a tired, shivering, damp, disheveled, polite, affable, engaging young man setting out with a small sack of groceries — compassionately amplified by some day-old freebies.

As the story goes, it was dark and the victim was hard to see. The community's primary question would be: what are people like that thinking?

His grandmother is quite a lady — a foothills farmer's daughter, an accomplished nurse and a senior hospital executive. In her grief, on each anniversary of the tragedy, with all her faculties and limbs in order, she tries a daylight walk from motel to market. Annually she concludes — it cannot be done. Each year incrementally more concerned friends, family and citizens join her. All agree — devoid of the marvels of world-class engineering, you cannot get there from here.

---

6. *Alex, while humbly striving towards a worthy message, the search for phrases and words takes me away.*
7. *I wish to emphasize that it is hard to get away — to escape. It takes deliberate, practiced effort.*
8. *I am remembering a drive from the airport to a favorite Florida vacation venue, burdened by incessant bad-news emails. Although I was on vacation, I was not away. I had not escaped. For me, escape required being consumed — as in anticipating, playing in, thinking about, dreaming about and preparing for the annual member-guest golf tournament.*
9. *With only weak apology on my part for including, you may skip this story, but please heed the message — escape requires being consumed...*

2017 Member-Guest 2018

Like you, I belong to a historic country club that was designed a century ago by a legendary, sadistic, master golf architect — ours by Mr. Donald Ross. Like yours, each summer my club conducts a sacredly serious member-guest tournament.

Formats vary. At our club, a full field provides for 42 member/guest teams, that's 84 golfers. These teams are divided by handicap into seven six-team flights. On Thursday, there is a practice round. Misguided compassion places pins favorably on slow-running greens. Among light-hearted *Bons Amis*, gimmes are generous. Post-round beverages and conversation are superb. Arrogant optimism abounds.

Five nine-hole, best-ball-of-two matches are played on Friday (3) and Saturday (2). On each hole, the winning team is assigned a point. When a hole is tied, each team is assigned a half point. A perfect score for 9 holes would equal 9. A perfect score for the tournament would equal 45. After all matches are played, the winners of each flight enter a playoff with the other six flight winners to determine the tournament winner. Throughout, plentiful food and drink and exceptional playing conditions are ideal — easy peasy.

There are complications. First there is the spouse who has to annually be convinced that three days of adolescent debauchery in the guise of competitive golf at the cost of a minor mansion's mortgage payment is a logical, permissible family expense. If relentless petition is started in the early autumn, wear down is complete (i.e., all objections are eroded) before the field is closed (i.e., before other less-skilled hopeful participants have overcome spousal objections).

Spouse assuaged, choice of guest playing partner is complex. Considerations include: love for the game, stamina, equanimity, competitive drive and handicap. After review, an on-the-surface amiable but sub-rosa pathologically competitive friend in possession of hitman glare, aplomb and an unconscionably inflated handicap who is likely to reciprocate with an invite to Augusta National approximates the ideal.

Then there is the golf...

- Thursday night into Friday's wee hours, residents living near the course complain of the incessant din of rough being fluffed, bunkers buffed and greens thrice cut and double rolled,
- Diabolical pin placements are conceived and executed,
- At inception (9 AM Friday) heat and humidity are consistent with an Oakmont US Open Sunday late afternoon pressure cooker. As play evolves, conditions deteriorate from cooker to fire,
- In the heat, consciousness wanes. The progression: "This game is easy," "I am having a bit of difficulty concentrating," "I now see two balls," "Perhaps another beer is in order," "Where am I?" "Who am I?" And finally, "911 we have an emergency,"
- Each 12-foot putt may only be lightly nudged two feet. If, despite all cautions, it should not go in, it will roll 6-feet by. Downhill putts are exponentially trickier and

- High handicappers (other than your guy) have "career shots" on every hole. Winners extol the rectitude, probity and integrity of the handicap system. Losers mumble cynical lament.

A play by play of one hole of our final round is revealing…

With conceit, my partner and I approach a par three. Our re-adjusted adjusted goals, 1) to not come in last in our flight and 2) to (especially) not to come in last in the tournament. Despite our magnificent potential, at this late juncture, we are pushing both envelopes. Our final opponents are our major competition in both regards.

They are delightful competitors — true gentlemen both. They represent a typical good golfer/bad golfer tandem. Conditions have their bad golfer moving beyond the "who am I?" stage and verging on a mercy call to 911.

Their good golfer is in the rough to the left. He then misplays into the rough on the far side of the green. For all intents and purposes, he is out of the hole. Our good golfer (a legend in his own mind) is on the green with a 12-foot uphill putt for birdie and is assured of a tap-in par.

Their bad golfer (who deservedly gets a stroke on the pare three) is in the rough unpredictably close to the left of the green. He predictably chili-dips it into hopelessly 'worser' rough and faces laughable odds for an up and down. Smelling blood in the water, we circle. With his wits further departed — if this were a boxing match, he would be declared concussed — our tremulous, woozy combatant addresses an invisible ball in deep, snarly rough. His tasks, 1) hit the ball firmly to get it out of the rough (improbable) and 2) stop the ball near the pin — a mere 15 feet from its starting place (impossible). Dangerously rocking back and forth, with shaking hands and closed eyes he smashes at it, dissonantly tops it, careens it into the rough six inches before the fringe and spins it out with perfect English that stops it two feet from the hole — a "good miss" for the ages.

Shaken, our over-coached-by-his-partner legend of a golfer blows his first putt four feet past a pie plate. Missing a return downhill bender towards an indistinct thimble, he three putts for a four. Recognizing he and his partner deserve the ignominy and justice of a well-won last place, he removes all doubt by graciously conceding the two-foot winner to their barely conscious opponent.

Exhausted and irate (the technical golf term is pissed), the non-winners (aka the "biggest losers") make their way to the parking lot. Genial observation of the play-offs and affable toleration of good-natured ribbing — the "good sports" thing — is not in them. Lost in coulda, shoulda, woulda recriminations — chief among their many mortifications, their hubris had bet the ranch they would win their flight and the tournament — they pack up and slither home.

A week goes by and a lame excuse is found for good friends to communicate, "I have an extra ball-mark in my bag, is it yours?" The next week, there is a breakfast meeting. Per code, all four-letter words (especially golf) are verboten. At the end of the month, there is a friendly two-dollar Nassau — as usual winner remains in dispute — and all is again well.

As the days have shortened and the evenings cool, I, on the jot, have begun chatting up the spouse about the obvious favorable cost/benefit ratio of a 2018 re-do. At this time, her enthusiasm and encouragement are muted (read, on schedule with all systems go).

—————◆—————

10. *Alex, avocations are encouraged. Escape is required. At the same time, heed Phyllis McGinley's caution, "The trouble with gardening is that it does not remain an avocation. It becomes an obsession."*
11. *Other thoughts?*

Respectfully submitted,
Dr. Mike

Dr. Ed Drawbaugh Comments

Balance in one's life can be a difficult thing to achieve, especially for physicians. Work and family time are naturally the most important, with each individual having to decide where the balance point between these two should reside. Early in one's career, there is little time for anything else. Yet, as soon as possible, it can be very rewarding and refreshing to develop one or more outlets for mental and/

or physical rejuvenation. Whether these take the form of hobbies, sports, travel, writing (as for Dr. White) or whatever else is immaterial, as long as the individual finds relaxation and fulfillment in them.

I have found tremendous satisfaction from the study of photography. The technical aspects make perfect sense to my left brain while the artistic component constantly challenges the under-developed right side.

Regal Ms. Lion, Tanzania
EJDMD

238

60

Dying

"Death never comes at the right time,
despite what mortals believe.
Death always comes like a thief."

CHRISTOPHER PIKE

The FountainHead WhiteHouse
Alex,

1. *Good morning.*
2. *Thank you for all you do daily so well for so many.*
3. *Sometimes life taught me that which I should reasonably have learned in my training...*

———————

One day while conducting teaching rounds I was interrupted by a frantic call from my wife, Jackie, who is not given to such things. I immediately knew a great tragedy had befallen. Between sobs, she told me our 3-year-old beagle, Abby, had cried out, taken a few last breaths and died in her arms in our living room.

Jackie was distraught and inconsolable. I immediately left work and made the 30-minute trek home. I found my wife and her neighbor friend having tea in the kitchen. Our pooch was on the living room floor where she had lovingly been covered with a comforter. She appeared to be in a peaceful asleep.

Although my wife had collected herself, she was still a wreck. She was doubly troubled. She had lost her good best friend and, with dread, she was anticipating the scene that would unfold in a few hours when the children, ages 14 and 12, would return from school to find their devoted friend stolen from their lives.

I carried the body to the basement, set her up for viewing, consoled my wife and returned to my hospital duties. As I drove back, part of me wondered about the big deal. OK, so our dog has died. In time, we will get another. Surely, it is not the end of the world as we know it.

The kids came home and their reactions were worse than anything that could be imagined. The oldest daughter chose to accuse my wife of lying and simply refused to accept the death. The younger boy fell apart. Both realized that, in Abby, they always had an unconditional friend. With Abby, even in their darkest moments — unjustly grounded on a Saturday night — they were never alone. Through all this, I was lost in the so important work that could not wait at the office.

Eventually, I returned home. I willingly made it my responsibility to dig the grave; to carry Abby to and place her in her resting place; to lead a ceremony and to cover the grave. As I did so, the enormity of the situation began to catch up with me. The irreplaceable loss of devotion, joy and warmth love and the onset of coldness, stiffness, lifelessness, darkness and finality — so clear from the beginning to the wife and kids — overcame me. That night, with the others, I cried myself to sleep.

In two weeks, the daughter began to consider another beagle. In four weeks, the son was willing to begin to trust that there is a God. Abby was replaced by Sadie — the adorable beagle puppy from hell. Soon she began to do things that helped all of us fondly remember and mercifully forget our good friend.

These many years later, I remain impressed that my wife and children intuitively understood so much more about the realities of death and dying than I, the professional, did. I am grateful that they so patiently and skillfully taught me.

After review, I should have learned what they knew so well in medical school and residency. When my patient died, I should have, at least once, worked with nursing to physically, respectfully and lovingly prepare the newly deceased for viewing by the family. Then I should have stayed on to mingle and converse with the family. Finally, upon their departure, I should have assisted nursing with the physical movement of my patient from her/his room towards a final resting place.

———————

4. *Alex, perhaps Juli Fraga's New York Times article, "When a Pet Dies, Helping Children Through the Worst Day of Their Lives" should be mandatory reading for the medical student.*
5. Other thoughts?

Respectfully submitted,
Dr. Mike

Dr. Ed Drawbaugh Comments

I agree with Dr. White's idea about including medical students or interns as a part of the team dealing with the immediate aftermath of a patient's death. To fully understand the finality of the event and its impact on the deceased's loved ones would be a powerful learning experience, and assistance in the preparation and transport of the body would be a final show of respect for the individual. These perspectives would be invaluable in the formative experience of a physician.

Yet, the young clinician would need an experienced guiding hand to steer her/him away from the family at the appropriate time. The same mentor would also have a powerful role in helping the pupil learn how to appropriately grieve for a lost patient while still maintaining sufficient objectivity to render care at the highest level for her/his remaining patients.

Surveying the Plain, Tanzania
EJDMD

61

In Search of Affordable HealthCare

"The Affordable Care Act is not that affordable."

Al Redmer

The FountainHead WhiteHouse
Alex,

1. *Good morning.*
2. *Thank you for all you do daily so well for so many.*
3. *As you step forward into a medical career, it important to understand health insurance in 2017 — which will certainly morph to something very different within the next decade.*
4. *The Cliff Notes: in 2017 those with Medicare are, for the moment, in a health-care sweet spot. The indigent with Medicaid are provided "free" healthcare (but hospitals and physicians are underpaid and are often unwilling participants). Those with traditionally "great" insurance now often face massive deductibles and the risk of financial ruin if illness intervenes.*
5. *Combining concepts: healthcare and avocation, consider an article I wrote for consideration by a local newspaper...*

———

Perusing our local newspaper, a recent a headline grabbed me — premiums for Obama Care might rise 30% for 2017. Understanding that premiums will rise in 2017, let us appreciate 2016 as a baseline.

I have run into many ladies in this same situation: an older husband has retired and qualified for Medicare coverage; the younger spouse has several years to go prior to Medicare eligibility; and the spouse is no longer covered by her husband's corporate healthcare coverage. To avoid being uninsured, the spouse must find coverage through Affordable Care Act /Obama Care (ACA/OC).

Let us consider one lady's not-entirely-hypothetical excursion into (ACA/OC) that was shared with me:

- Relief — thanks to ACA/OC, healthcare insurance that recognizes preexisting conditions is available.
- Pain — coverage is going to be expensive. If lucky and she seeks no care (an improbability), she will pay $7,000 in premiums in 2016. If major care is required, she will pay an additional $5,000 in deductibles before insurance coverage first begins to kick in.
- Feeling healthy, invincible and bullet-proof, she considers going uninsured in 2016 and pocketing a cool $7,000. Oops #1, their accountant says she will have to pay the IRS a penalty of about $1,500 for being uninsured and Oops #2, one serious illness or accident will make $12,000 look like chump change.
- With premiums paid: tough decision #1, she will daily pay meticulous attention to diet and exercise; tough decision #2, prescription medications will be kept to a minimum; tough decision #3, preventative care will just have to wait for Medicare and tough decision #4, she will keep her organized and personal medical record in order and at her fingertips (just in case) to facilitate safe, efficient compassionate care.
- Remembering that life is what happens while making plans, her strategy is: 1) to hope for the best — staying healthy and avoiding major and preventative care — and spend about $8,000 on premiums and unavoidable care and 2) to prepare for the worst — $12,000 plus.

- After review, she is most grateful for the opportunity to purchase healthcare insurance as a bridge to Medicare and she feels most fortunate to be positioned to address premiums and the threats of deductibles and co-pays.
- She worries. Based on her experience, how can those working paycheck to paycheck manage? She surmises that they may just be able to pay premiums but will be crushed attempting to address co-pays and deductibles if/when illness intervenes.
- She was prepared to swallow hard for an increase in 2017. The numbers are now in. Choosing a plan with lesser benefits, her premium will be $7900 and her deductible $6500 — totaling $14,400 to first dollar of insurance coverage.

The good lady has conflicting emotions regarding Medicare. She hungers for the coverage but is in no hurry to meet prerequisites (age 65).

Time has passed and blessed Medicare has caught up with the lady. Alas, Medicare is not free. For her first year of Medicare (2017 figures), her expenses will approximate:

- A quarterly Medicare premium of $402: $1,608
- A Medicare Supplemental ($2,200 deductible) premium: $442
- A prescription plan ($400 deductible) premium: $365
- Potential deductibles: $2,600

After review, her worst-case Medicare scenario is $5,000, which equates to $9,400 better than her Affordable Care alternative. Through good fortune and hard work (diet and exercise), she intends to spend less than $5,000.

She is thrilled and relived to have the privilege of "affordable" Medicare. She wishes all were as fortunate.

6. *Alex, how do I process this information?*
   - *Healthcare is unaffordable,*
   - *We will move towards a single payer system (Medicare for all),*
   - *Premiums and deductibles will rise for all,*
   - *Reimbursements for physicians will decline and*
   - *The truly rich will find and participate in a separate system of care.*
7. *How did we get here? An insightful insurance executive (Ms. Gaye McGovern) shared this with me, "healthcare dollars are important regardless of whether they are from insurance, government programs or something like Medicare for everyone birth to death. The latter seems to be where the US will eventually end up. Recently I read a reprise of healthcare changes in developed countries following WWII. Most had government health programs for all citizens by then. But the stated reasons that the US did not follow included our tradition of capitalism and competition as hallmarks of a balanced economy, fear of anything seeming like Socialism (we were in the Cold War at that point with fear to be fingered by McCarthy as communist) and surprisingly to me, the objection of the AMA and the hospitals. So here we are in the US, stuck with politics at the heart of the national healthcare discussions at the Congressional level.*

   Patient safety is what healthcare should be about. CMS seems to be directing insurance and providers in this direction. In the end, the outcome for the patient is what matters. Thank you for your patient safety efforts."
8. *Therefore, as I advocate for a career in medicine, I again advocate the student leave medical school relatively debt free — thereby making the joy of practicing medicine primary and massive income requirements a secondary consideration.*
9. Other thoughts?

Respectfully submitted,
Dr. Mike

Dr. Ed Drawbaugh Comments
I am not as certain as Dr. White that America will move to a single payer (i.e. federal government) health system, but I think that is most likely correct. The one

certainty is that the delivery system of ten years from now will be decidedly different from that which exists today. Those entering the medical field will need to be adaptable, but will also have the privilege and excitement of participating in molding the new system. Hopefully it will serve us all better than what exists today.

Vervet Monkey Family Portrait, Tanzania
EJDMD

62

THIS DID NOT HAPPEN?

"I would get my student loans, get money,
register and never really go.
It was a system I thought would somehow pan out."

RAY ROMANO

The FountainHead Whitehouse
Alex,

1. *Good morning.*
2. *Thank you for all you do daily so well for so many.*
3. *It was not until midcareer that Dr. Grover's words would resonate with me (see Jaguar letter above), "The physician should have but four financial goals: her/his education, her/his family's educations, her/his home and her/his retirement."*
4. *From that point forward, I began to introduce pre-meds, medical students and physicians-in-training to his wisdom.*
5. *Let us again find power in a story. Its ending will be left up to you…*

———◆———

There is a rumor out there that I cannot validate. It seems so outlandish that my instincts would have me just ignore it. However, it continues to circulate. The version I have heard goes something like this:

A blue-collar kid went after the American dream. She was the first in the family to go to college. Then, she went on to medical school. What a great country we live in.

She was always in the top echelon of whatever she attempted: good student, good athlete, nice personality and a favorite among friends. She was insightful and realized any success she enjoyed stemmed more from hard work, passion and persistence than from natural ability. Therefore, she was always dedicated to go the extra mile to ensure success.

Unlike many of her suburban high school peers, she had to work to make ends meet. From age 16, she worked at the neighborhood pharmacy evenings and weekends, caddied at the country club on the weekends (proudly the only female AA caddy) and loaded trucks at the newspaper mailroom from 2:00 to 5:00 a.m. twice a week. This allowed her to support a modest private (parochial) school education and have a semblance of stylish clothes, etc. It also gave her a priceless feel and appreciation for the real world and real people that would stay with her forever. Her schedule did cut into her social life and sleep. Although she sometimes had to say no to things, she never seemed to mind.

She was the oldest of four children. Her parents were bright and driven but had not gone to college. To provide a comfortable home, they both worked several jobs. Family values were strong. Standards were high. For the more gifted, more was expected. After review, it was a good environment to grow straight and strong.

From the beginning (first grade actually), it was anticipated that she would go to college and medical school. However, when the time came, there were no savings for a college education. This vacuum was more reality than oversight. Her family was making it day to day — the proud middle-class thing.

She was early admissions at the local small private college (great reputation, strong pre-med program, beautiful campus, expensive). With scholarships and loans, it was doable. To keep expenses reasonable, she lived at home and commuted as a "townie/brown bagger" — sobriquets not always meant to be endearing. Although she continued to work at the pharmacy and newspaper, she rarely had two spare dollars in her pocket. She was unable to remain stylish so it became unimportant to her. In those instances when she felt she had less time to devote to her studies than her peers (and feared she may not be competitive for medical school), she would just sleep less and work more. Academic breaks were opportunities to double-up at work. Travel or time off, were never a consideration. Although there were many interested suitors, she determined she would not complicate the complicated by exploring a serious emotional relationship.

In final analysis, she was all about meeting her primary goals — a solid education and admission to medical school. As she observed, almost as an outsider, her more traditional classmates revel in graduation, she did privately admit to having some regret for missing much of the once in a lifetime experience of campus life.

Then it was on to medical school. Application and interview expenses allowed her to only pursue two interviews. She was accepted at her expensive regional private medical college. With a vague understanding that things work out, she matriculated to this closest to home school. Generous loans were made available to make it financially possible — with no counseling that physicians such as her were forever doomed to a high income/low wealth existence. Despite the rigors of her studies, she worked nights in the hospital chemistry laboratory. There was little in her life out of the medical school culture. Avocations she truly enjoyed and was good at (skiing, golf, photography, theater) were set aside.

She did well and was consistently in the upper third of her class. As her clinical years progressed, she came to understand she was definitely not a surgeon but she did immensely enjoy family practice, internal medicine, psychiatry and pediatrics. Although she preferred psychiatry, she feared she would be unable to make a living in that field so she chose internal medicine and matched with a well–respected university program.

She fit right in. Given her background and work ethic she became one of the program's most accomplished residents. She enjoyed her work, and loved for the first time, having, however modest ($12,000/year), an income and the rare luxuries (for example, a fast food dinner out) it enabled. Her faculty mentors advocated fellowship training (infectious diseases and rheumatology were attractive to her); however, she enjoyed general medicine and was, at age 30, frankly anxious to have an income and a life. When she was heavily recruited to sign on with an HMO associated with her university, she did so.

Based upon an identified need among graduating residents, her enlightened residency program director — "it is my responsibility to prepare you for success in life as well as for success in medicine" — offered to review her financial situation with her. She took her up on her offer. After review, they determined:

- She had realized a $180,000 (tuition) education,
- When she left medical school, she had $40,000 in college debt and $100,000 in medical school debt at 8% interest,
- She was proud that, given her hard work, her indebtedness was not, like some of her resident peers, much greater (a scary thought),
- She was disturbed to confront the fact that as she left residency, her debt had already grown to $163,000,
- She was required to enter a 10-year repayment program. They calculated a monthly loan payment of $1977,
- General internists were entering the marketplace at $90,000 to $120,000. She signed on for $105,000 plus benefits (health insurance, disability). No retirement plans other than a 401K with a modest employer contribution were offered,
- The contract was for two years with 90 days cancellation by either party. Painfully her program director explained she had signed a 90-day contract,
- She could reasonably expect to work a 50-hour week plus call from home every fourth night and every fourth weekend call,
- There was little likelihood of significant bonus or salary advancement in the next several years,
- She had no other significant debt; however, she had no savings, furniture, or clothes to speak of. She envisioned a wardrobe for work, a

reliable new car, a starter home and a significant vacation (Europe) in her first year. She understood it was important for her to begin to save for her retirement (401K). Given her big job and princely salary, her parents were pressuring her to assist her youngest sib with his college education and

- She was stunned to find that the loan payments (neither principal nor interest) would not be recognized as business expenses for tax purposes.

She and her program director ran the numbers and in 15 minutes they understood:

I. Monthly income:		*$8750*
II. Monthly expenses:		
• *Loan repayment*	*$1975*	
• *IRS*	*$1940*	
• *State tax*	*$260*	
• *Car payment*	*$350*	*($16,860@9% X 5 years)*
• *Condo Mortgage*	*$600*	*($90,000@7% X30 years)*
• *401k (voluntary)*	*$525*	*(6% maximum contribution)*
• *Insurance*	*$125*	
• *RE/school taxes*	*$210*	
• *Social Security*	*$375*	
• *Parking*	*$65*	
III. Monthly expense sub-total	*$6425*	
IV. Monthly disposable income		*$2325*

She very much appreciated the program director's analysis and she became a bit realistically despondent. After review, she began thinking about the exigencies of paint, carpet, necessary furniture, too-long delayed orthodontics and professional wardrobe. Violating Einstein's law (the most powerful force in the universe is compound interest), she began to trim her 401k savings.

Any thoughts of vacation were put on hold. With a 50 hour plus work-week, she was stunned to find herself wondering out loud about moonlighting opportunities.

Although she never approached a career in medicine as a business deal, for the first time she wondered, with some angst and anger, if her college and medical school deans understood these numbers. Physicians in her circumstance were high-income, low-wealth individuals with education loans and taxes making it impossible to get ahead for many years. She felt betrayed that her deans had not shared some truth in lending as they encouraged her to borrow dearly to finance her medical education and at the same time take herself away from gainful employment for almost a decade.

Her anxiety and anger were additionally fueled by the question — having sacrificed her youth to get to personal and professional life at the end of the tunnel, could it be there was no end to the tunnel?

6. *Alex, it is my intent to inform you — "forewarned is forearmed." Although it is not my intent to frighten you from a medical career, this outlandish rumor intensifies...*

A few months after settling into her position and community, her institution pursued cost cutting and her position was eliminated. Although her work was exemplary, their policy was last in first out. Finding her community totally over-doctored, she picked up stakes, headed towards home and latched onto a similar circumstance. Her condo was placed on the market but did not sell so she could not qualify for a mortgage or afford rent. Therefore, she moved in with her parents. As the story goes, shortly thereafter she was downsized again. At last report, she was contemplating her options.

7. *Alex, I choose to first believe this story but not allow it to end here. I give it two endings...*

#1 The young doctor picked up stakes and sought out a community that needed a general internist. Although she had to make some family and geographic compromises, she was soon gainfully employed and reasonably compensated in a place that needed and appreciated her. Her condo sold (putting the lie to old infectious diseases joke: Q: What does not belong: syphilis; herpes; or, a condo? A: Syphilis — you can never get rid of herpes or a condo.

She connected professionally and personally with a spectacular peer (whose finances were actually worse than her own). Recognizing Thoreau's wisdom, "A man is rich in proportion to the number of things he can afford to leave alone," they lived sensibly — Holiday Inn Express versus the Four Seasons was their private joke. After a decade, their education debts were behind them and they were addressing souls, home, college educations and taxes. They loved the honor and privilege of their careers. They were doing meaningful work and making a difference. Life was good. Provided their too little, too late start towards their retirement planning, they good-naturedly resigned themselves to the honor and privilege of doing their good work and making a difference well into dotage.

#2 Given her back-to-back double fiscal traumas, the young physician ran the numbers. After review, she recognized the straight line shortest distance between her and solvency was a gastroenterology fellowship. She applied, was accepted and within three years was handsomely employed. She connected professionally and personally with a peer who her father fondly called "the trust fund kid." *(Author's good-natured note, "I shall never forgive my father-in-law for not being independently wealthy").* They enjoyed the honor and privilege of their profession and made a difference. When the children came along, she was able to cut back at work and give them the attention they deserve. Three decades later when they became empty nesters, they opened a government-supported free clinic in the Caribbean and today they continue to "enjoy important work and make a difference."

———◆———

8. *Alex, if you have waded through Physician Finances I, II and III, then I owe you my bias. Having been there and done it, there is no greater honor and privilege than being a physician. Having said that, I cannot advocate that a young person signs on to give up her/his youth and live in poverty for 15-20 years. Therefore, I advocate that you pursue a medical career only if you can begin your professional life reasonably debt free. As the kids might say, use OPM (other people's money). Find others (for example, encouraging family, military, public health, community, major scholarship) to proudly subsidize, enable and share in the honor and privilege of your devoting your life to medicine.*

9. *Alex, I shared this chapter with a surgical colleague, Dr. Push Senan. He fears I have been too harsh. He states, "Although the finances of a medical career have become more complex, Medicine is still the noblest profession. So If the aspiring physician is attracted to a vocation that provides opportunity for meaningful work that makes a difference then, with eyes wide open, he/she must merely consider her/his education as, what will ultimately be recognized as, a modest first mortgage and step up to a second mortgage for home when propitious circumstances allow. But, at all costs the aspiring physician must follow her/his dream."*

10. *Dr. Senan convinces me there is a definite middle for consideration. In fact, I have always said, "My (huge) educational debt was merely my first mortgage." Therefore, please consider two related thoughts: speaking to the compensation of professional athletes, retired NFL All-star Eric Davis states, "You are not paid what you deserve. You are paid what you negotiate" and his observations had me remembering my negotiations when I was leaving Arizona to step up to a leadership role in Western Pennsylvania. While completing phone negotiations with the President/CEO (Mr. Howard Jones), I had seventeen requests. He said yes to each. Hanging up I was stunned. I shared my confusion with my Arizona/life mentor (Dr. Wm James Howard) who immediately concluded, "Your list was not long enough." So true — especially regarding my salary request. Years later (and way late), as a physician executive I went to a seminar conducted by Mr. Roger Dawson — "Mastering the Art of Power*

Negotiation." My major take away: (although humans always do) never underestimate the power you have in the negotiation process.
11. Other thoughts?

Respectfully submitted,
Dr. Mike

Dr. Ed Drawbaugh Comments

I have little to add to this important lesson. However, I will mention that I have worked with a number of superb physicians who were trained in the military, and I highly recommend this route as a consideration.

Zebra Portrait, Tanzania
EJDMD

63

Technical School

The FountainHead WhiteHouse
Dear Alex,

1. *Good morning.*
2. *Thank you for all you do daily so well for so many.*
3. *Many years ago, I was asked to present at a small breakout session at a national assembly of internal medicine program directors. The purpose of the session was to demonstrate efficient teaching/learning. The participants' assigned task was to present an important concept of their choice in a memorable way in 5 minutes or less. To this assigned task I added a personal requirement — the presentation would also be memorably funny.*

    At the time, a new phenomenon was being noted in the recruitment of United States medical students into residency. Fewer and fewer students were choosing internal medicine and more and more were choosing the surgical specialties. After review, a major reason for the shift was massive college and medical student debt and the enhanced income potential of the surgeon.

    As I made my presentation, I was, give or take, forty years of age. By all appearances, I was finding success: career, family, income, etc. Less apparent, I would still be paying of my educational debts for several more years. I told an audience of department chairs, program directors, faculty and chief residents the following fiction as if it were fact...

———◆———

I, T. Michael White MD, am blue-collar kid from Schenectady, New York. I have an identical twin brother Mr. T. Jonathan White — my beautiful, younger brother Jack. As identical twins, we had everything genetically in common; yet, our lives and career paths could not have evolved differently.

A thumbnail of my early life — I was mature, studious and driven. From early on I had my sights on pre-med at a fine school and a career in medicine. Finances were tight so I scrimped and saved. Hard work at part-time jobs and sacrifice were the norm. Time and sleep, as in never quite enough, were always an issue. I received a great deal of positive feedback from parents and teachers and, for many I was the "darling." Jack alone would lovingly provide counsel, "Get a life."

In contradistinction, Jack floated through life as the golden boy. In fact, in the privacy of our double room in the attic of the family homestead — tidy on my side and less so on his — with admiration I called him "Horning". He gladly left the manifestation of any and all obsessive-compulsive behaviors to me. Grades seemed unimportant. Athletic pursuit, politics and social events were his sweet spots. Time and money were never an issue. Sleep — "the 'rack monster' adducted me," he would say — was his specialty. Despite his equanimity, he would often be counseled to be "a bit more like Mike."

Twenty-two years ago, we went our separate ways. I went onto to a prestigious (read expensive) college; medical school; internship; residency; chief residency; and, fellowship. Nine years ago, I signed on as junior faculty and scored my first paycheck. In three years, I will have retired my education debt (my first mortgage). At that time, with Pittsburgh home, cars, etc. in order, I hope to begin to begin to fund family educations and consider a retirement plan.

Twenty-two years ago, Jack went to electronics technical school where he distinguished himself. Twenty years ago, IBM hired him. Immediately he began to climb the corporate ladder. Along the way, they funded his bachelors and MBA degrees. Twenty years ago, IBM and he began to fund his retirement plan. Was it Einstein who said, "The most powerful force in the universe is compound interest?" — I chose to believe so. Anyway, Jack and family are living large (with home, cars, boat, educations and retirement in order) in Florida.

Just last month my parents, my family and Jack's family assembled at his truly lovely home beside Boca Ciega Bay. After dinner, as the sun set, all, except my mother and me, made their way from the poolside table to the end of the dock. For years, she has been embarrassingly sure to let everyone know about "her son the doctor." For all those years, I have been a source of pride and joy. As she and I sat looking beyond Jack's pool to the tops of the distant sailing masts touched by the setting sun, she asked, "Why didn't you go to technical school like your brother Jack?"

———————

4. *Alex, it is fair to say the audience loved the story. With the punch line there was riotous, uncomfortable laughter. Years later, they still want to talk about it.*

5. *The audience provided the following feedback:*
   - *This humorous fiction conveys painful truth,*
   - *Our profession represents a long slog,*
   - *We are very much into delayed gratification,*
   - *Many medical students do accumulate significant debt,*
   - *Career decisions must take economics into consideration,*
   - *The requisite investment of time and money in our careers sets us up poorly for addressing the big four: our education, our children's educations, our homes and our retirements,*
   - *It is possible to convey a complex message in five minutes and*

- *The message was entertaining and the entertainment was critically important to successfully conveying (and remembering) the message.*

6. *For several years thereafter I worked to make it my responsibility to make aspiring physicians aware of the fiscal reality of the career choices. Partnering with others, the physician finances became part of our residency's curriculum. Medical students and residents were most attentive and appreciative.*

7. *I was invited to speak regionally and nationally. Although I was making a difference, I realized the audience I was addressing was already too far down into their career pipeline to make decisions that would enable dramatic impact. The better audience would be the mature pre-med student — students to whom I did not have ready access. Soon I became distracted by other responsibilities, gave up the ghost and went onto other endeavors — until now and this privileged dialogue with an aspiring physician.*

8. *Other thoughts?*

Respectfully submitted,
Dr. Mike

———

V. Hollywood

"There is no great genius without some touch of madness."

ARISTOTLE

64

NURTURED GENIUS

"Once we accept our limits, we go beyond them."

ALBERT EINSTEIN

The FountainHead WhiteHouse
Alex,

1. *Good morning.*
2. *Thank you for all you do daily so well for so many.*
3. *I want to put up a warning flare: even though you may have your humble head on straight, for inexplicable reasons, otherwise very kind and compassionate colleagues will find it necessary to work to diminish your success.*
4. *A brilliant internal medicine resident, Dr. Ravindra Godse, comes to mind. When I told him a hundred years ago, I wished to write a book, he began to write magnificent books, screenplays and produce, direct, act in, film and distribute movies.*
5. *I am remembering: 1) he was really talented (genius actually) and 2) rather than to jump up and offer support, good people inexplicably went out of their way to diminish his early work.*

6. *Now that he is a cinematic icon, I submitted several thoughts that he may use as niduses for tales to be told. As I was contemplating my messages to you, he and I had the following catch-up communications...*

Dr. Ravi,

Hello.

Jackie and I are contemplating moving from our empty nest. So, I have begun to thin my library — no point moving tons of unread/unreadable fungus growing parchment to Florida. As you might predict, as I remove three books, Jackie returns two.

In the process, I came upon a keeper — your first book, *2 guys; 3 girls* and *A MAD PROFESSOR*. As I reviewed a chapter or two, I immediately remembered a classic worthy of P.G. Wodehouse —a wonderful, humorous story well told. I also remembered inexplicably jealous medical colleague naysayers.

And I am wondering — is there another book in the works; is there a new movie in the works; and where stands your artistic career?

Dr. Mike,

It is always good to hear from my mentor.

I just came back from India where I finished directing my fourth movie. It is called Remember Amnesia. You had read and given feedback on the script. It stars Tovah Feldshuh who has been nominated for two Primetime Emmys and is a Broadway star with several Tony nominations and Drama Desk wins.

At this time, I am remembering a story you told me about a hero pilot, a dysfunctional workplace impacting aircraft safety, workplace courage, a workplace lawyer (the story's hero), effete human resources response and a happy ending. Converting this to a serious script followed quickly by a movie, would be interesting. Of course, I would make it funny without losing the intensity. Before I get my teeth into my next film — Honey, I Changed the Past — this could be a pleasant distraction.

I like to write the whole 90-minute script in one sitting. Then it goes through about 11 drafts worth of polishing. Let's find time to meet so you can add some color to the brief story you shared with me.

*Note: my internal medicine practice flourishes. My clinical work keeps me grounded. Spouse, partner (and fellow mentee) Dr. Madhuri says hello. She still observes that I am "famous for writing, producing, directing, shooting and **watching**" my own movies.*
Dr. Ravi

———

7. Alex, the (wrong) adverse opinion of others did not influence him — please refer again to Toltec Master #5. Remembering Mark Twain, "Keep away from people who try to belittle your ambitions. Small people always do that, but the really great make you feel that you, too, can become great."

8. A hidden message: I am confident his artistic work is enhanced daily by the honor, privilege, responsibility and perspective of his medical training and career.

9. An obvious message worth emphasizing — his practice of medicine remains important to him.

10. Personally hoping to be discovered by Hollywood, I sent the good doctor/writer/producer/director/actor (what do we do to good people? —we punish them) four more fictions possibly worthy of exploration:

———

65. Not Mister

I don't care to belong to any club that
will have me as a member."

GROUCHO MARX

The FountainHead WhiteHouse
Dr. Ravi,

1. *Good morning.*
2. *Thank you for all you do daily so well for so many.*
3. *Many ask me why I insist on addressing them with their title (Attorney, Coach, CEO, CNO, Doctor, Judge, Mister, Professor, Reverend; etc.) and signing Dr. Mike.*
4. *To explain, please consider a decidedly unpleasant fictitious encounter with an esteemed (in his own mind) fellow physician that may help to explain why I believe there may be a story for you to tell...*

The evening was a country club delight — a candlelight dinner in celebration of the holidays. Every detail was meticulously addressed. Those responsible had successfully placed the event over the top.

As the evening was concluding, a physician was approached by a colleague who went *ad hominem,* "in this community we do not introduce ourselves as "Dr. Smith or Dr. Jones." Rather we say, "I am John Jacob Jingleheimer Schmidt a physician at the hospital." He then went on to say "your insistence on being called "doctor" and not "mister" make you a deserved pathetic object of ridicule." Resembling those remarks (and remembering Toltec Master #5 — do not be affected by the perspectives of others) unhurt he explained:

- "I have had the privilege of being a member at golf clubs around the country where the staff had been meticulous, without coaching, to use the prefix, doctor, for appropriate members,
- I belong to the club for three reasons: 1) social (minor), 2) golf (major) and 3) venue to entertain business associates — primarily healthcare types (major),
- When I first joined and would invite business associates who are members of distinguished national clubs, they were surprised to hear me called "mister. They shared five observations:
  1. Despite reasonable tenure, the golf club did not know who I was,
  2. Despite reasonable tenure, the golf club did not care who I was,
  3. They have been invited to a most peculiar golf club,
  4. #1, #2 and #3 troubled them and made them uncomfortable and more likely
  5. They felt compelled to (with glee) to take the opportunity to make me uncomfortable.
- So I have consistently advocated that staff:
  1. Address me by my first name or
  2. Address me as doctor and
  3. Never (did I mention never) call me mister or the even more dreaded fumble — "mister doctor."

Note for emphasis: calling me by my first name is entirely acceptable.

- Since I have stated my preference, I note that the staff meticulously meets my expectations. More importantly, I observe they now address all physician members and professors as "doctor."
- Finally, our fine club would tremendously benefit from more members. Our community tremendously benefits from our club — for example, it is "the" venue for weddings. Its health and well-being as a community treasure is important to many. Sadly, only the smallest percentage of doctors in our community belong to and support our club. They seem to be more comfortable elsewhere. Something feels

wrong to th*em. I observe your mean-spirited assault this evening contributes to their being ill at ease."

He calmly listened. Unmoved he stated, "I continue to disagree." Respecting John Jacob Jingleheimer Schmidt's, a physician at the hospital, prerogative, the "real doctor" carried on.

———

5. *Dr. Ravi, moving from fiction to reality, my message to you begins:*
    - *(minor) — it should appear to my guests that staff know me,*
    - *(minor) — it appears that some, who readily observe they "can buy and sell me" are made uncomfortable at the distinction between mister (them) and doctor (me),*
    - *(major) — doctors in fact are different. The sacrifices we make (11-15 years of arduous training and a life-time of unremitting responsibility) distinguish us,*
    - *(major) doctors impact lives daily in ways others cannot,*
    - *(major) — if we aspire for young people to follow us into our profession, they must be aware there is something special about our profession worthy of demonstrative respect and*
    - *(major) — when the time comes for a club member to seek my care, it is important for he/she and me to know, although we may belong to the same social setting, our professional relationship is special.*
6. *I find myself recalling my first communion — age six. It was a beautiful spring day in our humble backyard. Friends and relations came early and made for quite a party. Then Doctor/Uncle Jack Sherman and his family showed. Elvis was suddenly in the building. I immediately understood, I had been the warm up band. He, as humble as a cloistered monk, was royalty — a status assigned by those who admired and depended on him.*
7. *Finally, remembering Groucho, despite my desire to support my community, if this fiction had happened to me, the next golf season would find me joining*

my medical colleagues at the first over the border course where they seemed to be comfortable with doctors as members.

8. *A trusted senior colleague, Dr. Ed Drawbaugh, observes, "Aspiring physician — you will soon learn that the road you have chosen is an arduous one, and you should take immense pride once your training is complete. The title of "Doctor" is recognition of all that you have sacrificed to reach that point. Be proud of the title and use it to the degree that you feel comfortable. Always, in all settings, comport yourself such that you continue to deserve the honor associated with it."*

9. *Dr. Ravi, while I have your (busier than God's ear), please consider another fiction perhaps worthy of your magic touch. As you are most aware, the physician is often in a leadership role. As you the artist are most aware, there are often clinical, emotional and ethical tensions. I sense the following fiction may prove script worthy…*

———

66. Tension

"The manager administers, the leader innovates. The manager maintains, the leader develops. The manager relies on systems, the leader relies on people. The manager counts on controls, the leader counts on trust. The manager does things right, the leader does the right thing."

FORTUNE MAGAZINE

———

This may have happened thirty years ago. This may have happened yesterday. This may happen tomorrow. Hopefully, this has and will never happen.

As Chief Medical Officer, I was notified. The hospital's safety officer called me on a late Monday afternoon to report that preliminary information suggests a fifteen-year-old girl who died in our emergency department may have died unnecessarily. I alerted the President/Chief Executive Officer of the concern; made plans with the safety officer to substantiate the concern; and, if indicated, to initiate a process to determine the root cause.

The following information became readily available:

- The girl a good kid who was headed for ninth grade. Because of some family financial distress, she was in a new neighborhood and heading for a new school. Despite challenges, she was making his way.
- On Friday, she was practicing cheer leading gymnastics with friends in the neighborhood park. She took a tumble and injured her elbow and shoulder. A few hours later, her parents had her in the emergency department. After a meticulous evaluation, it was determined that she, luckily, had only soft tissue injuries that would respond to ice, heat and watchful waiting.
- Her temperature, however, was inexplicably elevated to 102.2. Therefore, despite a chaotically busy ED, her thorough emergency medicine physician went back in, took another detailed history, re-examined the young man from tip to toe and did some "probably unnecessary" lab tests. After review, he/she could not ascertain a cause for the fever, decided it was likely viral, advised regarding flu-ids and analgesia, meticulously instructed parents to "come back if condition changes" and sent her home with her informed, attentive family.
- The next morning radiology called the emergency department and reported an abnormal test as a "critical value."
- Within the chaos of the emergency department, the emergency medi-cine team lost sight of the critical information.
- Monday morning, an EMS ambulance team brought the girl in in full cardiac arrest. After a heroic and prolonged resuscitation (code)

attempt by the same emergency medicine physician who had cared for her on Friday, the young lady was pronounced dead.

- During the resuscitation, the unreported critical value was discovered.
- A link between the critical value and the patient's fatal presentation was determined to be clinically plausible.
- As per protocol, the case was discussed with the Medical Examiner's Office. The case was accepted for autopsy.
- The father who had called EMS and accompanied his daughter was inconsolable. Soon a disbelieving, hysterical mother and the child's dazed siblings came to the bedside.
- In caring for the girl and then her family, the emergency medicine physician and his support staff, as second victims, became visibly overwhelmed with grief.

At her request, I had an emergency meeting with the President/Chief Executive Officer (P/CEO), a seasoned executive, to provide a detailed update. I shared the facts of the case as I knew them:

- I anticipated that, after review, this case might have to be reported to the Department of Health and the Joint Commission as an unanticipated death,
- I would convene a formal root cause analysis, synthesize events and design and implement a plan to avoid a repeat and
- I expressed concern that, if the coroner concluded the unaddressed critical value contributed to the death, our self-insured institution may be at risk for a significant financial settlement with the family.

At this point our patient safety and patent advocacy professionals went to work to ascertain if our hospital had met its mission — safe, timely, efficient, effective, and equitable/just patient-centered care — or if opportunities for improvement existed.

Our patient advocacy officer, compassionately checked in with the parents to understand their story and ascertain their immediate needs. She reported:

- She spoke with the dad by phone. The mother was incapable of conversation.
- The family was devastated by grief.
- This very nice and already accomplished — scholastically, athletically [cheer leading and soccer] and artistically [voice and keyboards] — lady had become the center of the family's hopes and aspirations. Her parents were proud of her. Her two younger brothers idolized her.
- The family had fallen on hard times. When his industrial plant cut back, the father was laid off. The mom commutes by bus 30 miles to a factory in a neighboring community. The dad is underemployed with two part-time service jobs.
- In a fiscal death spiral, they lost their home. Embarrassed victims of circumstances, they moved to a two-bedroom apartment in a rough section of the city. Despite this, they remained unbowed.
- The girl was well until Friday's tumble. Saturday, she was uncharacteristically under the weather and laid low. Sunday both parents were working long hours. Their girl had been sleeping when they left and was sleeping when they arrived late in the evening. They both were experiencing inconsolable guilt for not checking her more closely on Sunday and for not doing more, sooner.
- On Monday, the mom had returned to work and the dad was preparing the girl's breakfast when he found her unarousable with labored breathing and called 911.
- In their neighborhood, thoughts of illicit intravenous drug abuse would be in the differential diagnosis; however, the parents were adamant — this young lady had no interest in experimenting with drugs.
- Their former community and church has come forward and they were being assisted with the funeral and burial expenses.
- They are most appreciative of all the fine care their daughter received in the emergency department. They expressed great appreciation for

the emergency physician and the nursing staff who did everything possible and wept with them when all had been lost.

- They showed no insight that critical information, available Saturday, had been available.
- They understand that you (VPMA/CMO) and I (patient advocate) will be pleased to meet with his wife and/or him at any time should they ever perceive a need.
- He had no specific request of the hospital at this time.

At my direction, our patient safety officer conducted a formal root cause analysis. A meticulous process was undertaken that had the right people assemble and brainstorm the case, provide a draft report to the President/CEO and outline recommendations. After review, opportunities for improvement were identified regarding the reporting and adjudication of critical values (expected) and emergency department staffing (a surprise). Recommendations addressed both root cause concerns.

The coroner's report concluded the mortality was due to a massive infection. There was no mention of illicit drug use or of an unaddressed critical value.

I was sadly proud of the analysis and synthesis of a complex circumstance. Our approach demonstrated, in the worst of times, an enlightened, ascendant institutional culture dedicated to safe, timely, efficient, effective, equitable/just patient-centered care.

I was totally unprepared for a meeting with the health system's chief legal counsel. He (the CEO's proxy?) came at me with six shooters blazing:

1. "Your approach to root cause analysis is most interesting and unusual."
2. "Your root cause analysis is not raw enough. Heads should have already rolled." *Note: he was erroneously merging two processes: root cause analysis (a continuous quality improvement process) and peer review (a just culture/accountability process). Although related, these are distinctly separate processes that must be addressed separately. Contaminating root cause analysis with punitive action would create a culture of fear and forever make reporting and root cause analysis impossible within the hospital's culture.*

3. "You state that we must tell ourselves the truth; however, it is just the truth as you want us to know it."

4. "Your root cause analysis process is much too transparent. Your process has created an institutional consensus that a saint has unnecessarily died on our watch with blood on our hands. You have created a most dangerous fiscal crisis. *Note: emphasis has switched from making the hospital safer for the next patient to diminishing the self-insured hospital's risk-management exposure.*

5. "Do you really believe that this kid from that neighborhood is so perfect? Surely dirt is available to obfuscate the pristine picture your root cause analysis has painted."

6. "Your root cause analysis process may have exposed us to a $300,000 settlement." *Note: I silently calculated a cost of error ten times that.*

7. Then he got to the point: "if you want your career to continue:
    a. Recognize that as a VPMA/CMO you are a renegade "weird duck,"
    b. Recognize the VPMA/CMO is here to protect the hospital,
    c. Cease all VPMA/CMO patient safety root cause analysis. From this point forward, they will be conducted by our risk-management department,
    d. Meet with the parents and tell them you have completed a full investigation,
    e. Express regrets for this unfortunate act of nature,
    f. Do not advance disclosure to the family,
    g. Do not introduce the concept of equitable/just compensation,
    h. Do not disclose process concerns as there are just too many unknowns for us to be certain of causality, culpability and/or any change in outcome and
    i. Find reason to be critical of the emergency department physician, so that if there is a settlement, other deep pockets will be implicated and forced to contribute."

Confronted with a perilous moral and ethical chasm, the VPMA/CMO proceeded as if the meeting with the lawyer had not occurred:

- The state's department of health was notified of an unanticipated death,
- The Joint Commission was notified of a sentinel event leading to an unanticipated death,
- With compassion, the concept of unaddressed critical values/information was disclosed to the parents,
- Lines of communication between the VPMA/CMO, the patient advocacy officer and the parents were left wide open and
- Talented professionals partnered to make the hospital safe for its next patient.

---

10. *Ravi, enough said. You get the gist. I will leave the denouement of this story to you.*
11. *This fiction has me remembering Thomas Carlyle, "Make yourself an honest man, and then you may be sure there is one less rascal in the world."*
12. *A trusted senior physician, Dr. Ed Drawbaugh, brings us back to his considered experience, "This sad and lengthy story contains several important teaching points. First, despite the best efforts of all of our 'Better Angels' on the healthcare team, mistakes still occur on a too frequent basis. Many (almost all) are the result of system errors far more than personal ones. Modern techniques such as root cause analysis seek to find the point of error in the system and correct it so that the same mistake cannot be made again. The old "heads are going to roll" mentality does nothing to prevent the same problem from harming future patients. It simply changes the faces of those who will commit the error.*

    The second issue revolves around "doing the right thing." The COO in this fiction was inappropriately attempting to protect the institution from the truth of the error which contributed to the boy's demise. Failure to disclose would be an egregious omission — an omission that, when discovered, would vastly compound the institution's liability.

    Perhaps in a bygone era that would have been standard behavior. Today, however, he and the institution would be expected to quickly step up and

277

inform the family of the error. In my experience as physician executive and hospital board member, leadership would do so with regret but without hesitation. In medicine, doing the right thing is always the right thing to do."
13. Dr. Ravi, a third fiction for your consideration...

67. The Non-Participating Non-Physician

"I will remember that I remain a member of society,
with special obligations to all my fellow human beings...."

FROM THE ORIGINAL HIPPOCRATIC OATH

A hundred years ago, his medical school's university teaching hospital served its geographic region. All patients were cared for regardless of ability to pay. Residency and fellowship found him trained in similar circumstances in disparate regions of the country. When he entered practice in small-town America, although most patients were insured, it was his honor, privilege and responsibility to care for all comers.

As a teaching physician responsible for the resident medicine clinic, he was stunned one day when a resident announced that he did not have to waste his time "learning social-work techniques for caring for the indigent" as his practice would be "on the right side of the tracks" and he would only care for (insured, paying) "patients with means." When the supervising physician, clearly unsettled, asked if he did not have an obligation to the community, without hesitation he said:

- "My father is a physician,
- He has paid for my education,

- He has taught me that medicine is a business,
- Indigent care is to be provided by county, state and federal programs; therefore,
- I will have no obligation to the indigent."

It occurred to the supervising physician that he might point out that his admittedly expensive education was in fact significantly subsidized and/or that indigent patients had provided the student and physician-in-training the opportunity to refine his craft. Perhaps a mention of the spirit of the Hippocratic Oath was in order...

"I will remember that I do not treat a fever chart, a cancerous growth, but a sick human being, whose illness may affect the person's family and economic stability. My responsibility includes these related problems, if I am to care adequately for the sick."

But recognizing an unsalvageable sorry lost-cause (to whom he could not begin to relate) who had chosen to make medicine a joyless business, he demurred.

Years later, as a senior physician, he began to hear rumors in the national media of a mature beast that was roaming the land. As an example, the stories went like this:

- At a community hospital, surgeons were compensated to cover the surgical and trauma services. The hospital and community were well served to have 24/7/365 surgery/trauma coverage available.
- All was well and good until some surgeons in the rotation announced that they would not participate in or accept insurance plans.
- Into this setting stepped a patient who required emergency surgery (an acute gall bladder). Although she presented to a hospital that participated in/accepted her insurance, the surgeon stated: 1) her/his fee for the gall bladder surgery would be $4,000, 2) he/she would not accept insurance and (3) the patient/family would be responsible for the full amount. Alternatives offered — find a local surgeon who accepted their insurance (none available for this crisis) or transfer (at great expense and some clinical danger) to a university hospital several hours away.

Alternatives unavailable or impractical, the patient agreed to have her emergency surgery. After review:

- Fortunately, emergency medicine and anesthesia physicians accepted her insurance,
- Her insurance company agreed to pay $1250 of the surgeon's fee. The remaining $2,750 was her responsibility,
- Gainfully employed but living paycheck to paycheck (her husband was underemployed), the physician's fee for her emergency surgery threw her family into financial crisis,
- Her outstanding surgeon's bills were aggressively pursued and sent to collection,
- She appealed for assistance to hospital and insurance advocacy systems and state and national regulatory agencies to no avail and
- Lives were changed.

———

14. *Dr. Ravi, picture the financial ramifications if emergency medicine physicians and the anesthesia team did not accept insurance.*
15. *if this scenario were to be true, somewhere along the way, a fine, gifted physician lost sight of her/his professional big picture.*
16. *Please recognize that tragic, unfortunate, misdirected usurers can, against all professional and ethical standards, cause harm. In the process, they may earn the disdain of colleagues, hospital executives, hospital boards, patient and families and the communities they serve; rob themselves of the important, meaningful joys of making a difference and, no longer be entitled to the reverent designation — doctor.*
17. *Dr. Ed Drawbaugh weighs in, "Sadly, the field of medicine is not immune to the presence of misguided individuals whose primary purpose in life is to maximize personal gain. Those who pursue this path cast a shadow which falls upon the reputations of their innocent colleagues and taints the long-cherished*

vision of physicians as healers and protectors of their patients. They have be-come businessmen first and physicians a distant second."

18. *Now (recycled — see #41 — for the attention of your Hollywood eyes) a fourth and final draft script for your consideration...*

---

68. Acute Epidural Hematoma

"Heroism is not only in the man, but in the occasion".

CALVIN COOLIDGE

It was the third-year medical student's first surgical rotation. He had been arbitrarily assigned to neurosurgery.

To that point, his medical career had been a panoply of mixed experiences:

- When he came home from first grade with a straight A report card, his letter-carrier father announced, "you are going to medical school."
- As the oldest of all the sibs and cousins, he was often left in charge at family functions (a scary thought) and his Aunt Marie declared "you will be a pediatrician."
- When anxious regarding the prospects of confronting "blood and gore," his mother invented "they make you wash your hands in blood and you get used to it."
- He worked evenings and weekends at the local pharmacy and toyed with going to pharmacy school rather than medical school until his horrified pharmacist boss and mentor disabused him of such folly.
- In college, the thought that he might not be accepted to medical school made him determined to succeed (whether he actually wanted to or not).

- In his arduous first two years of medical school, he came to enjoy and appreciate both the science and the glimpse of the art of medicine he was exposed to.
- Having rotated through pediatrics, he understood that caring for seriously ill precious little ones who had no understanding that his well-intentioned painful interventions were in their best interest was not for him. Along the way, he observed that surgeons are born (not made) and he had not been born to be among them. Therefore, his career would fall to the cognitive adult side of the profession — medicine, neurology or psychiatry.

Already he recognized a sine-wave pattern to his career. Having been accepted into pre-med, he was among the elite in high school but as a freshman in college, he was relegated to the basement. Having been accepted into medical school, he was again among the elite in his college class but his first day of medical school returned him to the basement. Two years of success in the basic sciences had separated him from the pack; however, each third-year clinical rotation started him back in the basement. And the roller coaster rides the future would hold were becoming clear to him: medical school graduate, intern, junior resident, senior resident, junior attending, attending, chair, dean — a relentless series of hard won peaks immediately reverted to basements.

His ego was nonetheless sound. He had no trouble with this sine-wave. He appreciated that, as a an supernumerary third year medical student, he had been granted a position of great privilege — to each day join senior physicians in their complex work attempting to advance the circumstances and lives of their complex and vulnerable patients and, with this granted privilege, he understood his responsibility — to take it all in and use it to find his unique place in medicine--- to find the career that would have him be his most productive, do his most meaningful work and make the greatest difference for those he was privileged to serve.

His neurosurgery team's rounds started in 5:30 a.m. darkness. The chief resident and his senior residents were finished with 'oversight rounds' and in the OR by 7:00 a.m. where they would be sequestered until 4:00 p.m. The work of 'grunt' rounds, orders and notes was left to the intern (not yet OR worthy) and the novice third-year student (never OR worthy).

Neurosurgery was the most competitive surgical field and attracted only the best, the brightest and the most dedicated. It also attracted those with the most stamina as their seven years of training required every other night on call in the hospital. With sardonic sadness, they would lament "so we must miss half the good cases." Unsurprisingly, his intern was brilliant. As he supervised and taught on meticulous rounds, the student learned exponentially — basic post-op care, complex neurosurgery concepts and major organizational skills.

Unbelievable as it will sound, the day before the intern had had significant surgery (pilonidal cyst). By all accounts, he should have been home medicated and recuperating. But, as was clearly implicitly expected, he was there taking one for the team. Nevertheless, he did have to excuse himself to go to his call room and change his dressing and, as he did so, he left his intern beeper (covering all neurosurgery outside of the OR) with his paralyzed-by-fright student.

Unbelievably, the beeper immediately went off. When the student called the number, he was (unbelievably) speaking with the chief resident in the OR via speaker phone who said, "A painter fell off his ladder, had a concussion, is now alert and has been admitted to the floor to our service by ED assholes who don't know chicken shit from chicken salad. Run down and make sure he is OK."

This first day on neurosurgery third year medical student found his way for the first time to the neurosurgical floor and found the patient in his room being admitted by a third year, soon to graduate, nursing student. He was stunned to find a head injury patient who was unconscious and demonstrating deep sonorous respirations. From his meager classroom clinical medicine conferences, he recognized a syndrome (head injury, unconscious, alert and again unconscious) consistent with an acute epidural bleed and understood that only immediate acute neurosurgical intervention could save this patient.

Unbelievably, this lowest figure on the totem pole told the 'powerful' nursing student to find the head nurse, send her in and then set up for an IV. As he placed the IV, he told the 'more powerful than God' head nurse to call the OR and inform the neurosurgical 'thinks he is God' chief resident that his patient is on his way with a likely acute epidural hematoma. Within moments an unconscious patient, a head nurse in a state of shock, an impressed nursing student and a determined first-day-on neurosurgery third-year medical student had the patient in the OR elevator.

As the doors opened an angry OR head nurse, an angrier anesthesiologist and a frankly bewildered neurosurgical chief resident confronted the inexplicable scene: bed, patient, head nurse, student nurse and medical student. After only a moment with the patient, the chief resident flew into action. Within minutes the patient was undergoing emergent craniotomy.

At about this time, the intern found his beeper and his student in the OR men's locker room. The student was shaking and weeping. He was all apologies, "I am so sorry but I thought it was my responsibility to do what was best for my patient." He was convinced of impending doom, "Surely the Chief of Surgery will demand my ass and the Dean will bounce my ass." A flummoxed intern listened and consoled without understanding. Then, a beaming chief resident appeared with good news, "A most fortunate patient will likely survive an assuredly fatal, brilliantly diagnosed and courageously managed acute epidural hematoma."

Within minutes, the service was back to normal. Rounds were completed and the pecking order was appropriately re-established. As predicted, there was regression to the third-year medical student neurosurgical mean — for every right answer proffered by the medical student there would be two wrong. And, soon all would be forgotten until almost two years later at awards day when the head nurse would retell the story and the painter would hand the graduating medical student the Patient Advocate Award — presented to the student who most nearly approximates the ideal doctor/patient relationship.

———◆———

19. *Ravi, remembering David Bromberg, "What I do is not universally appealing. It is not my goal in life to be famous, but I would not run away from it." When you make me famous, I will struggle to make the most of it.*
20. *Other thoughts?*

Respectfully submitted,
Dr. Mike

———

VI. Closure

> *"The two most important days in your life are*
> *The day you are born and*
> *The day you find out why."*

MARK TWAIN

69

Echoes

"Wishing I didn't know now what I didn't know then."

Bob Seeger

The FountainHead WhiteHouse
Alex,

1. *Good morning.*
2. *Thank you for all you do daily so well for so many.*
3. *Thanks for giving me the opportunity to set this table for the aspiring pre-med physician. I hope you have found a morsel worth tasting.*
4. *Closer to the end than you, I have encountered and been affected by the words of a retiring surgeon, Dr. Bibhas Bandi, who at age 76 and after 40 years of practice leaves practice with these thoughts for colleagues, staff and patients, "From the distance, I shall wave my hands with my silent message from my heart to everybody — so long and farewell. I wish better than the best to you all."*
5. *As you look forward and I look back, what do I wish I didn't know now that I didn't know then...*

G iving you every encouragement to pursue a career in medicine — if that is what you decide is for you — looking back I recognize some retrospective hard-earned cautions. Letters in this book have fleshed out many of these. Let me concisely echo a few points. If I had had a magic wand...

- I would have started with a clear spiritual philosophy. For me, from the beginning, I would daily strive to be a Toltec Master. As time went by, I came to increasingly appreciate the daily power in this,
- Close behind, I would only have matriculated into a vocation — and not onto a career (job) path. For me, this was never an issue,
- I would have arranged for others (for example, family, community, military) to fund my education — with a promise to pay them (not the bank) back through pride, service and/or treasure over many years,
- I would have had enough funds to live comfortably — neither elegantly nor in poverty. From ages 18-32, [18-22 (pre-med), 22-26 (medical school), 26-29 (residency) and 29-32 (fellowship)] there must be adequate funds to support both hard work and a semblance of a modest comfortable life — car, apartment, dinner, theatre, vacation,
- I would have deferred major life decisions (for example, marriage, family and home) until after growing into myself (the me I would become) — i.e., until after completion of training and the successful start of career,
- I would have made an early decision about specialty and career path and pursued it with unrelenting gusto. My story has me, the born psychiatrist, letting life and finances take me from psychiatry and leadership into a career of general internal medicine and leadership. Although it has all worked out and being cognizant that we should "watch what we wish for," I so want a Mulligan on this,
- I would have chosen career settings where they recruited team members in the manner of U Conn's women's basketball coach Geno Auriemma:
  - Top priority — a winning team,
  - Talent,
  - Those who are supremely confident in their own abilities and
  - Those who impact whatever team they are on in multiple ways, making those around them better on and off the court.

Looking back, those are the leaders and environments to which I would entrust my career,

- I would have become an expert within my specialty — a subspecialist (for example, having chosen psychiatry I might have trained in both psychiatry (major) and internal medicine (minor) and concentrated on (i.e., become a national expert in) liaison psychiatry addressing the psychiatric needs of the admitted medical and surgical patients). As a corollary, I would have avoided being a generalist — for me, an unsatisfying, insurmountable, exhausting, infinite task,
- From the beginning, I would have striven to be on a path towards master clinician and residency/division/departmental/medical staff leader,
- From day one (age 18), I would have been adept at carving out time entirely away from patients, institution and career — time to allow for the development of brain synapses, personality traits, social skills and physical prowess beyond the professional me — traits that influence and enhance both the professional and personal me and
- I would have begun and ended each day back at the beginning — striving towards my spiritual philosophy — the Toltec Master.

———————

6. *Alex, that's the big picture to which the echoes of a career take me — a good place for the aspirant to start.*
7. *With couldas, shouldas and wouldas in focus, I would not change a thing.*
8. *If, with eyes wide open, a career in medicine is for you, I give you joyful encouragement.*
9. *Other thoughts?*

Respectfully submitted,
Dr. Mike

Dr. Edward Drawbaugh Comments

There is quite a lot of deep thought in this letter. However, as a surgeon, I find my brain inclined to think on a more incisive, pragmatic level. So, I would emphasize the points about finding a way to finish training with as little debt as possible, delaying major life decisions, seeking the best training available and striving to be the best that you can be.

Vervet Monkey Portrait, Tanzania
EJDMD

70

A Score of Fellowships (22 and Counting)

"Professionals with stimulating careers
have lived their life in chapters."

David Brooks

The FountainHead WhiteHouse
Alex,

1. *Good morning.*
2. *Thank you for all you do daily so well for so many.*
3. *As promised/threatened, some of what I submit will appear over the top to you. In your busy-ness, this final letter is, unapologetically, heavy lifting. So do what any good physician would do — just give it a speed read.*
4. *Let us end at the beginning — please take a moment to review the oft ne-glected dedication. For me, my journey has been and your journey will be the joy of relentlessly moving forward on the Dreyfus brother's model for skill acquisition: from the novice's "rigid adherence to taught rules" to competence, proficiency, expertise and onto mastery and the "intuitive grasp of situations based on deep, tacit understanding."*

5. *Cutting to the efficient, effective Alex chase — the following enumerates one physician's boundary-less journey. This example of endless opportunities and challenges is at the heart of my message — why the gifted aspirant, you, might/ must pursue a career in medicine.*

6. *Three patterns of inquiry give me confidence that sharing this timeline is important:*

   - *From time to time, physician colleagues would send their most precious high school/college school daughters or sons to me so that I (why me?) may explain to their precious children why they might consider a medical career,*

   - *As I was stepping away from the position of vice president medical affairs/ chief medical officer, three magnificently established mid-career physicians independently stopped into my office to ask what they needed to do to emulate my (why mine?) career path and*

   - *As I was stepping away, several late career physicians, whose careers had followed most successful straight lines sought me out to inquire, "how did your eclectic career evolve?"*

7. *My answer to the three sets of career colleagues (early, mid and late) has been:*

   - *As a perpetual student, I have always found myself most comfortable on a new, challenging, uncomfortable, steep learning curve.*

   - *I have consciously studied people, positions and processes. Like those who enjoy tinkering with cars or clocks to understand what makes them tick, I have reveled in tinkering with healthcare and hospitals to understand how concepts and functions (patients, families and clinical care and administration, board, medical staff, nursing, pharmacy and support staff) all come together.*

   - *I have been comfortable in living my life in chapters — yes, some might observe I have had trouble in keeping a job. However, in listening to two heroes in conversation, Charlie Rose and David Brooks, (as a redundant aside, it is important to have heroes), they observe that many professionals who have enjoyed fulfilling careers have divided their lives into chapters.*

- *I have been comfortable in uncomfortably stepping up to try the next level of leadership and mystery for four reasons:*
  - *Ennui: having unexpectedly successfully sort of mastered one harrowing challenge and plateaued, I would become a bit bored and ask the Peggy Lee question — "is that all there is?"*
  - *Challenge: to see if, in giving it my all, I am up to a tougher task. Can I do it?*
  - *Threat: recognition that if I do not step up someone else will — and thereafter that individual will be in control of my destiny.*
  - *Judgment (or lack of): frankly, I may not have placed enough weight upon the "what ifs of failure" and failure's potential professional and personal consequences.*
8. *Physicians think of the chapters in their professional lives in terms of their training: pre-med, medical school, internship, residency and fellowship (specialty). I will take some license with that progression and, anticipating more to come, briefly describe what I recognize as 20-plus fellowships that have formed, nurtured, prepared and hardened me along the way...*

---

1. Schenectady

Growing up in a proud blue-collar circumstance under the nurturing guidance of parents, Sisters of Saint Joseph, Irish Christian Brothers and coaches and mentors, I was provided a foundation of confidence that enabled a kid from "the city that lights and hauls the world" to go forward and have a go of it.

2. Applied Psychology

While working at the pharmacy (age 16 to 22), I was significantly introduced to human nature. Mr. Henry Aumiller, a caring, erudite pharmacist and world class entrepreneur "adopted me," became my first mentor (an early important lesson — have mentors and when the time comes be a mentor) and ran me through his master's degree level applied psychology course.

Under his tutelage, there was little about humans and their private lives to which I was not exposed. Importantly, Mr. Aumiller insisted that I recognize, analyze, and synthesize each event and apply each lesson learned to my own development — "Mike, I want you to learn from the lives of others — you do not need to personally make each mistake yourself to understand consequences and alternatives."

My work as a clerk in the pharmacy proved to be superb training for a physician-to-be. When the time came, my physician listening and actually hearing skills were astute. Near my journey's end, I consider this to be my most significant fellowship.

3. Undergrad

When it came time to consider college, I became aware that for financial reasons I would find the nearest to home pre-med education that would have me. I matriculated to Schenectady's Union College — a fine liberal arts, engineering, pre-med institution.

In preparation for medical school, I studied Science and English. Unlike many of my pre-med peers, I worked my way through college (keyboards, newspaper mail room and pharmacy). After review, I do not advise it as I left much (academics and social life) of what college had to offer on the table. More to the point, the consequences of working my way through college were nearly devastating. If not for the serendipity of an organic chemistry mentor's (Dr. Howard Sheffer) dedicated interest, I would not have matriculated to medical school — a story perhaps for another day (see #21 The Horizon).

Through joy, pain and the compassionate care of those to whom my career and life was entrusted, college provided requisite rapid growth.

4. Medical School

I matriculated to Union University's Albany Medical College. I entered contemplating pediatrics and moved on to consider psychiatry, then neurology and, provided the exigencies of life, ended up in internal medicine — Emerson's "Things are in the saddle and ride mankind."

I worked my way through medical school (chemistry lab from 11:00 p.m. to 7:00 a.m.) — absolutely not recommended as medical school is rigorous enough. Depending on circumstance, I was both the sharpest and dullest tool in the shed as I was interested in the first 90% of everything and bored with the final 10%.

Heeding Satchel Paige, in general I don't look back as "Something might be gaining on me." However, as I contemplate the aspiring physician, I regret not more proactively considering my next career/life steps during medical school. Life drifted me from psychiatry to neurology to medicine. Although all is well that ends well, I do wonder "what if." For this fellowship, I assign a grade — incomplete.

5. Residency

I planned to do my internship at Rochester's Strong Memorial. At the last-minute, life (Emerson again) had this small-town lad sign on at New York Medical College's Metropolitan Hospital (Manhattan).

I fell into magnificent on- the-job training where dedicated residents and interns did their best with scarce resources. At times, I was simultaneously as much nurse, respiratory therapist, radiology tech and lab tech as physician. Supervision, teaching and learning were, however, unconscionably deficient.

Since attending supervision, formal teaching and therefore care were not up to my standards, I moved on to two years of residency at Greenwich Hospital in affiliation with Yale. Known as the "country club," care, supervision, teaching, support services and facilities were unparalleled. In a nurturing environment, master physicians and expert leaders mentored my clinical, teaching, leadership and interpersonal skills.

After review, residency training was the fellowship that identified and ameliorated my flaws and amplified my strengths. Looking back, residency is the fellowship that formed me. Although education, experience and maturity would change me (note: this old dog takes pride in continuing to change), the changes are mere refinements on where residency positioned me.

6. Private Practice

Saddled with debt, I decided to go into private practice in small town Connecticut instead of pursuing a fellowship (by nature and nurture I was naturally attracted to Pulmonary Medicine, Infectious Diseases and Rheumatology).

For four years, I awoke each day at dawn feeling late for ICU rounds. Each day would end when my last patient was ministered to.

Leaving residency, I perceived I was a complete and brilliant board-certified physician. After two years in practice, I understood I was beginning to approach being a proficient physician.

Senior physicians, country doctors each, mentored me. Subspecialists guided me. I had a minor academic relationship with the university (their students rotated through my private office). In this setting, I refined my outpatient and in-patient clinical skills and learned the business of medicine.

I am often asked, why did you leave the celebrity and riches of a successful private practice? Consistently, I provide two answers:

- The community's practice model was flawed. It did not provide for vitality — a balance between professional and personal lives. I was either "on" or out of town — there was little in between and
- Some internal force urged me to move on to the privilege of caring for precious physicians-in-training as they cared for their precious patients.

7. Leadership

As a most junior physician, I unexpectedly (a vacuum existed and I filled it) became an important physician partner with administration, board, nursing and pharmacy leadership at our small community hospital. Our task was to align the hospital with The Joint Commission and Department of Health regulatory requirements.

Fortuitously, this placed me on a steep hospital administration learning curve — for which I am forever indebted. It turns out, if you understand how a small hospital works, you understand how a hospital works. Within four years, my mentors/partners had provided me with a mini Master's in Health Administration.

Having stepped up, I learned:

- Vacuums need to be filled. Be prepared to step up and fill them,
- Many physicians abhor the thought of non-clinical administrative processes. It truly is different strokes for different folks and
- Although I did not see it coming, four years as a country doctor enhanced my clinical, teaching and administrative skills and opened career paths to me.

Often residents and fellows stop in to chat, in general terms, about pursuing a MPH, MHA or MBA. I share a consistent bias: go and practice for three to five years. As a foundation, move from proficiency in your clinical skills towards expert. As you do so, explore the healthcare environment and find that which fascinates you. Then choose and step into a targeted program (administrative, clinical, technical, and/or research) that will efficiently advance your very unique and very personal career.

8. Faculty/Administrator

In the fifth year of my Connecticut practice, my internal medicine residency program director (Dr. Jim Bernene) moved to the Southwest and encouraged me to join him as junior faculty, medical director of the internal medicine clinic and administrative director for the graduate medical residencies' (Cardiology, Gastroenterology, OB/GYN, Pediatrics, Plastic Surgery and Surgery) out-patient clinics.

I agreed. In stepping forward, by necessity I was forced to advance — under the careful supervision of able academic (DIO Dr. Wm James Howard) and administrative (CNO Rhonda Anderson) mentors my clinical, teaching and administrative skills.

In stepping forward, for the first time outside of clinical medicine, I assumed the responsibility of significant executive decisions — decisions that would impact the care of patients and families and influence the work environment of the assembled healthcare team.

Right here, a career line can be drawn. Right here, I crossed out of my clinical, academic, administrative and leadership comfort zone. Right here, the doctor/teacher/executive me had to actively begin to recognize, accept and step up to responsibility.

9. Chair and Program Director

After six years in Arizona, at the tender age of 41 (may seem ancient to you, but still just a kid), I successfully competed for the privilege of serving as department chair and residency program director for medicine at a large sophisticated hospital in Western Pennsylvania. In one fell swoop, I took a giant step into medical staff leadership, medical staff politics, graduate medical education and hospital administration. Suddenly academic, care, quality and political issues were owned by me.

Wonderfully capable superiors (CEO Howard Jones and VP Medical Affairs John Moyer) and kind faculty and colleagues helped me navigate through a touch of Valerie Young's "Impostor Syndrome" and overcome self-doubt. Partnering with many, I enjoyed a modicum of success. Communicating with you today is testament that I survived. After review, this jump in responsibility and experience was the fellowship that placed me on my steepest learning curve.

10. Quality and Safety

While serving as chair and residency program director, my prescient master President/Chief Executive Officer (Mr. Howard Jones) provided me the opportunity to pursue formal industrial engineering quality training at the Crosby Quality College. I came to appreciate quality from the perspective of the customer, the supplier, the manager, the chief executive and the board. As I have written elsewhere, this fellowship was responsible for greatly enhancing both my professional and personal lives.

11. Teacher

While chair and residency program director, I graduated from Michigan State's Primary Care Faculty Development Fellowship. Its focus was to teach clinicians how to teach. The formal fellowship advanced my teaching, research, leadership and interpersonal competencies. Please take note: while serving as chair and residency program director — far beyond a full-time position — my enlightened President/Chief Executive Officer, Mr. Howard Jones, again was allowing/encouraging me to carve out time to advance my repertoire — to add arrows to my quiver. I shall forever be grateful for his investment in me. In his honor, I have constantly striven to pass his favor and wisdom forward to those reporting to me.

12. Vice President

Next, I served as residency program director and vice president for quality at a large Pittsburgh hospital. I used the opportunity to utilize my continuous quality improvement skills to retool a residency program. It was my laboratory for refining these skills. This experience took me from talking continuous quality improvement (theory) to walking continuous quality improvement — the design, implementation and maintenance of continuously improving processes. This experience represents my maturation as a care and safety leader.

13. VP Medical Affairs/Chief Medical Officer

After seven years, I moved on to a community teaching hospital within a major national university healthcare system. My position was responsible for graduate medical education, medical staff affairs and quality and safety. Hospital leadership provided me with a blank canvas and the university provided me with unlimited exposure to genius and resources. In this setting, enabled by a master administrator (Mr. Ron Ott) who had enabled an ideal healthcare culture, I was able to begin to bring it all together: care, quality, safety, graduate medical education, medical staff leadership and hospital administration. In my role in this ascendant, enlightened community teaching hospital, I was positioned to partner with other incredibly enlightened organizations (for example, the Pittsburgh Regional HealthCare Institute, the Accreditation Council for Graduate Medical Education (ACGME), the Association of Program Directors in Internal Medicine (APDIM) and The Joint Commission). Provided these robust circumstances, I began to go beyond being a cog in a hospital's culture to partnering to influence the culture of a hospital.

In retrospect, this healthy, vigorous experience encompassed several fellowships, but I will only claim one. After review, I recognize this to be my copacetic career sweet spot.

14. A Big Hairy Audacious Error

While in my own mind, approaching mastery of my domain, I proved capable of doing the wrong thing for the wrong reasons.

I was in the perfect situation in Pittsburgh. Loyalty had me do the wrong thing for the wrong reason. As a result, instead of being in a bit over my head at one fine institution, I positioned myself to be submerged at 300 feet — in pretend charge of two fine but very different institutions and two very different cultures which were, at 100 miles per hour, an hour commute apart.

All the joy I had experienced was dissipated by well-meaning over commitment. Try as I may, with loyalties divided, I could not disengage from one to the other. So, as empty nesters, it was time for spouse and me to move on to Maryland and proximity to children, grandchildren and golf.

Let me get back to a consistent plea: please learn vicariously. Although I have graduated Phi Beta Kappa from the school of hard knocks, I cannot recommend it. I advocate that you avoid the pain. Enumerating missteps:

- I should have remembered that less is more,
- If it was appropriate to say no, I should have said no,
- I should have recognized that my career sweet spot was my fine community teaching hospital and
- I should have recognized that a non-teaching medical center is a far different species — not for the likes of me.

As I convey acquired wisdom to the aspiring physician, my perspective on this fellowship, buried here #14 among 22, must be afforded prominence; therefore, the "big hairy audacious" nod to Jim Collins and Jerry Porras.

15. Senior Leadership
I moved on to become the VP Value and Chief Medical Officer for an important Maryland health system. After four years, I decided to step away. Here is what I think I know: win, lose or draw — I cannot pretend the engagement was entirely a success — the scope of the position did not allow me to address my passion for care and safety in a hands-on, bedside, granular way.

I did grow from having administrative responsibility for: care, quality, safety, infection control, risk management, patient advocacy, medical staff affairs and the interfaces with the Joint Commission and the Department of Health and Mental Hygiene. However, I was a step too remote from impacting care and safety.

In retrospect, this position was a wrong detour away from the care and safety trajectory of my career path. If it was indeed time to move on from the university community teaching hospital — without regret, this will always remain an open question for me — I should have moved ever more deeply into leadership of care, safety and satisfactionat the bedside and ever more away from senior management and the C-suite.

As I take stock and write this book, I clearly recognize my error in late career choice. Respected for careful executive decision making, I erroneously stepped/leapt from the wonder of important meaningful work that makes a difference to a job. For the first time, despite being nourished and sustained daily by brilliant, effective and caring colleagues, my day gig was not fun. Nevertheless, since I am one who learns best from my mistakes, it was most fruitful.

Confident my message is clear, let me emphasize — as you design and implement your career moves use your quality training. Just as you would for a complex operating room process, design and implement logical next steps. At all costs, avoid the cost of error in your career steps.

16. Author

After almost four years in a position made joyless by circumstance yet filled with the joyfulness of working with wonderful colleagues, I stepped away to my long-promised intent to write my book. I fell right into the delight of important meaningful work that makes a difference. *Unsafe to Safe — An Impatient Proposal for Safe Patient-centered Care* was soon published. Looking back, I had accomplished five goals:

- I had time to think,
- I had opportunity to network with colleagues and friends,
- I learned how to write, edit, and publish a book,
- In the process, I recorded concepts and lessons learned so they would not be forgotten (by me),
- In the process, I recorded concepts and lessons learned so they may be shared and
- (I did not see this coming) my undertaking qualified me for consulting positions that would follow.

17. Consultant

I took a turn at site visiting institutions for several fine national organizations. In that it was important, meaningful work that made a difference, I enjoyed it. In that it required complex, oft disrupted travel — which many might relish — I soon observed it was not/could not be for me. In fact, truth be told, I failed at it — uncomfortable details were provided early on in the letter *"Penultimate Fellowship."* Nevertheless, I recommend the experience to those both attracted to its trappings and, unlike me, physically prepared to address its rigorous requirements.

18. Mission

The lows of my failed consulting career rocketed me to new heights — the silver lining thing. I came to comprehend that as I matured in medicine and life and as I had significant personal patient and family medical experiences, I became a more complete physician. Suddenly, I was positioned to say to patients and families: "let me show you how I personally address complexity" instead of my old "you should, without prerequisites, go out and address complexity." Sharing personal examples proved to be vital for taking patients and families from where they were to where they desired to be.

A mission, message, partnership (with geriatrician Dr. Stephen F Hightower), book, radio program and seminars followed. The introduction to our book *Safer Medical Care for You and Yours — Six Tools for Safe, Effective Compassionate Care* explains:

"The Institute of Medicine has put forward a well-conceived and clearly articulated national goal — for each individual to be provided healthcare that is safe, timely, efficient, effective, equitable/just and patient-centered (STEEEP). Provided my training and experience, I emphatically concur with and endorse the Institute of Medicine's logic and goal.

The purpose of this concise brochure is to position each unique individual — you, me and those near and dear to us — to enable the 'Better Angels' assembled to care for us to provide us with safe, effective compassionate care.

This brochure accomplishes this by providing examples of six *(now seven)* gift tools for the individual to understand, appreciate and then emulate in her/his uniquely personal manner. The gift tools are as follows:

1. My (Unique and Very) Personal Medical Record
2. My Chief Complaint (my story — why I am here today)
3. My (Unique and Very) Personal HealthCare Values/Wishes/Desires
4. My HealthCare Power of Attorney (and My Advanced Directives)
5. My Personal Professional Patient Advocate (My P3A)
6. My Safer Medical Care Emergency Alert System
7. *My Hospital Portal*

These tools are gifts to you of the peace and tranquility associated with confidence that your care will be safe and effective and your unique and very personal values and wishes will be honored should complex healthcare circumstances arise."

19. Legend in Own Mind

Now I am in the process of writing my fifth book — that which you are reading — *Letters to an Aspiring Physician*. Each day approaches my personal ideal: arise, caffeinate, write for five hours, exercise (golf or beach) for three hours; eat rightly (preferably with spouse and friends), enjoy avocations (music, sports, cinema, poker) and find peace.

My astute, incisive really, favorite nurse and wife, Jackie, declares me to be a certifiable "legend in own mind (LIOM)." The children and grandchildren respectfully address me as Dad and Old Dad. At times, I hear reference to the 'Old LIOM.' Although they are, assuredly, trying to tell me something — I do recognize "nothing is said in jest" — I am comfortable with the assignation.

20. Patriarch

I did not see this coming. Although the matriarch (age 93) is living large and spending inheritances in Florida, she has, like Pope Benedict XVI, relinquished all leadership responsibilities. As the oldest in a large family, I have become an unofficial patriarch. My background as a physician has proven to be invaluable preparation for this role. As previously mentioned, maturity, seeing care from the perspective of the patient and advocating on the behalf of family and friends have made me a more complete physician — one prepared to partner with others in the patriarch's role.

21. The Horizon

I cannot imagine this long line of adventures will not continue. Understanding always that "life is what happens while making plans," going forward I foresee:

- Major: my mission and message (with Dr. Hightower), *Safer Medical Care for You and Yours — Six Tools for Safe, Effective Compassionate Care,* will continue to influence involved, informed and responsible care,
- Minor: this book, *Letters to an Aspiring Physician,* is recognized as an important and meaningful work that makes a difference,

- Minor: I receive an invitation to sit with, converse with and captivate my heroes, Mr. Charlie Rose and Mr. David Brooks, by waxing philosophically about the wonders of medicine and life,
- Minor: I "just once play my usual game" and become the senior club golf champion and
- Major: as a relaxed, wiser, mindful (undistracted) participant/spectator in events of those near and dear to me, I write meaningful important short stories that make a difference. Quoting iconic sportswriter Frank Deford, but changing his word 'sport' to 'medicine,' "But I also believe that the one thing that's largely gone out is what made *medicine* such fertile literary territory — the characters, the tales, the humor, the pain, what Hollywood calls 'the arc.' That is, stories. We have, all by ourselves, ceded that one neat thing about *medicine* that we owned."

22. Magic Wand

It is always good to have stretch goals. If I had a magic wand, I would, for an extended evening, take command of Mr. Charlie Rose's table and assemble Mr. Rose, Mr. David Brooks, Mr. Joe Madden and Mr. Charles Howell III. There I would explore Mr. Rose's ability to, after Professor Herma Hill Kay, "make trouble without being a trouble maker;" Mr. Brook's ability to accurately observe and authentically describe humanity; Mr. Madden's ability to teach the most gifted how to "do simple better" and request Mr. Howell share his grace in being among the best without obsessing about it.

———

9. *Alex, I excitedly imagine where your life and career may lead you.*
10. *Wherever that shall be, enjoy every moment.*
11. *Other thoughts?*

Respectfully submitted,
Dr. Mike

Dr. Ed Drawbaugh Comments:

It is appropriate that Dr. White has concluded with a final autobiographical sketch of his life and career, for they serve as the fabric from which much of this book has been woven. His journey through the medical world has certainly not been typical, yet it perfectly illustrates the tremendous variety of options open to those in the field. By sharing so much of his personal history, he also cements his credentials as mentor, teacher and confidant — he can speak from the most reliable perspective of all, personal experience.

Best of luck, young Alex. I sincerely hope that you follow us into the fascinating and rewarding field of medicine.

71

Afterword

The Bedside Trust
Dear Aspiring Physician,

If you've gotten this far, no doubt you are considering a career as a physician. Congratulations. I can think of no profession requiring the brightest minds, the greatest compassion and dedication to the common good that is more desperately needed than today's and tomorrow's physician.

Yet, in today's environment, this chosen career finds itself under siege from a variety of fronts:

- Legislation (i.e., the repeal and replacement of the Patient Protection and Affordable Care Act) threatening to drastically reduce our public safety net,
- Regulation and bureaucracy threatening to increase work effort without corresponding benefit to the patient,
- Malpractice action threatening to question our every professional judgment and medical decision,
- Reimbursement cuts from insurance companies which have the net impact of reducing our economic fortunes,
- Consolidation in the marketplace among healthcare providers which further reduce professional opportunities and choices,

- Changing financial incentives which emphasize doing things to patients instead of being there for them,
- Rising educational costs and growing debt burdens of our current physicians-in-training which disadvantage them financially relative to their friends and peers and which further
- Distort career decisions toward increased specialization and away from primary care.

Before going further, it is important for you to understand the principle of "informed consent." The following working definition from "Wikipedia" is a reasonable starting point:

"Informed consent is a process for getting permission before conducting a healthcare intervention on a person. A healthcare provider may ask a patient to consent to receive therapy before providing it, or a clinical researcher may ask a research participant before enrolling that person into a clinical trial. Informed consent is collected according to guidelines from the fields of medical ethics and research ethics.

An informed consent can be said to have been given based upon a clear appreciation and understanding of the facts, implications, and consequences of an action. Adequate informed consent is rooted in respecting a person's dignity. To give informed consent, the individual concerned must have adequate reasoning faculties and be in possession of all relevant facts."

In many respects, Dr. Mike White's book, *Letters to an Aspiring Physician*, serves as a vital component of an informed consent process for your career decision-making process.

Through engaging stories, testimonials, actual letters, and other first-person accounts, Dr. White lays out the entire journey ahead of you, largely in sequence, from beginning to end. As a former practicing physician myself, I could readily identify with the general theme, if not the actual events in my own evolution, matriculation and experience over my own 40-year career in medicine. I appreciated the fact that these were not just his stories, but also a compilation of actual experiences from a number of other well-respected physicians across the country. Adding further credibility to these accounts is the expert editorial commentary at the end of many sections by Dr. Edward Drawbaugh, who insightfully adds his perspective, often in agreement, but occasionally with a slightly different spin which contributes to the depth and realism of the total experience. In my estimation, this journey as described is as real as it gets.

Thus, if after reading this, you continue to desire a career as a physician, then you have given your fully informed consent to this choice. I say, "double congratulations." We definitely need people with the proper sensitivity, requisite intelligence and indomitable will to carry on against these odds.

I will close by citing the "Modern Hippocratic Oath." This was written in 1964 by Dr. Louis Lasagna, Academic Dean of the School of Medicine at Tufts University. It is used in many medical schools today.

HIPPOCRATIC OATH, MODERN VERSION

I swear to fulfill, to the best of my ability and judgment, this covenant:

- *I will respect the hard-won scientific gains of those physicians in whose steps I walk, and gladly share such knowledge as is mine with those who are to follow.*
- *I will apply, for the benefit of the sick, all measures, which are required, avoiding those twin traps of overtreatment and therapeutic nihilism.*
- *I will remember that there is art to medicine as well as science, and that warmth, sympathy, and understanding may outweigh the surgeon's knife or the chemist's drug.*
- *I will not be ashamed to say "I know not," nor will I fail to call in my colleagues when the skills of another are needed for a patient's recovery.*
- *I will respect the privacy of my patients, for their problems are not disclosed to me that the world may know.*
- *Most especially must I tread with care in matters of life and death. If it is given me to save a life, all thanks. But it may also be within my power to*

take a life; this awesome responsibility must be faced with great humbleness and awareness of my own frailty. Above all, I must not play at God.

- I will remember that I do not treat a fever chart, a cancerous growth, but a sick human being, whose illness may affect the person's family and economic stability. My responsibility includes these related problems, if I am to care adequately for the sick.
- I will prevent disease whenever I can, for prevention is preferable to cure.
- I will remember that I remain a member of society, with special obligations to all my fellow human beings, those sound of mind and body as well as the infirm.

If I do not violate this oath, may I enjoy life and art, respected while I live and remembered with affection thereafter. May I always act so as to preserve the finest traditions of my calling and may I long experience the joy of healing those who seek my help.

———————

This is the oath you will take at the completion of your journey. It well-summarizes the promise and the possibility alongside the duties and awesome responsibilities of today's physician.

Should you persevere and succeed, I have no doubt that you will find the benefits far outweigh the risks. Good luck, aspiring physician, and Godspeed.

Respectfully submitted,
Brian D Wong MD MPH
Founder and Chief Executive Officer
The Bedside Trust: Patient Driven Leadership
Seattle, Washington

———————

VII. Appendix

"In preparing in haste for the Joint Commission,
one, at her/his own peril,
ignores the flotsam and jetsam of introduction and appendix."

T MICHAEL WHITE

72

Acknowledgments

Some suggested potential. Some expected perseverance. Some shared their fascination with observation. Others shared their captivation with words.

Doors were opened for me. Unguent was applied and tonics were administered. Victories were snatched from defeat.

Many encouraged transformations. Transformations yielded experiences. Experiences provided for an interesting passage.

As I acknowledge these truths, I see their faces — a long line of individuals who have guided me (sometimes successfully) from where I was to where I needed to be: Dr. Sherman (paradigm); Pharmacist Aumiller (wisdom); Professor Sheffer (kind advocacy); Drs. Cassidy, Firth, Goodman, Lamb, Scharfman, Steinhart, Tartaglia and Cantone (art and science); Dr. Bernene (probity); Dr. Alfonsi (judgment); Dr. Howard (vitality); Mr. Price (friendship); P/CEO Jones (enablement); Dr. Crosby (quality); Dr. Moyer (structure); Professor Anderson (learning/teaching); Ms. Kleppick (resolute); P/CEO Ott (culture); Dr. Leach (shift); Dr. Ahmad (grace); Ms. Navarra (faith); Dr. Roth (horizons); Mr. Lieber (fortification); Mr. Studer (implementation); Mr. Hirsch (mindfulness); Dr. Wong (consummate); Drs. Kellis, Ghobrial, Godse, Condit, Drawbaugh and Hightower (constancy); Editor Theriault (balance); Artist Haught (images); Reverend Dodson and Dr. Leff (connections) and Nurses Forsythe, Lasek, Theriault, Anderson, Como, Gaudy, Rotz, Lyons, Williams, Towe and Amalfitano (safe, timely, efficient, effective, equitable, patient-centered care).

As I remember their faces, I envision and acknowledge the faces of those standing by you, the aspiring physician, and know they are there to see you through.

———

73

Bio — Edward J Drawbaugh MD FACO-HNS

D r. Edward Drawbaugh was born and raised in Hagerstown, Maryland. His undergraduate work was done at the University of Maryland, culminating in a BS degree in Zoology. Duke University School of Medicine was the next stop on his journey. After graduating, he remained at Duke for a surgical internship followed by subspecialty training in Otolaryngology-Head and Neck Surgery. He returned home to establish a solo practice which was eventually built into a four-person group. He retired from active practice in 2005 and then enjoyed an eight-year part-time career as Medical Director of a surgery center and an inpatient surgical service. Since 2013, he has been pursuing his passions for travel and photography, frustrating himself with golf and enjoying his many friends and family.

—————

74

Bio — T Michael White MD FACP

D r. T (Thomas) Michael White's formative years were spent in Schenectady, Saratoga, Bolton Landing and Albany, New York. He went to college (Union) and medical school (Albany) in that region. He trained in internal medicine in New York City (Metropolitan/Flower 5th Avenue Hospitals) and Connecticut (Greenwich Hospital in affiliation with Yale). His career has addressed private practice, teaching (residency program director) and administration (vice president for medical affairs/chief medical officer). He has practiced in New York, Connecticut, Arizona, Pennsylvania and Maryland.

Dr. Mike White is the author of *Unsafe to Safe — an Impatient Proposal for Patient-centered Care.* It addresses healthcare quality and safety. He has also written *Safer Medical Care for You and Yours — Six Tools for Safe, Effective Compassionate Care.* It provides tools that assists patients, and the family members that advocate for them, to be informed, involved and responsible regarding their healthcare.

Dr. White lives in Hagerstown, Maryland. When not writing, his professional energies are spent assisting complex, vulnerable patients and their families partner with the 'Better Angels' who care for them so well to enable safe, timely, efficient, effective, equitable/just, compassionate, patient-centered care. His avocations include family, competitive golf and poker and visiting or going to visit Saratoga and Lake George.

The best way to contact Dr. White is via email — drmikewhite@tmichaelwhitemd.com. He will be pleased to hear from you.

———

75

DR. ED DRAWBAUGH'S PHOTO ALBUM

Baby Rhino, Botswana, page 43
Calculating Evil Baboon, Botswana, page 66
Cheetah Brothers, Tanzania, page 72
Curious Baby Elephant, Botswana, page 76
Golden Eagle, Tanzania, page 92
Grooming Lion Cub, Tanzania, page 105
Just Waking Leopard, Tanzania, page 116
Lunch on the Top Floor, Tanzania, page 126
Mr. Cape Buffalo, Tanzania, page 153
Mr. Zebra, Tanzania, page 160
Ms. Leopard, Tanzania, page 171
Pale Chanting Goshawk, Tanzania, page 181
Regal Ms. Lion, Tanzania, page 238
Surveying the Plain, Tanzania, 242
Vervet Monkey Family Portrait, Tanzania, page 247
Zebra Portrait, Tanzania, page 257
Vervet Monkey Portrait, Tanzania, page 292

To view Dr. Drawbaugh's photos in color, please go to www.tmichaelwhitemd.com. For information regarding his approach to photography, his photography collection and the availability of prints, etc., please contact him at e.drawbaugh@myactv.net. He will be pleased to hear from you.

76

Two Example Gift Tools from Safer Medical Care for You and Yours

- **Tool 1: My (Unique and Very) Personal Medical Record — a gift example**
- **Tool 3: My (Unique and Very) Personal Healthcare Values, Desires and Wishes — a gift example**

For your convenience and edification, Dr. Steve Hightower and I desire that you be provided with two tools for easy reference. They first appear in *Safer Medical Care for You and Yours: Six Tools for Safe, Effective Compassionate Care.*

I advocate that all seniors (i.e., anyone a day older than me) immediately emulate Tool 1: *My (Unique and Very) Personal Medical Record — a gift example.*

I encourage each senior and her/his healthcare power of attorney to consider Tool 3: *My (Unique and Very) Personal Healthcare Values, Desires and Wishes — a gift example* and begin to craft her/his own unique and very personal language.

The 6 X 9 format of this book does not present the tools in the most legible or user-friendly format. Should you:

- desire to discuss these tools or
- desire user-friendly Microsoft Word gift examples

please contact me at drmikewhite@tmicahelwhitemd.com. I will be pleased to hear from you.

Safer Medical Care for You and Yours: Six Tools
for Safe, Effective Compassionate Care

By: Stephen F Hightower MD FACP and T Michael White MD FACP

Amazon/Kindle

www.safermedcare.com drmikewhite@tmichaelwhitemd.com 240-291-2446

Letters to an Aspiring Physician

Tool 1: My (Unique and Very) Personal Medical Record — **a gift example**

My Identification:

- Thomas Michael Example MD; DOB: ##/##/####
- Paradise Bay; 555-555-5555; mikeexamplemd@zmail.com
- Career: physician, educator, executive, consultant, author radio host and golfer
- My HealthCare Power of Attorney: Ms. Jacquelyn F Example (spouse); Paradise Bay; 555-555-5555
- My Preferred Hospitals: Paradise Bay Hospital and State Capital Regional Medical Center
- My Hospital Portal — *MyParadiseBay* — https://www.paradisebayhospital.org

My Chief Complaint (my story — why I am here today):

For anticipated appointments, I will be prepared (in writing) to discuss the "O-P-Q-R2-S-T" of today's encounter: onset (when it started); place (what part of body); quality (what it feels like); related symptoms; radiation (where it travels to); severity (scale of 1-10); and triggers (what causes it, makes it worse or makes it better) — *after Dr. Orly Avitzur/Yale and others.*

My Allergies:

- Lifetime history of allergic rhinitis
- ACE inhibitors (for example, captopril) cause me to cough
- Respiratory depression with procedural sedation and analgesia
- No known allergies to medications or to latex

My Chronological Problem List:

Active

- 1952 allergic rhinitis
- 1978 actinic keratosis and removal of multiple basal cell carcinomas
- 1978 gastroesophageal reflux disease (GERD)
- 1995 hypertension
- 1995 intolerance to ACE Inhibitors (cough)
- 1998 rosacea
1. 2003 cystoscopy and partial prostatectomy for benign prostatic hypertrophy
- 2005 low HDL cholesterol
- 2011 pre-diabetes
- 2013 sleep apnea
- 2014 coronary artery disease
- 2014 left trochanteric bursitis; left sciatica (L5/S1); left cervical radiculopathy
- 2017 immunization and cancer detections: Influenza (2016); Pneumovax (2015/2016); Tdap; 2012; Zoster (2012); Hepatitis B (1995); gastroscopy (2000); colonoscopy (2010); PSA (2016)

Resolved

- 1961 appendectomy
- 2005 left inguinal hernia repair
- 2006 hemorrhoid surgery
- 2017 sinusitis

My Medication and Therapies List:

Morning Medications:

1. Metronidazole topical cream; 0.75%; apply to each morning (for rosacea)
2. Fluticasone nasal spray; 50 mcg; each morning (for allergic rhinitis)
3. Multivitamin; by mouth; each morning (for patient preference)

Evening Medications/Therapies

1. Allegra (fexofenadine); 180mg; by mouth; each evening (for allergic rhinitis)
2. Lipitor (atorvastatin); 20mg; by mouth; each evening (for hyperlipidemia/coronary artery disease)
3. Aspirin; 81mg; by mouth; once daily at bedtime (for hyperlipidemia/coronary artery disease)
4. Prilosec (omeprazole); 20 mg; by mouth; each evening (for reflux/indigestion)

1 |

5. Cozaar (losartan); 100 mg; by mouth; each evening (for high blood pressure)
6. CPAP; Nasal pillows (small); 7cm water; 3.5% humidity (for sleep apnea)

If needed medications:

1. Virtussin (guaifenesin/codeine phosphate) AC Syrup ; three teaspoons (15cc); by mouth; if needed for severe cough (rarely used)
2. Ambien (zolpidem); 5 mg; by mouth; once daily at bedtime if necessary for sleep (rarely used)
3. Tylenol (acetaminophen); 1000 mg; by mouth; every eight hours if necessary for aches, pains or fever (rarely used)
4. Advil (ibuprofen); 400-600 mg; by mouth; twice daily if necessary for activity related pain (used several times each week)

Note: as you construct your list, please remember to include: medications/therapies for: Behavioral Health Conditions (for example, depression or anxiety medications); Bowel Hygiene (for example, constipation); Ophthalmology Conditions (for example, glaucoma drops); and Pulmonary Conditions (for example, COPD inhalers).

My Pertinent Family History

My paternal grandfather suffered with late life depression (87). My maternal grandfather died with senile dementia (74). My maternal grandmother died of renal cell carcinoma (85). My father died at 89. He struggled with hypertension, minor strokes and anxiety/depression. My mother is a breast cancer survivor and is alive and well (93). She has atrial fibrillation. My siblings and children are alive and well.

My Personal Physicians/Caregivers:

- Cardiologist: Dr. Chester Paine/Paradise Bay/555-555-5555
- Dentist: Dr. Floss Daily/Paradise Bay/555-555-5555
- Dermatologist: Dr. U. V. Light/Paradise Bay/555-555-5555
- Gastroenterologist: Dr. Colin Reddy/Paradise Bay/555-555-5555
- General Surgeon: Dr. G. B. Stone/Paradise Bay/555-555-5555
- My HealthCare Power of Attorney: Ms. Jacquelyn F Example (spouse); Paradise Bay; 555-555-5555
- Interventional Cardiologist: Dr. Stent Thrombosis/Paradise Bay/555-555-5555
- Primary Care Physician: Dr. Wm. Osler Nodes/Paradise Bay/555-555-5555
- Optometrist: Dr. Venus Blind/Paradise Bay/555-555-5555
- Orthopedist: Dr. Cairo Practer/Paradise Bay/555-555-5555
- Otolaryngologist: Dr. E. N. Tears/Paradise Bay/555-555-5555
- Pharmacy: Dr. Phil Counter/Corner Drug Emporium/Paradise Bay/555-555-5555
- My Personal Professional Patient Advocate (My P3A): Dr. Grace Wisdom/Paradise Bay/555-555-5555
- Pulmonary/Critical Care: Dr. Stephanie O. Scope /555-555-5555

My HealthCare Documents (available upon request):

- 2016 and 2017 cardiac cath report; baseline EKG; latest lab studies
- 2017-01-11 My (Unique and Very) Personal HealthCare Values, Desires and Wishes
- 2014-01-05 My HealthCare Advanced Directives

From: *Safer Medical Care for You and Yours: Six Tools for Safe, Effective Compassionate Care*
By: Stephen F Hightower MD FACP and T Michael White MD FACP
Amazon/Kindle
www.safermedcare.com drmikewhite@tmichaelwhitemd.com 240-291-2446

Tool 3: My (Unique and Very) Personal HealthCare Values — **a gift example**

My Identification

- T (Thomas) Michael Example MD; DOB: ##/##/####
- Paradise Bay; 555-555-5555; mikeexamplemd@zmail.com
- Career: physician, educator, executive, consultant, author, talk show host and golfer
- My HealthCare Power of Attorney: Ms. Jacquelyn F Example (spouse); Paradise Bay; 555-555-5555
- My preferred hospital(s): (1) Paradise Bay Hospital and (2) State Capital Regional Medical Center

My Unique (and Very) Personal Medical Record

Please refer to an available separate document — *My Unique (and Very) Personal Medical Record* which provides you with an efficient, organized and accurate and up-to-date understanding of my past and current medical care. Thank you.

###########

My (Unique and Very) Personal HealthCare Values
A Gift Example

A very special individual (Ms. Jacquelyn F Example) has been thoughtfully chosen and has agreed to be appointed as my HealthCare Power of Attorney. I thank her for that. As important:

- She has given me permission to share my considered thoughts about my unique and very personal wishes for the end of my life with her and
- She has spoken with me to clarify the meaning of my wishes with me.

She is prepared to speak for me should I lose the capacity to speak for myself as she understands:

(1) Provided the wonderful coordinated care that has been afforded to me over the years, at this time I enjoy good health and I very much enjoy my life.

(2) If I were to unexpectedly become seriously ill and there were to be reasonable chance for my recovery, I wish to receive all indicated treatment to advance my recovery and

(3) At the same time:

- I comfortably recognize death as a part of life.
- If a meaningful recovery were to be unlikely, I would prefer a dignified death.

T Michael White MD

- For emphasis and clarification, I would place no value in preserving my life if heart, lungs and kidneys function but my wits, as I now know and enjoy them, have departed.
- For emphasis and clarification, very specifically, if two qualified physicians using an institutional protocol determine that I am brain dead, please recognize that I have died and proceed accordingly.
- For emphasis and clarification, very specifically, if two qualified physicians using an institutional protocol determine that I am in a persistent vegetative state, I place no value in preserving my life and desire interventions to maintain my life (for example, feeding tubes, antibiotics, transfusions, resuscitation, etc.) not be implemented and/or if already implemented, be withdrawn.
- For further clarification, I would recognize a prolonged existence in such states (brain dead or persistent vegetative state) as a major terminal indignity to a life well lived — an indignity to be avoided.
- Through the experience of family and friends, I have developed tremendous confidence in my regional palliative care and hospice teams. If and when appropriate, I advocate that these better angels be involved in my care. Confidence that palliative care and hospice teams will be appropriately involved is very important and reassuring to me.
- I request, in every circumstance (recovery or terminal), that my healthcare team continuously attend to and ensure my comfort. Confidence that my comfort will always be compassionately addressed is very important and reassuring to me.
- When the time comes, if donation of my organs would benefit the living, I wish to donate appropriate organs.
- My wishes for my religious/spiritual preferences and funeral arrangements have been made clear to my family. My understanding that these preferences and arrangements have been clarified and will be followed is very important and reassuring to me.

###########

Letters to an Aspiring Physician

Background Information

A. Purpose

The purpose of this document — *My (Unique and Very) Personal HealthCare Values* — is to efficiently and effectively convey in complex circumstances (for example, when I have lost the capacity to speak for myself):

- The very unique person I am and
- My unique and very personal healthcare values

to the fine, dedicated and caring healthcare team assigned to my care and to my healthcare power of attorney(s) designated in my available Healthcare Advanced Directives.

I anticipate that this will ensure that care is provided in accordance with my values and wishes. This is very important and comforting to me.

I have constructed this document with great care. It reflects in-depth conversation with my family, my healthcare power of attorney (Mrs. Jacquelyn F Example) and with significant others in my life. In constructing this document, it has been my intent to:

- Position myself to enable and receive safer, timely, efficient, effective and equitable (fair/just) patient-centered medical care by providing organized, accurate, legible and up-to-date information,
- Advance the professional effectiveness and vitality of the fine dedicated and caring healthcare team caring for me by saving them precious time and energy through removing ambivalence and uncertainty about my values and wishes,
- Do my involved, informed and responsible part to advance the HealthCare Value that my healthcare team provides to me (for me, HealthCare Value *equates* to compassionate medical care; quality outcomes; patient and staff safety; customer (patient, family and community) satisfaction; patient advocacy; and professional (medical, nursing, professional and support staffs') vitality *balanced by* resource utilization/cost) and
- Ensure that my very personal healthcare values and wishes are understood (by me, my family, my healthcare powers of attorney and my healthcare team) and honored.

B: My Personal Information — My Social History

It is important to me that the better angels caring for me in complex circumstances appreciate the unique and very special (to some) person I am — to that end:

I have had the honor and privilege to be a physician (general internist). My responsibilities have included private practice, residency program direction, graduate medical education (vice president value and education) and hospital administration (vice president medical affairs/chief medical officer). I have surveyed for The Joint Commission and the Accreditation Council for Graduate Medical Education. At this time, I am a HealthCare Value (quality, safety, experience, advocacy and vitality ÷ cost) author and consultant. I am on a mission to advance each individual's safer medical care by assisting her/him to be an informed, involved and responsible patient.

I grew up as a blue collar kid in Schenectady, New York. Along the way, I have been blessed to be influenced and nurtured by Union College, Albany Medical College, New York Medical College, Yale University, the University of Connecticut, the University of Arizona, Temple University, Michigan State University and the University of Pittsburgh. I live with my wife, Jacquelyn F Example RN BSN (555-555-

329

5555). We have four successful children of whom we are very proud. They live with their families in Santa Barbara (Benjamin), Louisville (Jessica), Arlington (Catherine) and Washington DC (Colin). In my spare time I enjoy studying medicine, writing, analyzing the New York Times, competitive golf, competitive poker, music, cinema, boating (Lake George) and thoroughbred racing (Saratoga).

C: Expectations

Through the creation and maintenance of this document, I have striven to provide the members of my healthcare team and my healthcare powers of attorney(s) with the necessary and accurate information required to address my care in a compassionate, efficient and effective manner.

Should additional information or complex decision making (for example, informed consent) be required, I anticipate you will approach me.

In the circumstance where I lack the capacity to communicate, I anticipate my healthcare team will address concerns with my healthcare powers of attorney(s) (identified in my available Healthcare Advanced Directives) who are well informed of my values and wishes.

I expect that my personal values will be respected and my wishes will be honored. I expect that my attending physician will write orders that are compatible with my values and that my healthcare team will follow those orders.

D: Informed Consent

I anticipate that my healthcare team and my healthcare institution will:

- Procure informed consent prior to the implementation of any complex procedure or treatment;
- As part of informed consent, assist with an informed understanding of complex financial implications of my care (for example, the hospital accepts my insurance but the physicians providing care do not);
- Whenever informed consent is required, ask me and
- If the circumstance is such that I have lost the capacity to speak for myself, then, obtain informed consent from my healthcare power(s) of attorney identified in my available Healthcare Advanced Directives. Through detailed dialogue with me, these individuals understand my very personal healthcare values and wishes; will respect them; and are entirely prepared to speak on my behalf with my interest at heart. Through detailed dialogue with me, they are prepared to work with my attending physician and complete my circumstance dependent end of life directives (for example, my State/Commonwealth Medical Orders for Life-Sustaining Treatment (MOLST) form) if I am unable to do so.

E: My Personal Professional Patient Advocate (My P3A):

Should I unexpectedly become severely ill, I anticipate that my healthcare process may become complex. Therefore, I anticipate that I or my healthcare power(s) of attorney may engage, at our own expense, a *My Personal Professional Patient Advocate (My P3A)* who:

- Understands the complexity of the healthcare process,
- Will be adopted/deputized/appointed as a family member (and not as a member of my healthcare team),
- Will, upon my request or upon the request of my healthcare power(s) of attorney, review my chart and participate in family meetings, etc.,

Letters to an Aspiring Physician

- Will assist me and and/or my healthcare power(s) of attorney in understanding my care (i.e., act as interpreter for the purpose of making the complex simple) and
- Will assist with the respectful, efficient, effective and articulate communication of my personal healthcare values and wishes to my healthcare team.

Should a My P3A be engaged, please welcome this very carefully identified and selected adopted/deputized/appointed family member into my family and into my care.

(Note for clarification: although my P3A's opinion may prove invaluable to my decision-making process, decisions will be made by me or, when necessary, by my healthcare power(s) of attorney.

F: Complexity

Through the process of creating this document — *My (Unique and Very) Personal HealthCare Values* — I have striven to diminish (and I do not anticipate) the possibility of clinical, ethical or legal complexity. I fully expect that my personal healthcare values and wishes will be respected and honored. I fully expect that my attending physician will write orders that are compatible with my personal healthcare values and wishes and that my healthcare team will follow those orders.

Should unanticipated legal or ethical complexity arise, I fully expect, request and insist the healthcare institution's ethics committee process:

- Review this document,
- Speak with me or if I do not have the capacity to communicate, speak with my healthcare power(s) of attorney,
- Upon my request or at the request of my healthcare power(s) of attorney, include *My Personal Professional Patient Advocate (My P3A)* in discussions so *My P3A* is positioned to offer perspective, advice and counsel to my decision-making process and
- Resolve any ambiguity in favor of my personal healthcare values and wishes by sundown (i.e., within 24 hours).

G: Gratitude

I recognize that my healthcare team is comprised of our nation's "best and brightest." I recognize that through dedication, sacrifice and experience you have become a "better angel" in my life. I am most appreciative of and confident in your care. I thank you for being here for me today.

Respectfully submitted,

Dr. Thomas Michael Example

Monday, January 23, 2017

From: *Safer Medical Care for You and Yours: Six Tools for Safe, Effective Compassionate Care*
By: Stephen F Hightower MD FACP and T Michael White MD FACP
Amazon/Kindle
www.safermedcare.com drmikewhite@tmichaelwhitemd.com 240-291-2446

331

Letters to an Aspiring Physician

Reflecting on a Career in Medicine

COMMENTARY BY Edward J Drawbaugh MD
FOREWORD BY Amy E Theriault MA
AFTERWORD BY Brian D Wong MD

T MICHAEL WHITE MD
A HealthCare Value Professional

Made in the USA
San Bernardino, CA
16 March 2018